David Warr was born just before the end of the Second World War. He attended a private boarding school in Surrey, leaving to join the Civil Service where he served in the War Department. On leaving the Civil Service he joined the police, serving as a CID officer. He left the police to work as an Insurance Inspector before setting up his own brokerage, and estate agency business. Due to a serious back injury, he had to give up work, and it was some years before he was able to regain a certain amount of fitness, before starting a renewable energy business. He has now retired from business and devotes his time to writing works of fiction.

David lives happily with Ann, his wife of thirty-five years, in a small village in Hampshire.

Visions of Death is David's second novel. The first novel, *Kaine's Chronicles – The Haunting of Jack Kent*, was released on St Georges Day, 2015.

Kaine's Chronicles

Visions of Death

David Warr

Kaine's Chronicles
Visions of Death

Vanguard Press

A CIP catalogue record for this title is
available from the British Library.

ISBN 978 1 78465 165 7

*Vanguard Press is an imprint of
Pegasus Elliot MacKenzie Publishers Ltd.*
www.pegasuspublishers.com

First Published in 2016

**Vanguard Press
Sheraton House Castle Park
Cambridge England**

Printed & Bound in Great Britain

This book is dedicated to the memory of Robin Gibson.
An adversary, a protagonist, and eventually, one of the best
friends that I have ever had.
27th September 2015.

ONE

October 2013

Professor Suzanne Kaine was going through her notes on a case involving twins who were having the same recurring nightmares. Not too unusual for identical twins but at the time of the nightmares they were separated by thousands of miles of Atlantic Ocean. Getting up from her antique mahogany inlaid desk, Professor Kaine went over to the bookcase under the painting of a Second World War Lancaster bomber flying in blue skies, presumably somewhere over England. The painting had hung there ever since she could remember, even as a small girl visiting her grandfather.

Suzanne selected a leather bound volume, checked the title, *Twin Telepathy* by Dr Marjorie Symens, and returned to her desk by the window. She looked out and viewed the bustling traffic of Harley Street.

Her mind wasn't on her work but on the events over the last few weeks, culminating in the acrimonious break up of her engagement with her solicitor boyfriend. He had failed to tell her he had been married before and that he hadn't obtained a divorce from his wife. A solicitor, for God's sake; what was the world coming to when you couldn't even trust a solicitor to tell the truth. She thought back to their engagement party, held at her grandparents' house in the Hampshire countryside, how happy she had been and how proud to have presented him to her family. Her grandfather seemed to have reservations about him right from the start, but wished them all the happiness in the world.

It was now ten years since she had earned her inheritance to this practice, started by her grandfather during the Second World War. Her own father had chosen civil engineering over that of the medical profession, and on the death of her mother, had emigrated from England to Australia, where he lived to this day. With the blessing of her father, Suzanne was the chosen heir of her grandfather when he retired, and who now lived in the Hampshire countryside with her grandmother.

Grandfather, Richard Kaine, had fled to England with his English mother from his native Austria in 1938. His father had been a lecturing professor of psychiatry at the Vienna Institute, until his death by torture at the hands of the Gestapo styled Austrian police. He had been a loud voice against the annexation of his country by Germany and was arrested for high treason, paying the ultimate price for standing up to the insidious Third Reich of Germany. Richard was raised by English relatives, sent to finish his studies at Oxford, before graduating out of medical school and choosing psychiatry over general medicine. With the inheritance from his mother, he was able to set up his practice here in prestigious Harley Street, where his reputation soon grew from successfully treating post-traumatic stress disorders from the many injured and damaged servicemen and women who were casualties of the Second World War. His success took him on the lecture circuits of Europe, as well as advising successive governments and other institutions up to his late retirement at the ripe old age of eighty two years, that was ten years ago.

Suzanne's grandfather had been the father she had sorely missed, making himself responsible for her education and welfare up to graduating out of the Institute of Vienna, like her great grandfather before her. It hadn't taken Suzanne long to earn her doctorate and settle into the Harley Street practice.

At the age of just thirty-six, she was indeed a very fortunate young lady and she knew it, but how miserable and bitter she felt now over this scurrilous solicitor. She could have him brought up before his own Law Society but that would make her look very foolish, no, it's best she just let the whole thing go and got on with her life, as her grandfather had advised her.

Suzanne was about to open the leather-bound volume in front of her when her buzzer sounded. She switched the intercom on. "Yes, Isabelle?"

"A Detective Sergeant Mike King is on the telephone asking for you. He says he's your cousin." Isabelle didn't sound sure, her voice rising at the end making it a question rather than a statement.

Suzanne smiled, immediately recalling her second cousin from the numerous weddings, funerals and other celebrations that took her into regular contact with her relatives.

"Put him through please, Isabelle." Suzanne picked up the handset of the telephone on her desk. "Hello, Mike, how's crime? To what do I owe the pleasure?" she asked, smiling to herself as she recalled the smartly dressed, very confident, bordering on the cocky, London policeman who always amused her.

"Professor, how lovely to hear your voice again," he almost purred. "Why would I need a reason to speak to the most beautiful one out of all my relatives, eh?"

"Same old bullshit, Mike," she laughed. "What do you want?"

"I'm serious, Suzanne, if you weren't my cousin I would be making serious advances in your direction."

"Second cousin, Mike, and much too mature for you," she corrected him. "And I'll ask you again, what... do... you... want?"

"Ouch, righto," he conceded, pretending to be hurt. "I work for a chief inspector on a murder squad at the Yard, who is also a very good friend as well as a colleague. He recently lost his wife, has gone through a lot of depression and I wondered if you would see him?"

Suzanne thought for a minute before answering. "I'm not really into bereavement counselling, Mike. These things normally sort themselves out in time. Has he seen his own doctor?"

"Yeah, I know that, Suzanne, but there are other factors involved in this." Mike started to press his case.

"Such as what, Mike?" she asked.

Mike hesitated, wondering how he could tell her. "Let me start off by saying I have never met anyone more sane, more stable or mentally and physically stronger than my boss at the Yard, until the death of his wife, that is." Mike paused before continuing. "Well, his wife spoke to him on her death bed but the thing is, according to the doctors, she was dead at the time." He knew it sounded mad, but surely that was what she was there for, wasn't it?

"What is she supposed to have said to him, for goodness sake?" Suzanne asked.

Mike picked up on the scepticism in her voice but continued. "Find her killer, that's what she said. Find her killer, and what is more, the supposed victim, a young girl, was sat in a corner of the room but disappeared without trace when he called the doctors." Mike waited for her to reply.

"It sounds as if you have a very interesting boss, Mike. Anything else?" she asked, her interest now slightly aroused.

"I know what it sounds like, Suzanne, and that's why I would like you to see him," Mike continued. "It has set him on a quest to find the girl, and you know what?"

"What?" Suzanne invited, as she turned the pages of the volume on her desk, her attention not yet fully with her cousin.

"We've discovered the identity of the girl who did, in actual fact, go missing some twenty-five years ago. We identified her from her missing person's file. I really need you to see him, Suzanne, he has reached the depths. He is able to function as a police officer, but it's when he stops, particularly in the evening and during the night."

Suzanne stopped turning the pages. It was normal for a bereaved person to feel the loneliness worse at night, but her professional curiosity was now aroused and she felt a certain tingling in her feet, as she always did when she got a little excited about something.

"Okay, Detective Sergeant, you've got my attention. Get him to telephone me for an appointment. What's his name?"

"His name is Jacks, Chief Inspector Jacks," Mike said, adding, "and he wants to keep this private, Suzanne, otherwise it will foul up his record."

"Okay, Mike, I don't have a problem with that," she confirmed.

"I knew you would see him, if only just to please me," Mike laughed.

"Bugger off, Mike." Suzanne put the phone down and returned to the volume in front of her. The tingling in the bottoms of her feet continued; she thought the chief inspector may just take her mind off of her present bitterness and self-pity.

***

Professor Suzanne Kaine first glimpsed Chief Inspector Jacks through her open office door as her secretary came in with some papers and placed them in her in-tray. His outward appearance was that of a confident, self-assured man. Tall, of rather athletic build, he faced the receptionist with a half-smile on his face. Suzanne's instincts, backed up by the tension she saw in the man's back and neck, told her that this man was as taut as a coiled spring, ready to snap. He had been, and was probably still going through, very traumatic times.

As he stood by the desk, Suzanne realised this was not the first time she had seen the chief inspector. She recalled watching the news on television sometime earlier; he had been speaking on the steps of some police station to the media gathered out front. Flanked by an enormous rugby full back type on one side and her detective cousin on the other, he was reluctantly reading a begrudged statement from a prepared script. Reluctant to impart knowledge about his case he may have been, but still very confident, a totally different man to the one she saw before her now.

"Leave the door please, Joy," she called to her secretary as she was leaving her office.

Joy, somewhat puzzled, looked at her questioningly with an eyebrow raised, but as no explanation was forthcoming, she did as she was bid. Suzanne continued to observe Jacks through the open doorway. Handsome, she thought, if not a little too rugged, his firm chin was jutting slightly forward and the smile was over clenched teeth. He could do with a good haircut, she thought as she noticed it hanging over his collar with an untidy shock of hair hanging over one eye. She guessed he was about to turn and face her but still continued to study him as their eyes met, catching her out. Suzanne, unfazed, rose from behind her desk, smoothed down the skirt over her flat stomach and went out of the door to reception.

Jacks had noticed her observing him and it was now his turn to watch and examine the woman coming towards him, tall, elegant, not pretty by his standards but very attractive none the less. She looked about thirty-six to thirty-eight years of age, and was dressed expensively in a tailored navy-blue suit, the skirt finishing just on the knee. Who did she remind him of? Jacks tried to think but couldn't bring the person to mind.

"This is Professor Kaine, Chief Inspector," the petite young receptionist introduced. "Professor, this is Chief Inspector Jacks, for his nine-thirty appointment."

"Thank you, Isabelle." A smiling Suzanne noticed the dark patches under his brown eyes as she stepped forward, holding out her hand. She was pleased that she received a firm but gentle handshake in return, no over exuberant machoism from this man.

"Come this way please, Chief Inspector. My cousin has filled me in with some of your details." She led him back into her office.

He couldn't help noticing the well-formed calves of her shapely legs, extenuated by the four-inch high heels. She indicated to a chair besides a walnut coffee table.

"Please sit, Chief Inspector," she invited, as she became aware of his interest in her legs. So, she was still attractive to the opposite sex after all. Stuff that bloody solicitor, she thought.

Before he sat down he looked round the office taking in the furnishings, wall paper, the various framed diplomas on the walls, and a very expensive looking leather couch alongside the far wall. Jacks was impressed. He also noticed the picture of a World War Two Lancaster bomber set high on the wall above a solid mahogany bookcase, which appeared out of keeping with the rest of the décor. His gaze stayed on the picture, and he wondered why a professional woman would have such an out of place piece of art on her wall.

Suzanne watched him scan the room, taking in the diplomas on the walls and noticed his gaze settle on the painting.

"Inherited with the office, Chief Inspector," she answered, reading his mind and anticipating the question. She became aware of the photograph in the smashed frame that still lay face down on the desk. She idly swept it off the desk and put it in the waste bin, but it did not go unnoticed by the sharp-eyed detective.

Jacks ignored it as a light bulb lit in his head, *Play it again, Sam. Play 'As time goes by.'* He suddenly remembered who

Suzanne Kaine reminded him of, Ingrid Bergman, the Swedish film star of Casablanca. A sort of awkward beauty, she even walked like her.

"Call me Jacks, please, Professor," he said as he sat down. "How does this work then? Do I stretch out on that leather couch?"

"That's what they do on the television, Chief Inspector, but you may sit where you are for this session, unless you would rather lie down?" she answered, with an amused smile showing in her eyes.

"No, I'm happy sitting here," he laughed, waving his hand to show how relaxed he was with it all.

"Do you have a first name?" she enquired, still with the amused smile on her face, high-lighting her angular features and showing the faint signs of dimples in her cheeks.

Jacks liked the smile, which showed through full red lips. He looked into her blue green eyes and said simply, "Chief Inspector."

Suzanne gazed at him with patient amusement. "You have been watching too much television," she said, observing his features and spotting the scar in his eyebrow. A warrior type, she thought.

"Chance would be a fine thing," he countered, "I prefer Jacks, if that's okay?" He smiled at her and said, "What do I call you? Do you have a first name?"

"Yes, I do. Professor," she answered grinning.

"Touché, Professor," Jacks responded.

"I'll call you Jacks if you call me Suzanne, okay?"

Chief Inspector Jacks felt a little more relaxed as his lips parted, showing a nice set of even teeth behind a more genuine smile. "Okay, Suzanne it is."

"I understand that your superiors don't know that you are here under these circumstances, is that right?" She waited and was surprised by his fairly quick answer.

"Yes they do. When Mike, your cousin, suggested it, I must admit I didn't want anyone knowing, but then I thought about it. If I hid it and they found out I would be in all kinds of trouble, so I decided to level with them and take the consequences on my record." Jacks casually crossed his legs attempting to show how relaxed he was about the whole thing. "As it happens, Carstairs, the Assistant Commissioner, was very good about it. In actual fact, he was downright pleased, said it wouldn't go on record and I could take time off as well."

"And are you?" she asked adding, "Taking time off?"

Jacks smiled at her. "I'm here, aren't I?" he answered, with his tone telling her that was all she was going to get on the subject.

"Do you wish you could turn the clock back to before your wife died?" Suzanne probed, trying to provoke a reaction to gauge.

Jacks just gazed at her and she waited patiently for his response. He eventually gave a sardonic smile before saying, "Not even God can change the past."

"That's very profound, you surprise me."

"Aristotle," replied Jacks. "Well, Agathon actually, but Aristotle quoted it in his Nicomanchean Ethics."

"Well, now you do amaze me. I wouldn't have taken you for a literary man, Jacks." Suzanne smiled at him, using his preferred name.

"The days of the flat footed peeler are long gone, Suzanne. These days some of us have even learnt to read and write."

"I'm sorry, Jacks, I didn't mean to patronise. I just took you for the action man, outdoors type, that sort of thing."

Jacks smiled disarmingly, his dark brown eyes showing his amusement. "It's okay, Professor. I've always liked to read and I pick up things quite easily along the way."

"Where were you schooled?" she enquired.

"I was sent to boarding school in Surrey, at the ripe old age of eleven and a half after winning a scholarship. We had good teachers, especially in English Lit, which I showed a penchant for. We learnt from the classics, as well as general sayings and their meanings, such as the 'crossing of the Rubicon', and a host of others. But you are right in a way, I was a sport fanatic, boxing, rugby, swimming, athletics, you name it, I did it. "

"Let's move on then," she said, not wanting to get bogged down too much at this stage. "I think we should start from the very beginning, before your experience of seeing any ghost and the death of your wife. Can you start with things that were happening in your life at that time?" she suggested as a starting point. "Try to memorize the events leading up to Leanne's death." Suzanne knew this would hurt, but she had to elicit as much as she could from him.

"*J'ai plus de souvenirs que si j'avais mille ans,*" Jacks spoke quietly.

"You have more memories than if you were a thousand years old," she interpreted correctly.

"Well done, Professor. You know your French," Jacks congratulated sullenly. "What about the author?" he asked with a raised eyebrow.

Suzanne just shook her head and waited for the answer.

"Baudelaire," Jacks said simply.

Jacks thought back over the short weeks leading up to the death of his wife, Leanne, and the circumstances that took him away from her side when he should have been with her.

"I could start with my latest case of murder and robbery at a jeweller's, that was ongoing at the time I first became aware of Leanne's illness." *Damn Brian Payne, damn his soul to hell,* he thought bitterly. "I was in the doctor's surgery with my wife when I got a message from your cousin, one of my sergeants, who told me that we had a robbery and murder on our hands…"

TWO

July 2013

Young and impressionable, pretty Lucy Barber was still daydreaming of the dishy man who had just left the shop sporting a brand new Rolex watch she had sold him, when her fanciful reverie was rudely interrupted by the sudden ringing of the telephone by her side.

To the appreciation of her boss, she answered the telephone on the third ring. "Jones the Jeweller, how may I help you?" she asked, in her melodic public school voice.

"Mr Howard Jones, please." The voice on the other end was clipped and sounded foreign; a Middle Eastern accent, Lucy thought.

"Who may I say is calling?" she asked, not daring to put through another cold caller to Mr Jones. She had allowed a sales representative to get through before, which had made Mr Jones very angry and bad tempered for the rest of that day.

"I am calling on behalf of a royal family who wish to visit your establishment. Can you put me through to Mr Jones please?" he persisted.

"Please hold for one moment, and I'll see if he's available." Lucy pushed the mute button on the phone and turned to her boss. "I think it's royalty, Mr Jones. He's asked for you by name."

"Okay, Lucy, no need to get excited. We've had them here before." Howard Jones appeared the epitome of calm yet underneath he was more excited by the call than Lucy. "I'll take it out back," he said, hurrying to his cubicle behind the display cases.

He paused in front of his extension to gather himself, cleared his throat before picking up the telephone and began speaking. "Jones here, can I help you?"

"Mr Howard Jones?" the Middle Eastern voice asked.

Jones puffed out his chest; they even knew his Christian name. He was getting known by the nobility, not only of Europe, but the Middle East as well.

He winked at his wife, who was listening with interest to his conversation. "The very same. How can I help you?"

"His Royal Highness is soon to wed and wishes to buy certain items of jewellery that will befit a new princess of the Royal House. He would like to visit you, if that is possible, Mr Jones?" the clipped accent requested.

"I am afraid the hour is late, sir. It is past our closing time as we speak," Jones answered. Friday night was always difficult at the best of times, with his squash court booked, Mrs Jones always having her hair done and none of the staff wanting to hang around with things to do towards the weekend.

"No, no, no, Mr Jones, not today, but the Prince is an early riser and wondered if you could accommodate him early tomorrow morning, say at eight o'clock, if that's all right?"

Mr Jones thought for a moment. His wife was frantically nodding her head, she didn't want to miss out on royalty visiting her shop.

"That would be quite in order, sir. Can we expect to see you at eight, then?"

"Yes, you can, Mr Jones. Please have some samples of diamond and sapphire rings, necklaces in gold or platinum, and anything else that would make perfect gifts for His Royal Highness's bride, or that you feel may be of interest to him. I think items of say between one hundred to two hundred and fifty thousand pounds will suffice, unless you have something really special, that is?" The voice was matter of fact.

Mr Jones thought, *how the other half live, he must do this every day on behalf of his royal master.*

"I am sure we can find items that will be of interest to your party and we, at Jones the Jeweller, will be pleased and honoured to serve you."

Mrs Jones was now holding her husband's free hand, squeezing it hard in her agreement and pleasure; even if it did mean her presence at the shop early on a Saturday morning, the last visit by royalty had led to a brand new outfit for her wardrobe.

"Until tomorrow then, Mr Jones," the Arabic voice continued. "I'll bid you good evening. Oh, one more thing, no fuss, Mr Jones," he added as an afterthought. "We would value your discretion." He didn't wait for an answer; the phone went dead.

Jones and his wife, Marjorie, smiled at one another. "Have we got sufficient stock of the best quality to show him?" Marjorie asked.

"I think I'll have to get on the phone and call in some favours," Howard answered. "I hope Herman can help me out."

Herman Gould was as old and as wise as Methuselah, and a very prestigious jeweller from Hatton Garden. He traded on the world's markets, often travelling to and from Amsterdam in Holland to Delhi in India. Jones and Gould had often helped one another out when something special was required at short notice. One never ventured to enquire where Herman obtained some of his 'special' pieces; it was rumoured he also travelled to Africa and dealt in 'blood' diamonds.

As the rest of the staff were leaving, not too pleased that they would have an early start on a Saturday morning, Jones and his wife were calling in 'favours' from his jewellery contacts across London. He would be busy most of that evening running about the city, gathering in the stock. He would miss his usual Friday night game of squash. No such inconvenience for Marjorie Jones, she was certainly not going to miss her hair appointment. She wanted to look her best for her royal visitor the next day.

Herman Gould was resplendent in his crimson velvet jacket. A skull cap placed on the back of his head seemed to keep in place wispy white hair, that joined his bushy sideburns that ran down to his chin. He looked the archetypal Hatton Garden jeweller. He had stayed open late to receive Howard Jones, and after an hour of bargaining, Howard was on his way home, more than satisfied with purchases that he had on a sale or return basis. Another smart outfit beckoned for Marjorie, thanks to Herman and the generous mark-up he was able to put on his merchandise for such elite customers.

The next morning, the lights inside Jones the Jeweller were on promptly at seven o'clock. Staff Lucy Barber, Glenda Ford and Neville James, together with the two proprietors, Howard and Marjorie Jones, were busy setting out items of exquisite taste on trays covered in deep blue velvet. They intended to show the merchandise off in its best possible light for their royal visitors.

"Only the best, please, everybody. I think five trays of diamonds, sapphires on gold or platinum should do the trick, if they are true to form." Jones smiled encouragingly at Lucy. "No need to be so excited, Lucy, he will be just another customer," he lied, trying to sound very cool about it.

Lucy Barber smiled back shyly. Although having been at Jones' for just three months, she had proved to be a willing, capable sales assistant and a valuable asset to the business. She was twenty-two years of age, five feet four inches in height, with a perfect figure. Her well-groomed hair was naturally dark black, offsetting her gorgeous dark brown eyes set under heavily mascaraed lashes, which brought the gentlemen in by their droves. She was also intelligent; whilst the men stared, mesmerised, she could carry out a lively and interesting conversation with them.

Glenda Ford, on the other hand, had been with the jewellers before Jones and his wife had bought the business, some four years previously, and they had accepted her as part of the package. She was forty-two years of age, starting to lose her figure in middle age, and did just enough to her appearance to pass as 'fairly smart'. Glenda pushed greying mousey coloured hair from her eyes as she handed Lucy the tray of gems she had been carrying. It would be Lucy and Mr Jones, watched over by Marjorie, who would present the pick of the bunch to any royalty.

Marjorie looked on the trays with pleasure and wondered what kind of outfit she would buy. She might even stretch to a nice piece of jewellery for herself.

Marjorie was in her early forties and still a very attractive woman. She kept herself in trim by weekly workouts at the local gym, visited the hairdressers at least once a week to have her hair revitalised in her favoured golden chestnut colour, and had her clothes specially tailored.

After twenty years of marriage, Mr Jones was still very smitten with his wife, and was determined to keep up with her by visiting the squash court at least twice a week. A distinguished-looking, middle-class man of fifty two years, his hair, although still full, was now grey at the sides, giving his light brown hair a 'salt and pepper' appearance. Trim and dapper, at five foot ten inches, he weighed about ten and a half stone.

He looked around the shop with admiring satisfaction at the appearance of the display cases and that of his staff around him. Jones caught the satisfied light in the eyes of his wife and beamed back at her.

"Neville," Jones addressed the male assistant. "Can you bring the tray containing the necklaces when they get here, please?"

"Of course, Mr Jones. It will be an absolute pleasure," the effeminate voice of Neville answered as he appeared at Jones's elbow. Neville had been with them for almost two years, and in his own way, had proven to be an asset to the business, dealing with gentlemen of a certain persuasion who Mr Jones, himself, found difficult to serve. Neville was of a very slight build, probably only weighing around seven and a half stone.

He wore clothes which fitted like a glove and Jones often wondered how he managed to get in and out of them. Neville was always willing to serve and got on well with the female staff, who seemed to accept him as one of their own.

Knowing how offended the Arabs could be, if they suspected someone serving them was a homosexual, Jones was keeping Neville at the back just to hand the trays to Lucy or him to present. Everything was ready for their distinguished shoppers' arrival, so they tried to busy themselves as they waited.

Jones looked up at the clock over the counter behind him. It showed eight o'clock precisely.

"Unlock the door please, Neville. Let's show the world Jones the Jeweller is ready for business."

Neville unlocked the bolts at the top and bottom of the door, turned the key in the lock, removed it and lastly, turned the sign showing OPEN, to the outside of the glass. He peered out into the street, which was showing a sluggish start to the day, quite unlike a weekday when the traffic would already be jammed down to the traffic lights at the junction.

The gleaming, highly polished, dark blue Bentley, with its yellow hazard lights flashing, glided to a halt and parked on the double yellow lines right outside the shop.

An Arab, dressed in flowing white robes, got out from the front passenger door, went to the rear and waited, whilst another large Arab came round the back of the vehicle.

The large Arab made sure there was nothing to threaten them and blocked the pavement, whilst the first Arab opened the rear passenger door. He bowed his head as the occupant seemed to flow out on to the pavement.

"Your Royal Highness," he said to the impressive and elegant figure, dressed in white robes edged with gold braid. They moved to the shop door, with the large Arab bringing up the rear.

The European chauffeur, smartly dressed in a grey uniform with a shiny black peaked cap, remained firmly seated behind the wheel.

Lucy Barber, looking outside, saw the occupants emerging from the gleaming vehicle and panicked.

"Mr Jones," she shouted. "Mr Jones, come quickly."

Mr Jones, alarmed by the urgency of the call, made an appearance immediately from a small cubicle just behind the solid, highly-polished walnut counter.

"What on earth is it, Lucy?" he anxiously asked, as his wife Marjorie joined him from the rear of the shop.

"I think it's the expected royalty, Mr Jones. They're at the door," Lucy answered excitedly.

Howard Jones panicked, his heart going into his mouth. "Don't panic, Lucy, everyone keep calm, it's just another customer." he said unconvincingly, trying to be very suave as the leading Arab started to open the door.

The Arabs stepped inside the shop and closed the door behind them. The leading Arab went to the counter, whilst the prince stood back.

"Mr Howard Jones?" he asked, looking directly at a beaming Howard.

Howard and his wife were impressed. He had addressed Mr Jones personally, even using his Christian name for the second time.

"How can I help you, sir?" he asked politely, with a slight bow of his head.

"As I said on the telephone, Mr Jones, His Highness does not want any fuss. He merely wants to select a few trinkets for his new bride. Nothing too ostentatious. Some items in the region of, say, a hundred to two hundred and fifty thousand pounds should suffice." The Arab spoke in a clipped voice, not quite able to sound the vowels of crisply spoken English. Typical foreigner, thought Jones.

"Of course, sir. We at Jones the Jeweller are very professional. What type of items is the Prince interested in viewing?" Howard smiled at his wife with an, 'it's going to be a very good day,' smile.

"If you set out a selection of rings, diamond, sapphire, that type of thing, set in gold or platinum. The Prince would also like to see any necklaces that you think would be of interest to him," he answered, turning to the Prince for confirmation.

The Prince nodded curtly his agreement.

"We would like a very private viewing please, Mr Jones." He turned and signalled with his hand to the large Arab standing with the Prince, who immediately moved to the door and turned the sign round.

"Is there a room or cubicle where the Prince can view the items with some privacy please, Mr Jones?" he requested politely.

"Of course. We have two cubicles where we can bring items to His Highness. If you would kindly follow me, please." Jones and his wife led the way, past the glass cases housing beautiful pieces of jewellery and watches, to one of the showing cubicles. They both stood outside the open cubicle and allowed the Arabs to enter.

"Please be seated, Your Highness, and I will have a selection of our best items brought to you."

When the Prince sat down, Jones left the cubicle, pulling the blue velvet privacy curtain across the entrance as he and his wife scurried off to collect the trays which they had prepared earlier. Five trays consisting of rings, brooches and necklaces had been selected. Jones reverently selected the best tray and waited as his wife, followed by Lucy and the other two assistants, picked up the others and fell in behind him. They marched in procession to the showing cubicle.

Mr Jones, tray in one hand, reached for the velvet curtain with the other and pulled it back to receive the biggest shock of his life. The pleasant smile on his face faded quickly as his eyes travelled down from the Arab's face to what was in his hands.

"Come on in, Jones. Don't say a fucking word." The voice was menacing and cold as the man, still with his Arab headdress on, took the tray from him whilst levelling a sawn off shotgun at his face.

The other two Arabs now reverted to crude London accents. They stepped outside of the cubicle, pointing their handguns at the rest of them.

"Shut up, behave and you won't get hurt," the leading Arab snarled. He had been so polite when he had first entered the shop. Moving quickly behind a shaking Neville he relieved him of the tray he was carrying. He clubbed him hard to the right side of his head with the butt of the gun. There was a loud sickening crack as the butt struck bone and poor effeminate, harmless Neville, slumped instantly to the shop floor.

Lucy and Glenda, terrorised, started to scream.

"Shut the fuck up, you little bitches," the distorted, twisted features of the robber screamed into their faces.

They stopped and froze immediately. Even in their terror they knew that if they didn't, the same fate or worse, would happen to them.

Marjorie was horrified and stunned. Numbed, she slowly and silently slid behind the mahogany counter, unnoticed by Neville's attacker, who was busy threatening the girls. She edged slowly towards the alarm button, just as the robber noticed her.

"Come back here, you old slag, or I'll let you have it."

Unfortunately for the terrified Marjorie, she wasn't thinking very clearly. Through her abject fear she ignored him and slammed the alarm button, setting in motion some very tragic events. The robber moved like lighting as the siren inside and outside of the shop sounded, hitting and hurting their ear drums. He reached her before she could move. She looked up at him with terrified wide eyes as his evil contorted face sneered down at her.

Marjorie opened her mouth to scream, but it had only just started to form in her throat, as he slammed the barrel of the pistol down across her horrified face, opening a gash down through her right eye and splitting her nose wide open. Mercifully, she fell slowly and silently to the floor behind the counter where she lay unconscious.

A horrified Howard saw what happened. His love and natural feeling for the defence of his wife rushed to the fore.

Howard lost all sense of reason and exploded. Screaming his wife's name at the top of his voice, he rushed forward, pushing past the surprised second robber, going straight for his wife's assailant. His hands reached out and grabbed the man's throat, tearing with as much might as he could muster. The robber was taken by surprise at this diminutive little man who started to choke him with such vehemence; it was the robber's turn to panic.

The 'Prince' and the other robber rushed forward to help, but they were suddenly halted in their tracks at the sound of the gun going off.

Mrs Jones' assailant had panicked. He had thrust the gun into Jones' stomach and pulled the trigger. Howard reacted as if he had been viciously punched by a giant. He lurched back, violently grabbing at his stomach before slowly slumping to the floor against a display case in front of the other two robbers. The glass case shattered as his head involuntarily shot back into it. He grimaced with the pain as the white shirt at his midriff immediately showed blood oozing freely from the fatal wound, as his life started to slip away. No amount of threats could stop the ensuing screams from Lucy and Glenda, which sounded above the deafening alarm.

The 'Prince' couldn't believe what was happening. A small little man, who they could have dealt with quite easily, now lay dying in front of him.

"For fucks sake, Treaders, what did you have to fire for? You stupid, stupid moron," the robber screamed.

"The bastard's shot me as well," the third robber groaned, as he held his hip. The bullet, fired at such close range, had travelled through the hapless Howard Jones and struck the robber, who was behind him.

"I had no fucking choice," Treadwell choked back at him, holding his throat. "She pressed the alarm and he wouldn't fucking let go of me." He looked around him in panic. "We've got to get out of here, and quick." He grabbed the tray of jewels he had put on the counter, and emptied the contents into a black sack he had been concealing under his white robes.

"No fucking choice? You fucking, low-life bastard." The 'Prince' was going red with rage as he levelled his shotgun at Treaders' stomach.

He turned to his injured companion. "How bad are you, Chalky? Can you manage?" the 'Prince' asked, hoping for the best.

Chalky tried a step. He managed to move, although he could feel the blood trickling down his leg. "I'll be okay if we can move out now, boss," he muttered through gritted teeth.

"Grab what you can and let's get out of here now," shouted the 'Prince'. "I'll be talking with you later, you witless bastard. You've managed to get us a fucking murder charge," he snarled threateningly at Treaders, as he lowered his gun.

The three of them grabbed what they could from the trays as they moved towards the exit, stuffing the contents into the black sacks they had been carrying. They exited the shop with Chalky trailing blood from his right leg, knocked over an elderly man on their way, and ran to the Bentley where the doors were already open.

They jumped inside, as amazed and stunned by-standers watched the almost comical flight of three Arabs, with their robes flapping round their knees, as they fled the scene. The vehicle was away before the doors had closed, causing the passenger door to smash into a street lamp on the kerb.

As the Bentley roared off down the street, the first police car, with its siren blaring, came screaming round the junction at the traffic lights. It went to pull up outside the jewellers but the old man, who had been so roughly bowled over by the robbers, pointed excitedly up the street at the fleeing car.

"Three Arabs in the Bentley," he shouted. "Go on, after them."

The police officer did not hesitate and flew up the road, overtaking the morning traffic. Cars up ahead saw the lights flashing and got well into the side or mounted the pavement to make way.

The Bentley careered dangerously down the road as the getaway driver lurched from right to left, weaving in and out of the traffic. He scraped down the side of a white van before bouncing off. The speeds they were now reaching became very dangerous as he suddenly braked, and then slammed down on the accelerator once again to overtake a vehicle, but it wasn't long before the police car was on its tail.

The driver made a series of turns up and down different streets, before finding himself behind two motorcyclists who were going in the same direction and abreast of one another. The Bentley sounded its horn, but they were either oblivious to the warning or were totally ignoring him. He went to move out to pass them, just as a lorry pulled out from its parking place a hundred yards ahead on the opposite side of the road and headed towards him.

Looking in his mirror, he saw the police car weaving in and out of traffic, gaining on them second by second. The driver cursed as he braked, and was forced back in behind the motorbikes. He pressed his hand hard down on the horn and held it there. The bikers saw the Bentley in their mirrors and in unison both lifted their right hands in the air, putting up two fingers at this arrogant toff behind. They failed to notice the flashing blue lights of the pursuing police car.

"Well, fuck you two bastards," the driver yelled, more to himself than at them, as he slammed his foot hard down to the floor. The automatic transmission of the Bentley's powerful engine screamed and responded as it leapt forward, sweeping the two cyclists in front of it. The impact forced them both from their seats and propelled them through the air like a couple of trapeze artists. They smashed head first through the front window of a furniture store, showering the plate glass onto the furnishings inside. An astonished salesman inside the shop covered his face, as the impact sent him flying backwards over the back of a settee.

The two motorbikes were pushed violently to the Bentley's offside, and into the path of the oncoming lorry, who couldn't avoid hitting and running over them.

All the traffic in both directions suddenly braked and came to a standstill.

The chase was over for the pursuing police car, which had to pull up sharply.

A police constable got out of his vehicle, and as he ran to help the stricken bikers he shouted into his radio, "Ambulance required control, two victims of a hit and run. The Bentley is continuing west at high speed with three Arab occupants."

The driver looked into his rear-view mirror and grinned. "Now to lose this vehicle," he said out loud, without a care or thought for the fate of the motor cyclists. They travelled on for another mile, cutting in and out of traffic and up and down various streets until they came to a multi-storey car park. The Bentley pulled hard over, entering the car park and driving down to the basement.

They started to strip off their Arab attire, revealing ordinary clothing underneath.

"What do we do with this lot, Boss?" Treadwell asked, looking at the pile of discarded clothing in the back of the vehicle.

"What do you suggest we do with it, you fucking moron? We have left a trail of DNA, thanks to you shooting Chalky here. No matter what we try to cover up now we are fucking sunk," the 'Prince' snarled at him. "Let's get the hell out of here. We'll decide what to do later. Can you move alright, Chalky?" he asked hopefully.

Chalky, in the rear of the vehicle, looked pale. It was obvious he was losing a lot of blood. "I feel a bit weak, Brian. I think I'm going to need patching up," he said to the 'Prince', using his real name.

Brian Payne got out, went to the back, opened the door and looked down at Chalky. "Oh, for crying out fucking loud," he said under his breath. "You'll be okay, Chalky, we'll get it sorted."

He turned to the driver, who had now joined him. "The vehicle up in the corner, the green Ford Focus, the keys are behind the driver's visor. Get it fast."

He turned to Treadwell with murder in his eyes. "No more slip ups, Treadwell, or you're dead."

Treadwell, as big as he was, didn't dare react or say a word.

The driver ran off to the corner of the basement, located the unlocked green car, found the keys at the back of the visor and drove round to the front of the Bentley.

Brian helped Chalky out of the back seat and steadied him, whilst Treadwell opened the rear passenger door and lowered him gently in.

"Have you left any evidence in either vehicle?" Brian asked the driver.

"No, boss. I'm wearing gloves and I shall burn the uniform," he answered.

"I'm afraid we're sunk. Chalky's DNA will be all over the fucking jeweller's floor and the pavement, thanks to Treadwell, but there's nothing to tie you in with us. I'll make sure I deposit your share in the usual box. I suggest you get lost." Brian Payne looked grim, but resigned to his fate. "I'll drive and drop you off."

The driver looked at the determined face of Brian and put out his gloved hand. They shook firmly as the driver said, "It's been a pleasure working for you, boss, and thanks."

Back at Jones the Jeweller, marked police cars, with sirens blaring and their blue light flashing, screeched to a halt outside the shop. Before the leading driver could get out, further vehicles pulled up noisily alongside and behind it. Uniformed police officers scrambled out of their vehicles and made for the entrance.

PC John Harper was first through the door. He observed the scene, seeing Lucy and the other female assistant cowering and trembling with fear. Just behind them, slumped between the counter and the display cases, he saw the unconscious, disfigured face of Marjorie Jones. His gaze went past the blood around her head to the body slumped against the back case with its eyes half closed looking down between its legs. PC Harper knew instantly that this was now a murder scene.

"Stay out," he shouted to the officers following him. They all stopped abruptly, looking at PC Harper for an explanation. "This is now a murder scene," he explained firmly. He went to the cowering Lucy and Glenda, gently took them by their arms and lifted them slowly to their feet.

"I want you both to come with me," he said softly, feeling the terror trembling through their bodies. He led them gently but firmly to the entrance of the shop, where they were handed over to the waiting officers.

"Take them to the nick and radio for the medical officer to attend, and then you had better contact the Murder Squad. Has anyone called for an ambulance?" he called out.

"On its way," a voice from the back called out. "Should only be a couple more minutes."

The two girls had just been taken away when the ambulance turned up, with its siren blaring and lights flashing.

PC Harper went back inside to make sure the medics did not contaminate 'his' murder scene as they removed the badly injured Marjorie Jones. Looking up at the CCTV cameras that overlooked the front door and the three shop counters, he went in search of the recorder, finding it in the back office with a television monitor. He checked the machine, opened the disc compartment, removed the disc and placed it in an envelope that was in the tray on the desk.

PC Harper sealed the envelope, looked at his watch, entered the time and date on the envelope and signed across the seal.

THREE

Detective Chief Inspector Jacks was sitting in the doctor's surgery when he received the call on his mobile.

As the phone vibrated and rang, faces turned, looked at him and then pointedly looked at the sign on each wall, 'PLEASE TURN OFF ALL MOBILES,' in large letters. His pretty wife, Leanne, sitting by his side, eyed him with disapproval and pointed to the door.

"Yes, love, I'll take it outside," he whispered to her, as he got up and made for the door.

"Jacks," he said, as he opened up his phone and listened to the voice of Detective Sergeant King on the other end. "How bad?" he asked, after listening to the message. "Okay, Mike, get me picked up at the surgery. Leanne can take my car and make her own way home." He waited for the answer and then said, "Yes, I'm sure, now step on it."

He closed the phone down. "Damn," he cursed to himself, placing it back inside the pocket of his brown leather jacket.

Jacks re-joined his wife inside the surgery. He sat down sheepishly beside her.

"If you have to go, then go," she said, without him having said a word. "Absence makes the heart grow fonder," she quoted as she smiled at him.

"The full quotation is 'absence makes the heart grow fonder. Isle of beauty, fare thee well,' by TH Bayley. He was saying goodbye to an island that he loved," he added with a wink.

Leanne was also a serving police officer, but in a different division. They had married whilst both were in the force, and they both accepted the call on their time from their chosen professions. Leanne was twenty-eight years of age, small and petite with blue eyes, her blonde hair tied back in a pony tail that bobbed rhythmically to the side of her neck as she walked. When Jacks walked behind her he always got the impression he was following a true thoroughbred filly. She was a big hit in the force, and he had to fight very hard to woo her from the clutches of his lecherous colleagues.

Jacks, in contrast, was six-feet one inch tall, and built like a super middleweight boxer. His dark brown hair, for the most part, looked fairly unkempt, reaching down over his collar and falling over his right eye at the front. The eyebrow above that eye had a deep scar running the length of it. His features were rugged, most moulded by his days of boxing and playing rugby, but he was still considered by the ladies as quite handsome and seemed to attract their attention wherever he went.

"Are you sure, love?" he asked, smiling down at her with his 'come to bed' smouldering dark brown eyes whilst handing her the car keys.

Leanne smiled patiently; she couldn't resist him when he smiled at her like that. "Bugger off, Jacks. Call me later if you get the time." Like everybody she still called him by his surname, his trademark, so to speak.

Jacks stood up, leant over his pretty, understanding wife and kissed her full on the mouth.

"Mmmm," she sighed. "Are you sure you have to go?"

Jacks smiled, looking round boyishly at the other patients, who appeared very interested in what was being said, and squeezed her hand. "Absence makes… I'll see you later, young lady," he whispered down at her, as he made for the door.

He waited on the road at the surgery's entrance, amongst the smokers trying to hide their habit from their doctors. The unmarked car pulled up at the kerb.

Jacks opened the front passenger door and climbed in, surprised to see the smiling face of Mike King in the driver's seat.

"I thought you would have gone straight to the scene, Mike!" Jacks queried. "Where's Bobby McQueen?"

"On his way to the scene, Guv. Robert Ludgate's holding the fort until we get there," Mike explained in his southern accent.

"DI Ludgate?" Jacks queried. "What's the Crime Squad doing on my patch?" he asked.

"It was a jewellery job gone badly wrong, Governor. Ludgate and his team have been after them for some months."

"Well I'm afraid he's going to have to take a back seat on this one, Mike. Murder trumps robbery every time."

"He's well aware of that, Guv; he knows he's just keeping things warm until you get there," Mike assured him, as he turned the blues on and put his foot down.

They were about five minutes away from the jewellers when news of the Bentley's escape came over the radio, also telling of a possible two motor cyclist fatalities.

"Bloody low life bastards," Mike cursed. "This lot don't care who they hurt."

DI Jacks, dressed in white overalls to preserve forensics and prevent contamination of the crime scene, entered the jewellery shop, carefully taking in the scene before him. No smashed display cases that he could see, no disorder at all really. He was expecting the place to be in a mess.

DI Ludgate, smiling grimly, came out of the side cubicle with Detective Sergeant Bobby McQueen, and greeted him with an outstretched hand.

"Hello, Jacks. I've secured the scene for you. There are four witnesses: the victim's wife, a male assistant, both who have gone to hospital with their injuries, and two young female assistants who have been taken to the nick for statements." Before Jacks could respond, he added, "By the way, PC Harper had the good sense to stop all and sundry from spoiling the scene, and even supervised the medics who took Mrs Jones to hospital. He also bagged his own shoes for you."

Jacks took it all in. "How bad is she?" Jacks asked.

"Pretty bad. She's going to be disfigured, but at least she's alive."

"Thanks, Robert. Do you know the gang responsible?"

"I think it's the bastards who are responsible for jewellery robberies all across London and the south of England. No names as yet, but we do have some in the frame," Ludgate offered hopefully.

Jacks knew DI Ludgate well, a good competent officer but lacking in originality and imagination. He didn't hold his breath at getting anything too helpful from him.

"You had better let me have those, and your thoughts on this, Robert. Let's have a look at what we've got here." Jacks moved round the mahogany counter and viewed the crumpled body of poor Howard Jones, slumped against a shattered display case in a pool of darkening blood. He spotted the various footprints in the blood.

"I think forensics had better have their go at this before anything else," he stated flatly. "What nick have the witnesses been taken to?"

The young police constable on the door interrupted, "Bromley, sir. The two shop assistants went to Bromley, the male and the proprietor's wife to hospital under guard."

Jacks looked up and noticed the CCTV cameras, "Anyone secured those?" he asked.

"I have, sir. Sealed, dated, timed, and signed," the constable replied.

"I take it you're PC Harper," Jacks responded, as he looked down at the young officer's white trainers. "Well done on securing the scene, Harper. I shall want to talk to you further."

"Thank you, sir, yes, sir." Harper replied sheepishly as he followed Jacks' eyes down to his replacement footwear.

***

An hour later, Jacks, King and McQueen arrived at Bromley Police Station. They booked and signed in with the police constable on the front desk, who immediately got on the phone to his sergeant, saying quietly, "Sarge, we've got the 'full house' at the front desk."

The three detectives were well known and often referred to in terms associated with playing cards.

The constable showed them to a small office at the rear of the station. Jacks waited impatiently, repeatedly tapping the desk with his pen, until Lucy Carpenter was shown in. Jacks and King stood up as she was led by her elbow to the desk by a female officer, whilst Bobby McQueen stayed on the door.

Lucy looked ghastly; her face was drawn and haggard, nothing like the vibrant young twenty-two year old of a few short hours before. She sat down in the chair that Mike King gallantly pulled back for her and looked down at the table in front as if in a trance.

"Hello, Lucy. I'm Chief Inspector Jacks and this is Detective Sergeant King," he started, feeling sorry for this wretched figure in front of him. There was no recognition of any sort. Jacks continued softly, "Lucy, I know you have had a great shock but it is necessary, no it's vital, that I ask you some questions. Is that OK?"

Lucy Carpenter nodded obediently without looking up. Jacks waited as she gradually raised her face to stare at him with haunted eyes.

"Yes, it's okay," she answered quietly.

"Thank you, Lucy. Is there anything I can get you first?" Jacks asked patiently with a sympathetic smile as he waited for her answer.

"Thank you, no, Inspector," she uttered finally.

"Call me Jacks, please, Lucy," he insisted gently. "Now I know this is going to be unpleasant, to say the least, but I need you to cast your mind back and remember all you can of what you saw and heard at the time of the robbery." Jacks waited, letting what he had said sink in. "Can you do that for me, Lucy?" he urged.

"Yes, I think so," she answered, fidgeting on her seat.

"Tell me what you saw when the robbers first arrived, Lucy. What kind of vehicle did they arrive in?"

Mike quietly took his notebook out and prepared to take down notes, as Jacks proceeded with his questioning.

"It was a dark blue Rolls Royce," she started, making the common mistake of getting a Bentley mixed up with a Rolls Royce. "A large saloon. A man dressed in Arab robes got out and bowed to the occupant in the back." Lucy was recounting what she saw in a dreamlike way. "When they got into the shop, he referred to his passenger as 'Prince'. Mr Jones, my boss, although he told us to keep calm, was very excited at the prospect of serving royalty and ushered the three men to a showing cubicle."

"How many men, altogether, Lucy?" Jacks pushed.

"Three," she answered quietly. "The prince and another man who had been sitting in the back and the one at the front. No, I think there were four, if you count the driver."

"What happened next, Lucy?" he asked.

"We took trays of samples, led by Mr Jones and his wife, to the cubicle, but when Mr Jones pulled back the privacy curtain they were waiting for him with a shotgun." Lucy looked back down at the desk in front of her. "It was horrible, Inspector, really horrible. One of the men went after Mrs Jones, who had gone behind the counter. He warned her to get back, Mr Jacks, he warned her but she kept going and pressed the alarm."

Her shoulders started to jerk as she fought to stay in control. When she looked up at Jacks, tears were streaming down her ashen face. "He went over to her and struck her viciously, cutting her face open. Poor Mr Jones went mad, nothing was going to stop him and he attacked the robber. He sounded like a wild animal as he grabbed the robber's throat, trying to strangle him. All of a sudden I heard a loud bang and Mr Jones was thrown backwards, holding his stomach."

Lucy was shaking badly.

"Would you like to stop for a while, Lucy, or can you carry on?" Jacks asked sympathetically, concerned at her obvious distress.

"I can carry on, Mr Jacks. I want to tell you what happened," she replied bravely. "The so called 'Prince' came over quickly and he said, 'What did you fire for, Treaders?' He said 'Treaders'. He referred to him by name," she said triumphantly.

Mike King scribbled on his pad, tore it off and slipped in it front of his boss.

Jacks picked it up and glanced at it. He nodded at Mike before continuing, "Did you hear anything else, Lucy?"

"The man behind Mr Jones at the time he was shot groaned, and said he'd been shot and was holding his hip. The man they referred to as 'Prince' asked him if he was okay and called him Chalky."

"What about the so called 'Prince', Lucy? Did you get a good look at him at all?" Jacks would have liked a name but would settle for a description.

"I didn't see his face properly, he had one of those headdresses on that Arabs wear, you know, like you see on

Arab sheiks in the films." Lucy was starting to cry; she tried stifling her sobs with her handkerchief.

"Good girl, and thank you, Lucy. I think it best that we stop right now and rest for a while I'll have someone take your statement later." Jacks nodded to the WPC, who came forward and gently took Lucy's arm, who rose from her chair and was led obediently out of the office.

As soon as the door closed, an excited Mike burst out, "We've got 'em, Guv. It has to be Gerry Treadwell, 'Chalky' Grahame White and... the Prince has to be Brian Payne. What a bloody coup."

"We've got 'em, Guv," Jacks mimicked his sergeant. "You're forgetting, your coup involves the bloody murder of the jeweller, Mike. No celebration in that, is there?" Jacks reprimanded sternly. He was the same at post mortems when those present came out with their black humour. 'There is no humour in death,' he would say, as he scolded them all.

"I know that, Guv, but all the same, a murder and about thirty odd robberies will be cleared up. I call that a result," Mike said, unapologetically.

Bobby McQueen came forward and sat down where Lucy had been sitting. "If it is Brian Payne we are going to have to move quickly, Guv. He won't hang about. We'll be lucky to find Treadwell alive. Payne won't like the murder implication he's been landed with. He's a violent bastard, but always knows where to stop and where to draw the line," he added ruefully in his Hampshire accent.

Bobby had joined his squad from the Hampshire Constabulary because he liked the London life. A rugby full-back who had trials for Scotland, because of his Scottish parents, he didn't take prisoners or suffer fools gladly.

Jacks had been searching for another detective sergeant since Ray Harris had retired due to injury on duty. Bobby McQueen was a worthy replacement; Jacks' gain was Hampshire's loss.

"Dig out the files on all three of them. I want present addresses, past addresses and all known acquaintances. Bobby, get round to Payne's last address. If you're lucky lift him, if there are others there lift them as well, and don't take any nonsense from anyone or any unnecessary risks. Draw firearms for all those qualified." Jacks turned to Mike. "Get hold of Robert Ludgate, I think he's about somewhere. I'll be in the Super's office upstairs."

Jacks made his way up the stairs and turned right along the landing. He stopped at the second door and tapped it with his knuckle, just to the right of the sign saying, 'Chief Supt. Campbell'.

"Enter," the Scottish voice commanded from inside.

Jacks entered to see his old pal, 'Jock' Bertram Campbell, sitting behind a desk in the middle of the large office. He was completely surrounded by paperwork.

"Come on in, Jacks, don't stand on ceremony, and sit ye-self down, man."

Jacks went over to the comfortable seat slightly to the side of the desk and sank down into the plush fabric, smoothing the sides of the arms. "Not bad, sir, not bad at all."

Jock Campbell, smiling broadly, leant over his desk as they shook hands. "How can I help, old mate?" he asked, almost knowing what Jacks wanted.

"I need an incident room, sir. It shouldn't be for too long, we have three pieces of scum in the frame for this. I also need my qualified boys to draw firearms. Can you authorise, please?"

"You can leave the bloody 'sir' out. Who are they?" Campbell asked.

"Brian Payne, Gerry Treadwell and Grahame White. I think you know Payne from old, Jock," Jacks ventured.

"If it is Payne, your boys should not only be tooled up but also go in with the Firearms Unit, Jacks."

"No time, Jock, Bobby McQueen's getting a team together and I'm hoping Robert Ludgate and his team will lend a hand, they're about here somewhere. Besides, I don't think we are going to find them in residence," Jacks confided.

"Okay, a bit like old times, eh! Take what you need, just mention my name if anyone objects. I'll ring down and authorise the issue of firearms." As Campbell finished speaking there was a knock on the door.

"Enter," he called out as the door opened and Robert Ludgate walked in. "Hello, Robert. I am hoping you can lend a hand here," Jock started.

"DS King filled me in, sir. Payne and his men were high on our list of the usual suspects, so no surprises there. I have my men assembled downstairs, so just say the word."

"Then go, Robert, don't hang about here," Campbell ordered with a grin.

"At the double, sir. My Crime Squad will be armed," Ludgate chipped in as he left the room.

As he left, Campbell turned to Jacks. "Use the office next door. The inspector is on leave at the moment. I'll also make the adjacent office available to you."

Jacks got up. "Thank you, Jock. I appreciate the expediency." He turned and went out to the office next door, but quickly popped his head back in. "You have an excellent young PC by the name of John Harper. Can you organise that I see him? He did very well at the crime scene for us."

"I'll see to it, but no bloody poaching, Jacks. By the way, how's the lovely Leanne?" Campbell asked, remembering the vision of loveliness the whole of the Metropolitan Police adored and coveted.

"Oh, for bloody Christ's sake," Jacks swore. "I've completely forgotten about her." He rushed out, back to the other office, as Chief Superintendent Campbell was left to scratch his head.

He flipped open his mobile phone, pushed one button on speed dial, and waited for her to answer.

"Hello, Jacks, busy day?" Leanne's voice answered.

"I am so, so sorry, Leanne. I've managed to get bogged down in Bromley," he apologised.

"I know, love, it's all over the news. Don't worry, we'll catch up as and when," said his understanding wife.

"What was the outcome at the Doc's?" Jacks remembered where he had left her before Mike King had called him away.

"Some more tests, I'm afraid. We'll talk about it when you get home, okay?"

Jacks thought about what she had said, but decided it was probably best to wait until he got home for further discussion on the subject.

"Are you sure, love?" he asked for reassurance.

"Back to work, Jacks. We'll speak later." Leanne rang off.

***

Bobby and his team, together with five members of the serious crime squad, all dressed with bullet-proof jackets and sporting dark blue baseball caps with police emblazoned on them, arrived at the smart address of Brian Payne. No blaring of sirens, unlike the television police programmes, they silently parked their cars as they sealed the building, back and front. They went up the stairs to the penthouse flat and waited outside the door. Not bothering to knock, and without any warning the door was unceremoniously smashed in.

Payne had been back and collected a few things. Bobby noticed the wall safe with its door wide open, Payne normally kept it locked behind a picture of a castle. It was empty, the man was running.

It was an hour and half later when Jacks received a message on his mobile from Bobby McQueen. No luck, they hadn't found anyone at their last known addresses.

In the meantime, Mike King and Jacks trawled through the known associates on the files of all three wanted men, until Jacks saw one name that stood out from the others; Jimmy 'the dip' Carter, on parole after serving four years of a seven year sentence.

"We need to put our thinking caps on for this one, Mike."

"Ludgate and his team have been after these boys for years, and he doesn't seem to have any idea," Mike answered.

"DI Ludgate puts me in mind of a quotation from Lord Bowen, 'A blind man in a dark room looking for a black hat which isn't there'. He's been looking at it from the wrong angle," Jacks smiled as he examined the files. "What do villains do with their ill-gotten gains, Mike?" he asked, raising his scarred eyebrow, which was turning slightly pink.

Mike had long since gotten used to Jacks quoting something or other, but recognised the signs and knew his governor was on to something.

"Fence," he stated simply.

"Who goes to a fence, Mike?" Jacks had a smile on his face. "Who goes to a fence with expensive jewellery and suchlike?"

"You've got an idea, Guv, haven't you?" Mike watched Jacks look down at the list of acquaintances and known accomplices on Brian Payne's file picked out from the three files in front of him.

"It's not just the big villains who lift precious things is it, Mike?" He tapped the file in front of him and then kept his finger under a name. "Jimmy 'the dip' Carter, one of the most successful pickpockets going. He was sent down last time for stealing a Cartier necklace off the neck of a rich Russian woman, valued at almost a quarter of a million pounds. What's more, he's on parole. Get Bobby when he comes back, and DC Arnold who knows the little creep well. Go and lift Carter, and bring him back here."

"What's he done, guv?" Mike asked stupidly, without realising what he was saying.

Jacks exploded. "I don't bloody care," he shouted. "Tell him he's been seen blowing his nose in public. He's on parole, he must have violated it ten times over by now. Just bring him in." Jacks was irritated, and as DS King made for the door he shouted after him, "And don't forget to search his gaffe."

***

Jimmy 'the dip' Carter was sitting in the interview room, nursing a deep red welt under his right eye which was already showing signs of deepening. He was flanked by Detective Sergeants King and McQueen, and wondering what Detective Chief Inspector Jacks of the Murder Squad wanted with him so urgently.

He was very nervous; he'd seen Jacks in action a couple of times. Once in the ring at the Thomas A Becket pub in the Old Kent Road, when he had given a local villain, who was tempted to take the opportunity to wreak revenge on the police, get the biggest hiding of his life. The other time was when he was witness to a bodged robbery when Jacks, King and McQueen routed and arrested the four armed blaggers on their own.

Three days growth covered his small pointed chin as he stared through nervous, beady little eyes, at the two way mirror on the wall. Was Jacks watching him? What the hell did he want?

He jumped at the sound of the door opening and his heart sank as he saw his nemesis, armed with files, enter the room and make for the chair opposite. Jimmy Carter felt like the proverbial sacrificial lamb. All of a sudden he had the strongest urge to go to the toilet.

"What's this about, Mr Jacks?" he asked, crossing his legs tight and watching nervously as Jacks placed the files on the table.

Jacks swept back the hair hanging over his right eye. He looked down at Jimmy before pulling out the chair and sitting down directly opposite.

It was then that he noticed the discolouring right eye that seemed to be closing by the second. He looked at Bobby, who turned away sheepishly. He looked anywhere other than at Jacks, as Mike looked on with a knowing grin.

"Who asked you to talk, Jimmy?" Jacks responded curtly, turning his attention back to him. "Speak when you are spoken to, do you understand?"

"I'm sorry, Mr Jacks, it won't happen again," he said with half a smile, which died on his thin face as Jacks stared at him across the table. As Jimmy looked into the hard black eyes opposite he gave an involuntary shudder, immediately lowering his eyes to look at the table in front of him.

Jacks examined the contents of Jimmy's pockets, laid out on the table in front of him, poking them about with his pen as if they were diseased.

"You're on parole, Jimmy. Three or four more years to go," he stated menacingly, as he turned the items over. He picked up the mobile phone and tried to turn it on. It was locked. "Unlock it," he demanded. "Now."

"Come on, Mr Jacks, its private, ain't it?" he pleaded, as he received a swift dig in his ribs from Bobby McQueen, causing him to lean over sharply in pain. He let out a stifled whimper and waited expectantly for the next one.

Jacks handed him the phone. Jimmy obediently pushed his code in, unlocking it. He shakily handed it back to the outstretched hand, whilst holding his painful side.

"No more back chat, Jimmy, or you're going back inside," Jacks warned. "Get this to forensics, Mike, will you? I want all numbers traced, checked and verified." He turned back to Jimmy. "If there's one dodgy person on there, you are straight back in for your full term."

Jimmy thought for a minute and began to panic, as he remembered that part of parole was not to consort with known felons. He had dozens listed in his phone.

"All right, Mr Jacks, what do you want?" Jimmy asked, guarding his ribs from Bobby McQueen's elbow.

"I'll come straight to the point. It's about the jewellery raid and… murder… that happened early this morning." Jacks emphasised the word 'murder' for effect, and waited.

Jimmy's beady little eyes widened in surprise, his mouth dropped open. "Nah, Mr Jacks, I had nuffin' to do with that, nuffin' at all," he whined. "You can't pin this one on me," he pleaded.

"Calm down," Jacks butted in. "I know who the heavies are. What I want to know is the fence who is taking all this high class jewellery from them?"

Jimmy, still guarding his ribs, looked pleadingly at Jacks from across the table.

He could smell the fear on the little weasel but was determined to press home.

"Please, Mr Jacks, if you know those involved, you know I won't last two minutes out there if they think I squealed." He glanced furtively at Bobby McQueen, half expecting another dig.

Jacks held his hand up to stop Bobby striking again.

"Nobody need know, Jimmy," he assured him. "You tell us what we want to know, you can have your phone back and piss off out of here." Jacks got up, leant over the table and stared into the frightened little man's eyes.

"If you don't, and I'm not going to ask again, you are going straight from here to the cells, then back to the Scrubs, and… we will let Brian Payne think you have told us anyway." Jacks let it sink in for a second, and then screamed at him, "What's it going to be, you little fart?"

"Big Al," he screamed out in panic. "It's Big Al, he's your fence for all the jewellery robberies. Don't tell Payne it was me, Mr Jacks, please. I'll be dead for sure."

"Well done, Jimmy, I hope for your sake you're right and not having me on. You know what I'll do if you are, don't you?" Jacks threatened.

"I'm not having you on, Mr Jacks, 'onest I'm not. I wouldn't dare," he affirmed.

Jacks nodded to Bobby who got up, lifted Jimmy up by his elbow and led him to the door.

"Your lucky day, creep," McQueen smiled malevolently, as he opened the door to take him out.

"What about me bloody phone?" Jimmy asked urgently, looking back at Jacks.

"What bloody phone?" Bobby McQueen asked, as he removed him roughly from the premises.

***

"Can you get me a phone tap on Alan Childs, Jock?" They were back in the chief superintendent's office. The two of them had been detective sergeants together in the Surrey Constabulary, before they both transferred to the 'Met' more or less at the same time.

"You had better be sure, Jacks," the ever careful and meticulous Campbell said. "You know the hoops we have to go through these days."

"I'm sure. It is a bloody murder case after all," Jacks wanted to press home the urgency.

"I'll rouse a magistrate and get it done." Jock looked at Jacks who wondered what he was going to say next. "I never cease to be amazed at you," he said. "Why do you keep turning down promotion? There's going to come a time when it won't be offered, you do realise that, don't you?"

Jacks smiled patiently at him but didn't offer any explanation.

"I suggest you get yourself home; nothing's going to happen tonight. Your team can call you if there are any developments." Jock got up from his seat and guided Jacks to the door. "Now go home," he ordered. Jock knew his reasons, but could never understand why a rising star such as Jacks wanted to stay at the sharp end of investigations instead of climbing the greasy pole.

FOUR

Brian Payne drove the Ford Focus in through the broken meshed gates of the disused factory he often used for cover when he needed it. The industrial estate was half empty of tenants and had become very run down, which suited him fine.

He drove round the back of the building and parked outside a set of double doors, which had broken windows at the top. He got out at the same time as Treadwell exited from the back.

"How's Chalky?" he asked bluntly.

"Looks really bad. He's lost a lot of blood, Boss." Treadwell was now showing real concern, as Brian Payne came round the vehicle and helped him lift Chalky off the back seat.

"Let's get him inside where we can see just how bad," Payne ordered.

They carried Chalky through the doors of the disused building with his legs dragging along the ground, until they reached a bay that had once been used for loading vehicles. He stripped the jacket off the unconscious figure, ripping his trousers apart at the crotch where, in order to stem the flow of blood, they had stuffed gauze and padding found in the car's emergency medical kit. The dressings were soaked with the blood still oozing through the padding.

Payne felt his pulse, it was weak, barely noticeable and he feared the worst.

"Do we get him a doctor?" Treadwell asked, fearing if he died something might happen to him.

"Shut it, you moron, I think it's past that now." Payne looked deep in thought before saying, "I'll see if there are any more dressings in the car."

He went out of the door to the car and popped the boot. Lying on an old tartan rug was the sawn-off shotgun he had used in the robbery. He broke open the gun, checking there were cartridges in both barrels before snapping the gun shut again. He laid it on the tartan rug, rolled it up before tucking it under his arm and closing the boot.

Treadwell watched him approach and noticed the rug.

"No dressings, Boss?" he enquired, thinking he had brought the rug in to make Chalky more comfortable.

Payne lent over Chalky and checked his pulse, nothing, he was dead. He straightened up and the tartan rug unfurled. He let it drop to the filthy floor to reveal the shotgun in his right hand.

As Treadwell looked into Payne's eyes, he saw the loathing hatred and knew there was no way out for him.

"No, Boss, no," he pleaded, as he put his hands out in front of him. With desperation he looked for a way to escape, but was faced with the sides and back of the bay. He remembered the pistol inside his coat which he had shot the jeweller with, and desperately reached for it. It was a race he was never going to win.

"This is for Chalky, you bastard."

The shotgun went off, putting a hole through Treadwell's chest which sent him and his pistol flying to the back of the bay.

Payne moved forward and pointed the gun at the contorted face of the convulsing figure, squeezing the trigger once again. The whole of Treadwell's face seemed to vaporise, as blood and bone flew in all directions. No one would ever recognise the man again.

"And that's for the murder charge you've landed me with," Payne snarled, as he stepped over the grotesque, deformed body and retrieved the pistol lying by Treadwell's side.

**

At about the same time as Brian Payne drove away from the industrial estate, Jacks drove the unmarked Volvo police car into his drive, and parked alongside their private black Audi saloon. There was just enough room to park the two vehicles in front of their modest, three bedroom, semi-detached house. He looked up at the closed curtains of the bedroom that over looked the drive. The lights were on.

"Bit early for bed," he muttered to himself, as he put his keys in the door.

"Anyone home?" he called up the stairs, closing the front door behind him.

Leanne, fully dressed, appeared on the stairs and started to come down. "And where else would I be?" she asked. She reached the bottom stair, holding her arms open for the embrace.

Jacks never needed a second invitation; he put his arms round her and they kissed.

"Sorry about earlier, I couldn't get away and just forgot to phone you with everything going on." Jacks smiled into her bright blue eyes, knowing he would be forgiven. "Have you been lying down?" he asked, concerned about her.

"These stupid headaches make me feel a bit sick, but I'm okay now," she said, as she kissed him again.

"I could get used to this. What's for supper?"

"Bastard," Leanne chided. "Always thinking of your stomach."

"Seriously, love, what did the doctor have to say?" The smile had gone from Jacks' face, which now showed his concern and worry.

Leanne let go of him and made her way to the lounge with Jacks following. "I have to have more tests. Doctor Edwards says I'm as fit as a flea and can't see why I am having the problems."

"You're not pregnant, are, you?" he asked, out of the blue.

"No I'm not, you silly man. I don't think you've got a good one in you, Jacks," she laughed, prodding him in the ribs. "They are booking me in for some tests, such as brain scans at the General, but I can't see it happening for some weeks, knowing the National Health Service."

"But you feel okay, or do you want me to book you in somewhere privately? And don't call me silly man." This had become her favourite term when she disagreed with anything he was doing or saying.

Jacks really wanted her to see a specialist, but Leanne always came back and asked the question, 'Specialist for what, you silly man?' He supposed she was right, until they knew what it was they couldn't decide what course of action to take.

"I'm fine. How was your day, murder and robbery I'm told? How is the jeweller's wife?" Leanne was interested to hear how he was doing.

"Let's have some supper, love, and I'll tell you all about it."

The telephone by the bed rang twice before Jacks snatched up the hand set. He looked at Leanne sleeping quietly by his side, before looking at the bedside clock; it was seven o'clock. Pulling back the duvet on his side of the bed he got up with as little noise as possible.

"Jacks," he whispered into the mouthpiece as he went out of the bedroom, closing the door quietly behind him and standing naked on the landing by the stairs.

"Sorry to disturb you, Governor," Bobby McQueen's distinct Hampshire accent came over the earpiece. "We managed to get a wiretap on Alan Child's phone late last night, and bingo! Brian Payne rang him and they have arranged to meet later today. Big Al wasn't too pleased about him contacting him. He knows about the murder and that the heat is on."

"What time are they meeting?" Jacks asked bluntly.

"Between five and six tonight at a café. I'll let you have all the details when you come in. I've rung Mike and let him know as well."

"Well done, Bobby, we'll organise things when I get there. I'll be in about eight-thirty this morning. Make sure you contact the whole team, I want everyone available for this." Jacks heard the click as Bobby rang off, and went silently back to bed. He placed the handset quietly back on the rest.

"Haven't got to rush off then?" Leanne was wide awake as she watched her naked husband get back into bed.

"I'll make you some breakfast, love," he said to his yawning wife.

"You'll do no such thing, Jacks. I'll cook the breakfast while you get ready for work, no arguments," she insisted.

As he was finishing his breakfast the telephone in the hall rang. Leanne got to it before he could react and brought the phone to him.

"Mike King," she mouthed quietly.

Jacks took the phone from her. "Hello, Mike, what's up?"

"Two bodies found in a disused warehouse, Guv. They think it's White and what is left of Treadwell."

"Give me the address, Mike, I'll meet you there." Jacks replaced the phone. "I have to dash, love. Two more bodies have been found. Looks like the robbers have fallen out and someone's cleaning house."

Leanne brought his jacket and handed him the car keys. She kissed him long and hard before breaking off. "You be very careful on this one, Jacks, do you hear?"

"Loud and clear, love, don't you worry," he assured her.

It took Jacks an hour to fight his way through traffic with his blue lights flashing, before arriving at the disused warehouse on the edge of a rundown industrial estate. The area had been sealed off, with police positioned everywhere. Jacks had to show his warrant card before he was allowed through the police cordon. Mike King with Bobby McQueen were standing talking to a couple of police constables just outside of the building. He got out of the car and went towards them.

"Morning, Guv," Mike and Bobby said in unison, as the two constables saluted him.

"They're both inside. I think White bled out from the robbery, but Treadwell received shotgun wounds to his face and chest," Mike filled him in.

"Who found the bodies?" Jacks asked nobody in particular.

It was one of the uniform constables who answered. "I was flagged down as I was passing the unit on a routine call of a break-in farther down the estate, sir. A vagrant was looking for a place to crash when he came across them."

"And what's your name, Constable?" Jacks enquired.

"Police Constable Jenkins, sir," Jenkins saluted, and Jacks made a note of his name.

"We've had him taken to the local nick, Guv. He'll make a statement and get some breakfast," Bobby chipped in.

Jacks ducked under the police tape held high by Bobby, and followed him and Mike into the building. Forensics and the photographer were busy doing their jobs, so Jacks stayed back. He could see the figure of 'Chalky' White laid out, almost reverently, on the filthy concrete floor. Treadwell had been blown back against the wall of the loading bay by the force of the shotgun blasts. Jacks winced; his face had been completely removed by one of the shots. His body lay in a hideous contorted heap, covered in blood and slumped with its back against the wall. It was obvious that both barrels had been fired close up, and had been very personal.

"Jesus Christ," muttered Jacks under his breath. "What a bloody mess." He turned to Mike and Bobby. "Let's get working on any witnesses, let's find out if anyone on this flea ridden site knows any of these, or Payne. Bobby, ask Diane and Len to visit the neighbouring units and the ones at the entrances at either end of the estate, they may have seen Payne or these other jokers."

Bobby went outside to see Detective Constables Len Baines and Diane Plant, both members of the Murder Squad team. Jacks watched from inside as they were given their instructions.

"Do you think he'll go ahead with his meeting with Big Al later today, Guv?" Mike asked.

Jacks turned to him and thought for a moment before replying, "I can't see he has any other choice. He's going to need all the money he can lay his hands on, and when I say money, he's going to want cash."

Bobby re-joined them. Jacks looked at his two sergeants and continued, "Bobby, you stay here and take care of things. Mike, you come with me, we have got some organising to do."

An hour and a half later, the murder squad, together with Robert Ludgate's team, were milling about with the tactical firearms unit in the main briefing room at Bromley Police Station.

Detective Chief Superintendent Cameron entered the room, followed closely by Jacks, Robert Ludgate and Inspector Blaine of the firearms unit, in his distinctive police combat uniform.

"Quieten down, everybody," Jock Cameron boomed out across the room, as they all stopped talking and made for their seats. "As you all know by now, we have at least two murders, possibly three, and the casualty rate could go higher if the two motorcyclists in intensive care don't make it." He turned to

Jacks. "It's all yours, mate, good luck." Cameron did an about turn and left the room.

Jacks went to the front with Inspector Blaine and eyed those present. "We are going to be staking out a café near Beckenham Railway Station this afternoon." He looked at the board behind him and pointed to the station. "Brian Payne, and for those who don't know the man in question," he pointed to a police picture of Payne, "is a ruthless villain. We believe, at this point, that it was Treadwell who killed the proprietor of the jeweller's shop and accidentally shot Chalky White in the process. I think Payne, in retaliation for getting him a murder charge, executed Treadwell in a disused warehouse whilst Chalky White bled out."

Jacks paused and looked round the room before continuing. "The man is dangerous, he is ruthless, he faces one murder charge at least, and most of all, he… has… nothing to lose."

Jacks turned to Mike King who was sitting at the front. "DS King and DS McQueen will be with me inside the café. If it is safe to do so, we will arrest him in there, together with the man he's meeting." he turned back to the board. "This is Alan Childs, otherwise known as 'Big Al', as you can see, he's earned his name. He is what we call a big man, or should I say obese, and it would be hard not to miss him. This is the man Payne's meeting."

"What if he spots you in the café, Guv, do we move in?" one of firearms officers asked.

"The three of us inside will be armed, but if there is any danger to others inside the café we will abort the arrest. It will be your job," he addressed the uniformed officer directly, "under the supervision of Inspector Blaine, either to arrest him or take him out once he's outside."

Jacks turned to Inspector Blaine, who had been standing patiently by his side. "I'll hand over to Inspector Blaine to brief you on how he wants to position you all and handle this operation. He is in charge of the whole outside operation, I hope that is clear."

Inspector Blaine thanked Jacks, and set about the deployment of his forces using the diagram on the wall. He finished by adding, "I don't want any heroes today, gentlemen. Let's have a successful operation but, most of all, we all go home safe to our loved ones."

Jacks immediately thought of Leanne and her parting words.

***

At four-thirty that afternoon, heavily disguised, Jacks entered Ron's Café, situated down a street near Beckenham's railway station. Not even his mother would have recognised him. Jacks was dressed in dirty jeans and a torn worker's donkey jacket that had long since seen better days.

The proprietor looked down at his muddied boots and the filthy footprints they were making across his floor as Jacks made his way to the counter. He had plaster tape over his right eye, which showed signs of blackening round the edges. Ron, the proprietor, didn't like the look of this rough house. He averted his eyes so he didn't have to meet Jacks'.

"What can I get you?" Ron tried to sound cordial as he pretended to mop the counter, he didn't want trouble with the likes of this one.

"Coffee," Jacks said brusquely. "Two sugars, and make it strong."

"Mug or cup?" asked Ron politely.

"What's this, twenty fucking questions? Oh, for fucks sake give me a mug," Jacks said, sounding very irritable.

Ron didn't say a word, he just poured the coffee, adding two teaspoons of sugar and left the spoon in the mug.

"Anything else?" he asked, tentatively.

"How much?" Jacks asked bluntly, already holding a handful of change.

Ron was going to say something like 'last of the big spenders, eh?' but thought better of it. "One pound," he offered.

Jacks dropped the coin in the puddle of tea and coffee on the counter and made his way over to a window seat, which enabled him to watch the whole street. As he slurped his coffee noisily, he glanced round the café noticing Mike and Bobby dressed in the blue uniform overalls of local gas fitters. They were sitting at a table in the middle of the room, talking noisily to two young girls. They seemed to be enjoying themselves, chatting the girls up, causing laughter to ring out across the café.

Jacks spotted Big Al at a table in the corner stretched over two seats. He was big, if you could call obese big. In spite of the cool weather, Al was sweating profusely, mopping his face with a large green handkerchief and looking around furtively. He noticed Jacks, and watched him as he slurped his coffee rudely before turning his attention to the rest of the room. Al seemed satisfied as he looked round, took his mobile phone out and dialled a number.

Jacks could hardly hear him over the noise his two sergeants and the girls were making.

"Yeah, it's all clear, Brian, I've been here sometime now and only the usual workmen and shop girls are in."

Jacks pushed the button on his radio in his pocket as a signal to the Firearms Tactical Unit to be ready. He hadn't spotted them when he came down the street and entered the café, so he was confident Payne wouldn't sus them out. The back of Brian Payne's head went past the front window. The hair on Jacks' neck stood up. How was this going to go down? How was Payne going to react? The handle of the pistol in the holster at his waist felt comforting as he gradually eased it out, keeping it out of sight under his donkey jacket. Payne had also been spotted by the other two but they ignored him, letting him open the door to the café and enter.

Payne, glancing round the room, had already satisfied himself everything was okay from outside. He went straight to Big Al's table and sat down.

"You got my money, Al?" he asked the sweating man.

"Have you got something for me?" Big Al responded.

"I don't have time to piss about, have you got the fucking money or not?" he snarled quietly with menace. "Or I'll leave you in a pool of your own fucking blood."

"Okay, okay, I've got the money," Al hissed, putting a package on the table. "There's one hundred K in there."

"They are worth five times that and you fucking well know it, you big fat bastard." Payne made sure that Al knew he was carrying by opening his jacket slightly.

Al spotted the pistol tucked into the top of Payne's trousers and sweated even more.

Jacks glanced outside to see the firearms officers closing into position behind cars parked in the street. He looked up at the offices opposite, noticing the rifle barrel slightly protruding from the window and directed at the café's entrance.

Mike King and Bobby McQueen glanced at Jacks, sensing how dangerous the situation was getting. Mike looked at the girls opposite, how could he get rid of them without raising any suspicions from Payne and the fat man?

"You filthy pervert," one of the girls suddenly shouted out, as she felt Mike's hand go between her legs under the table. "We are not that sort of girls, you bastard. Come on, Jackie, let's get away from these two creeps."

Both girls got up, gathered their belongings and without putting their coats on, headed for the door.

Brian Payne put his hand inside his jacket taking hold of the butt of his pistol. He looked round at the commotion, whilst Big Al watched him with alarm. Payne saw the girls hurriedly leaving, throwing insults at the two laughing gas workers who remained seated at the table.

Jacks watched intently, his hand on his pistol, the safety catch off.

"Fucking childish pervies," Payne hissed, turning back to Childs.

Jacks relaxed a little, he couldn't help the slight grin on his face as he continued to slurp his tea.

"It's all I could get my hands on at such short notice, Brian, honestly," Big Al pleaded, knowing this man could and would kill him if he thought he was being done over. "The jeweller's dead, I won't be able to get rid of the merchandise for some time," he pleaded.

Brian Payne took out a large packet from inside his coat and placed it on the table in front of Big Al. "Here you are, fat man. I hope you choke on the fucking stuff." He grabbed the other packet and slid it into his inside pocket, before getting up from the table and making towards the door.

Payne sneered at King and McQueen as he passed. He made it to the door, opened it and stepped out.

"Armed police, stand where you are and don't move," the megaphone shrilly echoed out across the street. The whole street seemed alive with uniformed men carrying guns pointing directly at him.

Payne slowly moved his hand towards the inside of his jacket. He knew if he was taken he was going away for life, did he want that, or would he prefer to die?

Inspector Blaine listened to the voice in his headset. "I have a clear shot," the voice of the marksman confirmed from the upstairs window of the office opposite.

He had Payne in the crosshairs of his rifle sight, but kept his finger away from the trigger.

"Hold your fire, on my order only," Blaine responded into his mouthpiece.

"Keep your hands in sight and get down on your knees," Blaine commanded through his megaphone.

Payne was still undecided and his hand was still going for the inside of his jacket. He was starting to sweat like the fat man, Big Al. Was this how it was going to end? He had such great hopes for the future, amassing a great deal of money from all the robberies he had carried out. Why hadn't he retired, always pushing for more?

"Fuck that Treadwell," he thought out loud. Payne was about to draw the gun out of his waistband.

Blaine, watching his every movement closely, prepared to give the order to fire, when he became aware that the door of the café was opening behind him.

Payne started to turn much too late. Jacks had launched himself at Payne like a locomotive with a full head of steam. He cracked his firearm across the side of Payne's head, sending him sprawling across the pavement.

The gun Payne was drawing out of his waistband, the very same gun that Treadwell had used to kill Howard Jones, clattered across the paving slabs and slid harmlessly under a parked car. Mike King and Bobby McQueen were over him in an instant with their arms fully extended, pointing their firearms at Payne's head.

"Everyone, hold your fire, hold your fire," Blaine screamed out through his mouthpiece and the megaphone. The firearms unit rushed in, pushing everyone aside and secured their prisoner.

An irate, red-faced Inspector Blaine came forward, deliberately standing right in front of Jacks, hands on his hips and legs wide apart. "So much for no heroics, eh?"

Jacks ignored him, turned round to Mike King and asked, "Where's Childs?"

"Oh, Christ! He's still inside, Guv." He turned with Bobby McQueen, falling over one another as they tried to get back through the café door.

The fat man was nowhere to be seen. Mike went over to Ron, the proprietor, who was trembling behind the counter as he stared at the gun in Mike's hand.

"Where's the fat bastard?" he screamed at him.

"He went out back, there's a back door leading to the yard," he shouted back in panic.

Mike and Bobby rushed to the back entrance leading to the kitchen, and then out through the open back door leading to the yard.

"Jacks will kill us if he gets away," Mike shouted to the back of Bobby. They had no need to worry; the fat man was spread eagled on the dirty ground between over-flowing upturned dustbins, with his hands firmly handcuffed behind his back and two firearms officers pointing their weapons at the back of his head.

Jacks came out of the back door and stood over Big Al. "Search the fat bastard, let's have those gems," he demanded.

Mike and Bobby heaved him to his feet and patted him down. After some frantic searching they gave up.

"Nothing, Guv," Bobby said lamely.

"Not a problem, lads, let's retrace his steps. They can't be far," a very cool and collected Jacks suggested. He led the way back through the kitchen and stopped at the toilets, Ladies on the left and Gents on the right.

"Search the toilets, and pay particular attention to the cisterns," he ordered.

Two minutes later, Bobby, who had been searching the Ladies, came out with a thick brown paper parcel still dripping with water, holding it out in front of him as if it had contacted the plague.

"Here it is, Guv, hardly had time to get soaked through," he grinned.

Alan Childs almost cried as he was led past a jubilant Bobby McQueen, packing the gems into an evidence bag. The armed officers, pushing for all they were worth, could only just get his big frame through the narrow doorways that led back into the café.

FIVE

"You'll have to make a statement, Jacks. I think the whole media is out there," Jock Campbell spoke as he looked down onto the forecourt of Bromley Police Station from his upstairs office window at the mêlée of photographers, cameramen and reporters that accosted everybody who tried to enter and leave.

Jacks joined him at the window. "They'll have to wait until we charge them tomorrow," he said, withdrawing from the window after being spotted from below.

"Just give them the bare details, man. You can flesh it out later. Tell them that you have arrested two men on suspicion of murder, robbery, receiving stolen property and, at this point, you can't say anymore," Jock appealed to him.

"Jock, as head of this division, why don't you do it?"

"Because it is your case, Jacks, not mine. Bromley nick is just the conduit for your operation. Now, for Pete's sake, go and do it," he commanded.

Reluctantly Jacks, flanked by Mike and Bobby, stood in front of the media with the constant irritation of flashes hitting him full in the face. Questions were fired at him in quick succession, which he ignored, making it quite clear to those present they weren't getting anything until they quietened down.

Eventually he started reading from his prepared script, which followed the lines of Jock Campbell's early suggestions. As he finished, the bedlam began again and as the barrage of questions came at him, he turned on his heel and re-entered the station with Bobby and Mike protecting his rear from anyone wanting to follow him. No one would get past the formidable bulk and power of Bobby McQueen.

Jock Campbell was standing in the foyer as he entered with his hand out. "Well done, Jacks. Wasn't so bad, was it?"

***

Jacks arrived home just before midnight. He had not charged the arrested men, and would only do that when the full extent of the charges were sorted out the next day, and because of his concern for Leanne.

The lights were on in the lounge which overlooked the lawn and driveway. Jacks could hear music coming from the hi-fi system as he inserted his key in the outside front door. Thank God for that, he thought, as he closed the door, no repetition of a couple of nights ago. He threw his case down in the hall and headed for the lounge.

"Hello, love," Leanne greeted him with a glass in her outstretched hand, before leaning in to kiss him on the lips. She had changed the music as she heard him come in to Queen's 'We Are the Champions', and turned up the volume.

"What's all this about?" he shouted over the music in feigned suspicion, eyeing her in a very seductive negligee. "You'll have the neighbours complaining." He went over to the music system and turned it down.

"Mike phoned to say you were on your way. I also saw you on the news about Payne and Childs, so did the neighbours, so they won't mind," she purred. "I thought a little celebration might be in order, especially seeing you didn't stop to celebrate with your boys."

"Plenty of time for that after we charge them tomorrow," Jacks said in matter of fact manner, as if catching a multiple murderer and clearing up over twenty eight violent robberies was an everyday occurrence.

"Oooooh, get him," Leanne responded, pulling a face and digging him in the ribs.

Jacks grabbed her wrists as she tried to back away.

"I'll give you, 'get him'. Come here, wench." he pulled her to him, kissing her passionately as his hands roved over her lovely rounded bottom. "Let's go up, love," he said, looking at her with his come to bed eyes.

Leanne could never resist him, and it was she who eagerly led him out of the lounge and up the stairs.

***

Jacks woke early, was there something not quite right? It was still dark as he put his arm out to feel the empty bed beside him. Raising himself up on an elbow he noticed the light coming through the half open bedroom door to the bathroom.

He got up and went to the bathroom door, opening it quietly, and went in. Leanne was sitting on the side of the bath. She looked up at him with tears showing in pained eyes.

"These blasted headaches," she said, looking pale. "I'm afraid I've been a little sick."

"Come back to bed, love, I'll go downstairs and get you a couple of aspirin," Jacks said, taking her by the elbow.

Unprotestingly, he led her back to bed and went downstairs, returning a couple of minutes later with a glass of water and two aspirins.

"Take these and lie still for a while," he ordered gently. He went into the bathroom and cleaned up the sick around the WC bowl and the hand basin. When he got back into the bedroom, Leanne was fast asleep.

Jacks returned to the bathroom, showered, shaved and then got dressed. He went downstairs to the hall telephone, took out their address book in the drawer of the desk and found the number he was looking for.

Jacks dialled, listened to the monotonous tone and waited. About three minutes later the call was answered.

"Surgery," the voice sounded tired.

He looked at his watch; it was now eight o'clock and the surgery had just opened.

"My name is Jacks, my wife, Leanne, is a patient of Doctor Edwards," Jacks stated.

"Yes, Chief Inspector, how can I help you this morning?" the female voice cheered up, as she recognised the now famous policeman who had appeared on her television the night before.

"My wife's been very bad during the night. She has been sick and experienced very bad headaches. Is it possible for Doctor Edwards to come out to see her, please?"

"Doctor Edwards will be in any minute, Chief Inspector. I will make sure he telephones you the moment he gets in," the voice assured him.

Jacks thanked her, put the phone down and went back upstairs to find Leanne sleeping soundly. He went back down to the kitchen and waited for the return phone call. It rang five minutes later.

"Jacks," he answered bluntly.

"Good morning, Chief Inspector. I understand that your wife has had a bad night," Doctor Edwards spoke in his soft Devonshire accent. "I will call out to see her. I should be able to get there about eleven this morning, is that okay?"

"Thank you, Doctor Edwards, I would appreciate it. These headaches of hers are concerning me. I have to go in to work today, but as soon as I have completed some urgent business I'll be back," Jacks explained. "My sister will come over and sit with Leanne until I am able to get back."

He rang off, immediately punching in his sister Maddie's number. Maddie promised to be there as soon as traffic would allow. He went up to the bedroom and gently woke Leanne, explaining about the doctor and Maddie. Leanne did not protest and kissed him goodbye.

He arrived at Bromley Police Station just after nine o'clock. Mike King was standing in the yard smoking a cigarette as Jacks got out of his car.

"Warned you about that filthy habit, Mike, it'll be the death of you," he quipped.

Mike grinned back at him. "Death will come way before that, Governor, probably through over work from a demanding boss," he joked. "We're all ready for you, even the top brass in the form of AC Carstairs have come down for this. They can't believe how quickly you've solved the murders and the robberies. Lots of kudos in this for you, Guv."

Mike stubbed out his cigarette under his shoe, falling in beside his boss as he strode towards the back entrance.

"What does Carstairs come all the way over here for? A bloody waste of time if you ask me. Don't assistant commissioners have anything better to do?" Jacks complained. "I suppose the press are in attendance and there's a photo opportunity to be had, eh?" he added sarcastically.

They went straight to the incident room, pushing past crowds of people milling about and blocking the corridors. They were even blocking the stairs.

Jacks turned to Mike. "Where's Bobby?" he asked over his shoulder.

"He's doing up the charge sheets with Robert Ludgate, Guv. Should be going to the custody suite anytime now, I'll go and see." Mike turned round and went back down the stairs.

Jacks elbowed his way into the incident room where he was greeted with loud applause accompanied by 'well done, Guv' or 'nice one, sir'.

He held up his hands to quell the noise. "Quieten down, you lot. If you're not supposed to be in here, people, out," he demanded, as he pointed with his thumb over his shoulder to the open door.

The room emptied out, with his murder team and Ludgate's crime squad boys remaining.

"Settle down," he ordered, making his way forward before standing in front of the incident board. "I want to personally congratulate you all for the hard work you have put in, with tremendous results."

Jacks was smiling, and the room warmed to him as he continued. "I am not going to mention any individual, because this has been a team effort between the murder squad, the crime squad unit, and not forgetting, the firearms boys. With the arrest of Payne and Childs we have removed a big threat off of our streets." The room erupted into instant applause, and he only just heard the phone buzzing on the desk.

Diane Plant picked it up; it was Mike King speaking from the custody suite.

"We're ready for the Governor. Bobby and DI Ludgate have completed the charge sheets and want him to look over them."

Jacks took the phone handed to him. "Thanks, Mike. How busy is it down there?" he asked.

"The AC's here with DCS Cameron, there's a couple of photographers, DI Ludgate I've already mentioned, and two others from the crime squad," Mike reported.

"Then there's room for some of our people as well," Jacks stated, and then put the phone down. "Pick four of you to come down to the custody suite and follow me down."

Detectives Diane Plant and Len Baines joined two members of the serious crime squad and followed him out. The four filed down the stairs behind Jacks, along the corridor, and entered the custody suite.

They were met at the door by the ageing and experienced custody sergeant, who Jacks thought had been in the force since the times of Robert Peel. He could just see him as a Bow Street Runner.

Jacks shook hands with him. "Sorry about the circus, Sam. I don't know where they crawl out from."

Sam Green grinned as he shook his hand, saying quietly, "You're famous, sir. They all want a piece of you." Flashes showed the presence of the photographers as Sam turned to show them his gleaming white teeth. "Make sure I get a copy to add to my collection, sir," he murmured behind smiling teeth as Jacks went forward.

AC Carstairs stepped forward with his hand outstretched, more flashes followed as Jacks grasped it, with the AC bathing in the limelight for as long as it was decent. Eventually he let go of Jacks' hand.

Jock Cameron, as an old friend, knew Jacks well and just patted him on the shoulder as he passed. He went up to the custody desk where Sam, the custody sergeant, was now entrenched with Bobby McQueen and Robert Ludgate on either side of him. Mike King was standing just behind them. Bobby offered Jacks the charge sheets, which he quickly declined.

"You've done the work. Detective Sergeant McQueen, you and DI Ludgate can charge them." The AC looked on disapprovingly as Jacks calmly asked, "Where are they then?"

The door from the cells opened, and Brian Payne was led through. He spotted Jacks standing to one side and grinned at him. Bobby moved behind the desk and stood alongside the custody sergeant, with Robert Ludgate flanking him on the other side. He noticed the grin on Payne's face as he looked at his boss.

"Take the grin off your face and keep your bloody eyes on me, son," he barked, as he leant over the desk. The grin disappeared, although Payne remained very composed. Dressed in a light denim shirt and jeans, he had shaved for the occasion, with his blondish hair well brushed. He had been well cared for in custody.

Bobby looked at Jacks for permission to carry on. Jacks merely nodded at him and stood back with Jock Cameron.

Bobby cleared his throat. "Brian Rupert Payne, you are still under caution, you are charged…"

Jacks didn't hear much of what was being said, comfortable with the fact that Bobby was a first rate copper. His mind was on Leanne. He was worried. What could be the matter with her?

He was brought back to the present by Jock tugging his arm and pointing to a police officer at the door.

"Sorry, Jock, my thoughts were elsewhere." He went over to the police constable, who had been trying to get his attention, and they went out, closing the door behind them. "What is it?" he asked.

"Your sister's been on the phone, sir. Your wife has been admitted to hospital, and could you phone her?"

Jacks didn't respond. He went straight outside to the back of the building to phone Maddie. The phone went to her answer service. Jacks thought for a moment, still at the hospital no doubt. He phoned the surgery, and after some ten minutes it was answered. Jacks impatiently explained who he was and asked for Doctor Edwards.

"Doctor Edwards, Chief Inspector," he answered. "I have admitted your wife to St. Peter's Hospital in Chertsey for observation and tests." His voice was neutral, matter of fact.

"What the hell is wrong, Doctor?" Jacks asked, desperately.

"We won't know that until the tests are complete," he answered truthfully. "Your sister was at home with her when I called, and has gone to the hospital with her."

"Do you have the number handy please, Doctor?"

"I'll get it for you, hang on." He came back a few minutes later with the number.

Jacks thanked him and closed his phone. He was about to dial when his sister returned his earlier call. Jacks told her he would be down straightaway, and then returned to the custody suit. The charging process was still going on, with Alan Childs now in front of the desk.

Jock Cameron saw him at the door, and without any explanation to those present, left the room. Jacks explained to him about Leanne.

"Get down there, now. I'll let those know who need to and if there's anything you want, phone me," he ordered.

Jacks drove out of the rear of the police station, headed towards the A307 Portsmouth Road into Surbiton Road, and made for the M3. He pushed the accelerator pedal to the floor. The Volvo responded, reaching speeds of over eighty miles per hour until he eased off, cruising until reaching Exit 11 of the Orbital Motorway a few minutes later.

He took the exit and turned off the roundabout, heading towards Chertsey before entering Saint Peters Way and into Guildford Road.

Jacks turned into the hospital, drove straight up to reception and parked. He quickly put a board in the front windscreen of the Volvo marked 'POLICE' and headed for the entrance.

The hospital was busy with a queue of people at reception. Jacks edged to the side, holding up his warrant card, catching the eye of one of the nurses.

"Yes, what can I do for you?" she asked in a soft, southern Irish accent, scanning the warrant card to make sure it was genuine.

"My wife, Leanne Jacks, was admitted earlier as an emergency. Could you tell me where she is please?"

"Wait one moment, Chief Inspector, I will look for you." The nurse went over to a computer terminal and pumped in the information.

A few minutes later, he was hurrying down the corridor, heading for the serious head injury department.

Maddie, looking quite distraught, was waiting outside the ward, drinking a cup of coffee. She spotted Jacks coming down the corridor, put her plastic cup down, which immediately fell over, and rushed to him.

They embraced and held one another tight as he asked her, "How is she?"

"The consultant is with her now," she said feebly. "I couldn't believe it, one moment I was talking to her in her bed and the next she screamed, held her head and passed out. I couldn't wake her, Jacks."

The door to the ward swung open. A uniformed sister and nurse, accompanied by a middle-aged man dressed in a dark navy blue suit, approached them.

"I take it that you are Mr Jacks, Leanne's husband?" the man enquired. "I'm Mr Graham Burton, the consultant dealing with your wife." The two men shook hands.

"How is she? What is wrong with her?" Jacks asked hurriedly.

"I have to be frank with you, Mr Jacks, it does not look good at present. I think your wife has a tumour on her brain, and I am sending her for a scan in a few minutes time."

Jacks was stunned. Maddie gripped his hand tight, started to sniff and struggled to hold back her sobs.

He looked at the consultant in disbelief not really understanding what was being said to him. "When will we know what it is?" he asked, not taking his eyes off the consultant.

Burton felt uneasy with the piercing stare he was getting from burning dark brown, almost coal black eyes. "I will accompany your wife for the scan. It won't be long before we have some answers. I suggest you and your sister go to the canteen for some refreshments, and I will come and see you as soon as I have any results."

Maddie pulled at his hand. "Come on, Jacks, we'll get a cuppa, it won't be long."

The consultant, accompanied by the nurses, went back inside the ward, conscious of the stare still being directed at his back. Thankfully the doors swung shut behind him.

SIX

There was plenty of room inside the canteen, with the main rush of diners now behind them. Nursing staff, mixed with hospital visitors and outpatients were sitting at small round tables, chattering between themselves as they sipped their teas and coffees. Maddie led Jacks to a table against a wall, where they could see the door and any one entering the canteen.

Jacks felt numb; he didn't say a word to Maddie until he was eventually seated opposite her.

"What the hell's going on, Maddie, Leanne is so fit, so full of life. What the hell is it?" he pleaded, more to himself than his sister.

"Let's wait and see what the consultant has to say, Jacks," she whispered, with tears still showing in her eyes, "Leanne is strong." Maddie, even in childhood and like everyone else, had always referred to her brother simply as 'Jacks'.

They remained seated in the canteen for another three quarters of an hour before the nursing sister came through the door and headed their way. Jacks saw her coming, he knew instinctively that it was not going to be good news.

"Mr Jacks, could you and your sister please come with me to Mr Burton's office?" she requested politely.

Jacks knew better than to ask any questions, knowing he wouldn't get any answers until he saw the consultant. He got up, waited for Maddie to pick up her handbag and collect her coat, and followed the sister out of the canteen. His knees felt a bit wobbly. He held onto Maddie's arm for comfort and support as she squeezed her elbow in against his hand to let him know she was there for him.

They stopped at the consultant's door. The sister knocked gently as she opened the door, and waited just inside, holding the door open, inviting them to enter. Jacks just stood in the doorway as Maddie entered. The sister smiled encouragingly at him as he slowly and reluctantly entered.

"Please, take a seat," Mr Burton offered, with a gesture of hand.

Jacks pulled a chair back for Maddie before sitting down gratefully, trying hard to compose himself. He did not want to be here, he did not want to hear this.

Get up and run, he thought to himself. He waited until the consultant looked up from his desk and looked him square in the eyes. Jacks knew. He put his hand up to his mouth and bit into the knuckle.

"I am very sorry, Mr Jacks," he heard him say, as Maddie fought back a gasp and sniffed again. "Leanne does have a brain tumour, a very aggressive one. I am afraid there is nothing we can do, other than to make her comfortable."

Jacks knew what was being said, but couldn't accept it. "Comfortable? What's that supposed to damn well mean? What about operating? Surely there's something you can do?"

Mr Burton looked sadly at Jacks and his sister. Shaking his head slowly, he answered, "I am sorry, but the tumour is inoperable. I'm afraid it is too advanced."

"How can that be?" Jacks asked incredulously. "What about her doctors? How come they haven't picked it up? We were… she was in the surgery only the other day."

"These things can be missed, I'm afraid. It is very unfortunate." Burton conceded.

"Unfortunate? Is that what you call it, you incompetent load of bastards? I'll make sure some heads roll for this," Jacks spat viciously, fixing Burton with his cold black eyes.

The consultant lowered his eyes and looked at his notes in front of him, not daring to hold the gaze of this very dangerous man on the opposite side of his desk.

"Jacks," Maddie's voice came at him from somewhere in the distance. He turned to her. "This is not the time, think of Leanne," she said, wiping tears from her eyes.

Jacks thought for a moment, before turning back to Burton. "I want to see her now," he demanded.

Burton remained seated behind his desk. "Sister Reynolds will take you to the ward, Chief Inspector," he said, using his rank to remind Jacks of who he was before nodding to the sister to go ahead.

Maddie hung back as she followed them down the corridor, and waited outside the ward door as Jacks and the sister went inside.

He was not prepared for what he saw as he went behind the curtain. Leanne was asleep with the bedclothes tucked around her neck. Jacks looked down at the ashen, gaunt face which appeared peaceful as Leanne lay oblivious to his pain. He clenched his fists and gritted his teeth at a loss as what to do next. He brushed her hair out of her eyes, smoothing it back across her head.

Leanne became aware of his presence as she slowly and sleepily opened her eyes. She tried a weak smile as she recognised him. "Hello, Jacks," she whispered. "How's it going?"

"I don't know what to say, love. You look so tired," he said helplessly.

"Thanks a lot, Jacks, I really needed you to tell me how wonderful I am," she smiled encouragingly at him.

"I'm so sorry, love. To see you in here is quite a shock. You will always look good to me, you know that." Tears started to form in his dark brown eyes, which now showed his concern and love for her, unlike earlier when they showed how dangerous he could be.

"Have you seen the consultant?" Leanne asked.

Jacks searched for her hand as he kissed her full on the mouth. He was lost, what could he say? He felt wretched and would willingly swap places with her.

"Yes, I have just come from Burton's office. He's told me," he whispered, as he squeezed her hand. "We'll get a second opinion, he doesn't know everything," he said desperately.

"No, Jacks, there is no need for second opinions. Two other consultants have also confirmed his diagnosis. I know the score," she whispered, as she resigned herself to her fate before adding, "To die will be an awfully big adventure."

"You can't give up, I won't let you give up," he said, as tears ran down his cheeks as he remembered the saying. "Peter Pan," he said gently.

Leanne nodded slightly as she smiled up at him. "I thought you would know that one, Jacks. No tears, not from you. I am going to need your strength to help me cope with this." Leanne stroked his cheek, wiping away his tears as she smiled gently at him, before slowly closing her eyes and going back to sleep.

Jacks remained where he was, with his head resting next to hers on the pillow.

The sister opened the curtain and signalled Maddie to come in. Maddie went to the bowed figure of her elder brother. Placing her hands on his shoulders she gently urged him upright. He reluctantly released Leanne, turned to his sister, embraced her and started to sob.

It was Maddie's turn to feel lost. This was her big brother, the one who had raised her, protected her; her hero. Now he was just a frightened little boy. She held him tight, and they cried together.

In the early hours, Jacks was awakened by a shout. He jumped at the sound, wondering where he was and what the noise could be. He was still sitting in the chair by Leanne's bedside, having fallen asleep through sheer exhaustion and worry; now he had cramp.

The night nurses were attending to another patient in the ward, who had woken wondering where she was.

Jacks looked at Leanne, who was sleeping peacefully after the medication she had been given. How could this be? She looked perfect. He stretched his legs out in front of him, turning his toes up to relieve the cramp before rising and gently stamping his feet on the tiled floor. The cramp subsided. Jacks went back to Leanne's bedside, took her hand and sat back down.

"Go home, Jacks," she murmured, without opening her eyes. "Go home and get some rest, love."

"Are you awake, or dreaming?" he asked her quietly.

Leanne slowly opened her eyes and tried smiling. "What do you think?" she asked.

He raised her hand to his lips and kissed it lovingly.

"Is that all I get?" she questioned, managing a smile.

He kissed her on her lips. "I didn't want to take advantage," he said, pretending to have hurt feelings.

"That would be a first, Mister. It's never stopped you before." They both smiled at one another as they had often done in intimate moments. "Still got those 'come to bed eyes', Jacks," she whispered.

Jacks watched as she closed her eyes once more and went to sleep.

At eight o'clock, Maddie pulled open the curtain. "How is she?" she asked quietly.

"She's sleeping, Maddie. She woke up early this morning for a brief talk and went off again. She's been sleeping ever since. Has Ron dropped you off?"

Ron was Maddie's husband and had become a good friend as well as a brother-in-law. He had fetched her from the hospital after he had finished work at his office the night before.

"Yes, and he will pick me up if I phone him later, so you can get home, shower, clean up and change."

"I don't like to leave, Maddie, what if…" he trailed off, not wanting to complete the finality of it.

"I'll ring you, Jacks, don't worry. You can be back in no time, now go on," she urged.

He got up reluctantly, kissed Leanne on her lips, turned to Maddie, kissed her on both cheeks, and without saying a word walked out of the ward, down the corridor and out into a cold misty morning.

Arriving home through the morning rush hour, he parked in his drive and sat for a while, looking at the cold empty building he once called home. It would never be the same, could never be the same.

Entering through the front door, he picked up the mail off the mat and entered the kitchen, where he put the kettle on for an instant coffee. He made it strong, probably too strong, but he was going to need his strength and to stay alert.

Jacks saw the red light flashing on the answering machine in the hall as he went by, he ignored it and climbed the stairs, cup in hand. He sat on the side of their bed, sipping his coffee before stripping naked and going to shower.

Half an hour later, he came down the stairs in his dressing gown and pushed the message button on the answering machine. The counter said there were fifteen messages left.

The first message was from Jock Cameron, offering to help wherever Jacks thought he could. The second message was from Assistant Commissioner Carstairs, offering similar help and telling him to take as much leave as he needed. The third message was from his mother, who had cried through the whole message.

"That's all I need, Mum," he said to himself. "Thank God I don't have to break the news to Leanne's parents." They had died a few years earlier, just before Jacks had met her.

He didn't bother with any more messages. He went into the kitchen to make himself another cup of coffee, before going back upstairs and changing, returning a few minutes later wearing a light blue pair of dungarees with a light grey denim shirt. He went into what they termed 'the boot room', selected a pair of pale brown soft leather shoes and looked round as he tied the laces. Everywhere he looked had Leanne stamped all over it.

Jacks put his head into his hands and tried to crush his own skull. Without her he was going to go mad.

He became aware of the door bell ringing in the background, got up and went out into the hall, waited for a moment, took in a deep breath and composed himself before opening the door. It was Mike King.

"Hello, Governor, can I come in?" He already had one foot on the door step as he smiled up at Jacks.

Jacks stepped back, allowed him to pass before closing the door, and followed him into the kitchen.

"Sorry to call like this, Governor, but I spoke to Maddie. She said you were home for a short while, I hope you don't mind?"

Jacks looked at his colleague who had become one of his closest friends. Smiling at him he said, "Forget the 'Governor' bit, Mike, we're alone for Christ sake. Thanks for coming. I think I'm going to lose her." Tears were forming in Jacks eyes as reality once again set in.

Mike took hold of his hand and embraced the man he idolised and respected more than anyone he had ever known.

"If there is anything I can do, Jacks, you only have to ask. I feel a bit lost as to what to say, and that's the truth," he whispered in his boss' ear.

Jacks pulled away from him, still holding his arms. He noticed the tears also forming in the eyes of this hard man in front of him, Mike King, smart, articulate and quite ruthless, when he had to be. "That's a first for you, Mike, nothing to say, eh?"

"Mac sends his best and said if there's anything he…" Mike trailed off and knew he was stating the obvious.

"Thank Bobby for me, will you? And the rest of them who have sent messages, but now I must get back to the hospital."

"Do you want me to run you?" Mike asked eagerly, wanting to be of further assistance.

"Thanks, Mike, but you had best get back to the Yard and keep an eye on things for me." They shook hands and parted.

An hour later, Jacks pulled into the visitors' car park of the hospital, and began the laborious hunt for a parking space. He managed to squeeze the Volvo in between a Jeep Cherokee and a brand new Range Rover. If the drivers had trouble getting in to their Chelsea Tractors, that's bloody hard luck, he thought as he headed for the wards.

Maddie had been crying again. Her eyes were becoming swollen with dark 'panda' blotches under them. She was starting to look as bad as Leanne, he thought. Then he panicked.

"What is it, Maddie? Has anything else happened?" Jacks stared into her swollen eyes, expecting to hear the worst as he looked down at Leanne, who appeared to be sleeping peacefully.

"No, nothing's happened," she muttered. "Two more consultants have been to see Leanne. Mr Burton wanted to see you as soon as you got here."

"I'll be back in a minute, Maddie, and then you had better ring Ron and ask him to pick you up. You look all in."

Jacks hurried down the corridor to Burton's office and tapped on his door. It was opened by another man dressed in a three piece grey suit.

"Come in, Mr Jacks, please," Burton called out, as he rose from his desk. "This is Professor Gideon, who has kindly agreed to examine your wife for me."

The three piece suit offered his hand; Jacks took it, shaking it briefly. "What is your verdict, Professor?" he asked accusingly.

"Well, Chief Inspector," the title did not escape Jacks, "Hardly a verdict. We only diagnose, it is not us who pass sentence."

Jacks was feeling irritable and it was showing. "Professor, I am tired and my wife, according to you lot, is dying. Spare me the niceties and tell me the bottom line."

"Very well, Chief Inspector," he cleared his throat and looked up at Jacks. "Your wife is not going to recover, I'm afraid. It is only a matter of hours, perhaps a matter of one or two days, before the end."

Even though Jacks had expected the worst, this still hit him like a bomb shell. He looked at the two men who were speaking to him in turns but didn't hear a word they were saying. Feeling cold, he shivered and shook before hearing the Professor's voice trailing off.

"…It is doubtful if she will wake again, I'm afraid."

Jacks didn't remember getting back to the ward until Ron squeezed his shoulder.

"You, okay, Jacks?" he asked softly.

He looked up, taking his eyes off Leanne to see Ron standing with Maddie by his side. "Hello, Ron. Yes, I'm fine. I am finding it rather hard to take in though. Look, take Maddie home, she needs some rest. I'll phone you if there is any change." Jacks got up and shook Ron's hand. "Thanks for your support you two, you've been great, now bugger off home."

Maddie bent over Leanne and kissed her gently on the forehead before kissing her brother on his lips. She left with Ron without another word.

At seven o'clock that evening, Sister Reynolds brought in a tray of sandwiches with orange juice.

"Eat something, Mr Jacks, or I will have to ask you to leave," she threatened.

"Okay, Sister, I hear you. Would it be possible to have a cup of strong black coffee, please?"

"If you eat your sandwich, Chief Inspector, I'll bring you a pot of the stuff," she cajoled him, with a rueful smile.

In spite of the coffee, Jacks fell asleep holding Leanne's hand. At nine o'clock in the evening he woke with a start, something was wrong. He bent over Leanne, who appeared to be breathing regularly.

Jacks still felt uneasy, like someone had left an outside door open letting in the cold, but without any draught.

Suddenly he became aware of someone else sitting in the corner, and looked up to see a pretty young girl in a yellow dress watching him.

"Who are you? What are you doing here?" he asked. "Visiting time was over some time ago, young lady, besides, do we know you?" Jacks thought she looked familiar, probably someone Leanne knew, but he couldn't place her. About to question her further, he became aware of Leanne looking at him. She was awake, in spite of what they said, she was awake.

"Oh, love, you have had me so worried," he said, holding her hand and bending over to kiss her. She seemed cold, so cold.

"Jacks, I love you," she said softly, almost inaudibly. "Find her killer, Jacks. She cannot rest until you do."

Jacks was dumbfounded. What on earth did she mean 'find her killer'? Leanne certainly wasn't referring to herself, so who? What?

"What was that, love?" he asked.

Leanne had closed her eyes. She lay very still and Jacks couldn't see any signs of her breathing.

"Oh, God, no." He shivered as he spoke and turned to the girl who had been sitting in the corner. "Get a nurse for God's sake, get a doc…" The girl had gone.

Jacks looked round the room; she had definitely gone. He called out desperately for a nurse.

A few minutes later, the duty doctor joined the two nurses attending to Leanne and Jacks was ushered outside. A few brief minutes later, the doctor came out. His face said it all.

Jacks fell back against the corridor wall, sliding down it until he rested on his backside. He was taken to an office with an examination table and given a sedative. Lying on the table with his eyes firmly shut, he ground his teeth in frustration, anger and a foreboding sense of loss.

Eventually he got up, took out his mobile phone and punched in Maddie's number. She answered sleepily on the sixth ring.

Jacks made no apology for waking her as he said simply, "Leanne has gone. Can you telephone those who need to know please, Maddie?"

"Oh, Jacks," Maddie cried.

"Not now, Maddie, can you do as I ask?" Jacks was abrupt, almost cold.

Ron took the phone from her. "We'll deal with things, Jacks. We'll make sure the family know. Is there anything else you need?"

Jacks hung up, he didn't want to talk further. He remained seated on the examination table with his legs dangling over the side. What could he do now? What should he do now? He lay back down to try and think clearly.

An hour later, Mr Burton entered the room; he didn't want to, he was unsure of the reception he was going to get, but he entered and faced this haunted man.

"I am so sorry, Mr Jacks. Is there anything I can do for you?"

"No thank you, Mr Burton. There isn't anything anyone can do for me now." Jacks looked up at the consultant, remembering that he had been told Leanne wouldn't wake up again.

"You were wrong about her not waking up though," he said to him. "She woke up to say goodbye and…" Jacks broke off, trying to remember what Leanne had said, but he was interrupted by Mr Burton before he could say anymore.

"I'm sorry, Mr Jacks, but that is not possible. Your wife died some hours before you alerted the nurses. I think you must have fallen asleep."

He tried to take this in. "No, you're wrong, she woke up and spoke to me. Ask the young girl who came to visit."

Mr Burton eyed Jacks with puzzlement before asking, "What girl was this?"

"A young girl, a girl of about sixteen years of age… pretty with long fair hair down to her shoulders. She was dressed in a bright yellow dress. She was sitting in Leanne's room, she heard her." Jacks assured him.

"I don't know about any young girl, Mr Jacks, but I can assure you, your wife died some hours before you called for the nurses," Burton insisted.

SEVEN

The internal hospital investigation proved fruitless. No girl had been seen by any member of staff, patient or visitor. It was decided by Burton and his team of investigators that Jacks had dreamt the whole thing. The post mortem also proved Burton right, Leanne had indeed been dead for at least three hours before the nurses were called, and they assured him that there was no girl either in the room or the near vicinity.

The news was relayed to Jacks at the same time that he was told Leanne's body was to be released for burial. Ron and Maddie had dealt with the arrangements, helped by Jacks' father and mother, who had temporarily moved in with him.

He spent most of the time in his bedroom with the curtains closed shut, only emerging to take possession of another bottle of whisky. Most of his meals remained untouched and were collected by his mother from his room.

"I don't know what he thinks he's doing, Lionel, staying in his room night and day. It's not healthy," his mother said to his father.

"What can we do about it, Doreen? If he doesn't want to come out, there's nothing we can do about it." Lionel was lost, it was his wife who normally dealt with any crisis that came up in the family, and he was always happy to go along with any resolutions to problems.

"You could at least try, Lionel. You are his father, you used to be so close," Doreen responded angrily.

Lionel got to his feet and took a deep breath. "You are right," he said firmly. "I will go up now."

He climbed the stairs, his legs feeling like lead. What was he to say? What could he say? He stood outside the bedroom door and rapped sharply, before boldly opening it and striding in.

Jacks was sitting upright on the bed, just looking blankly at the wall opposite. The room stank of stale whisky and body odour. He was still in the same trousers and shirt he had been wearing three days previously. He was dishevelled, unshaven and unkempt.

"My God, son, what on earth are you doing to yourself?" his father asked, disbelieving the sight before his eyes. He strode to the window, pulled back the drapes and opened the windows wide.

For the first time, Jacks became aware of someone else in the room. He looked up with haunted eyes to see his father standing over him.

His stare seemed to soften as he recognised him. "Hello, Dad. I'm sorry, I just feel so bad, so very, very bad."

Lionel smelt his foul breath and nearly baulked. "I know, son, I know," he comforted, as he sat down next to him. "I think you may feel better if you shower, shave and get into some clean clothes. What do you say, eh?"

Jacks nodded, he knew there were things to be done, things he had to do for Leanne. "I will, Dad. Tell Mum I'll be down as soon as I've cleaned up."

"Okay, son, I'll let her know. Don't be too long about it though, will you?" Lionel went into the en-suite bathroom and turned on the shower. "Your shower is running, son, get undressed," he ordered, as he left the en-suite and closed the door.

***

Mum and dad were seated at the kitchen table as Jacks came down the stairs. He noticed there were no messages on the machine in the hall, and entered the kitchen. They were pleased to see he had made the effort, but still horrified at the sight of their once athletic and handsome offspring.

"Dinner will be in half an hour, and I don't want any arguments about it, Jacks," his mother addressed her son in his favoured title, although what was wrong with the Christian name they had given him was still a mystery to her and dad.

Jacks sat down, resigned to the fact he would have to play the game. He gave a weak smile to his mother, who came round the table and kissed him on his damp head.

Jacks was sort of helped through the next two weeks by his family, a host of callers from work and the vicar who was going to conduct the funeral service. The Reverend Charles Sinclair had been a friend of his parents for many years, and had overseen Jacks' own confirmation.

"I will be conducting the service for Leanne, Hilaire," the Reverend Sinclair explained. He was one of the only people ever to use Jacks' Christian name. In fact, other than his parents and Leanne, not many others knew it. He remembered Leanne tittering by his side as the vicar, revealed it during their wedding vows. His father had named him after the French Anglo writer and poet Hilaire Belloc, much to the chagrin of the vicar because Belloc was a Roman Catholic. Jacks didn't take in anything being discussed, and was pleased when the vicar eventually left.

They came and they went, Jacks didn't recall who or when. On the 15th September, on a chilly morning for the time of year, the hearse pulled up outside the house, accompanied by two large black limousines. Jacks allowed himself to be ushered to the limousine behind the hearse. Before getting in, he stopped and stared at the polished wooden casket in the back of the vehicle just in front, noticing Leanne's solitary police hat placed on the top of it. His heart beat faster; his head seemed as if it was going to explode as he thought of his Leanne lying there in the cold. He started to sway a little but fortunately Ron noticed and rushed to his side, steadying and gently moving him into the rear of the car.

There was quite a crowd at the church, with his colleagues from the Yard and Leanne's friends and colleagues from her station. Mike and Bobby stood waiting for him and fell in behind as they entered the church.

The service was short and simple. Mike King gave a eulogy, followed by a tearful Becky McQueen, Bobby's wife, who had been Leanne's best friend. Jacks hardly heard a word that was said, keeping his eyes firmly on the floor in front of him. The coffin, decked with a wreath and Leanne's police hat, was laid on trestles before the altar. The loneliness of the solitary coffin in the middle of the aisle seemed to scream at him.

As the vicar completed the service, the pall bearers moved in, but stopped abruptly as Jacks came out from his pew to place both hands on the coffin and bend forward to kiss the name on the brass plate. Mike King moved forward and put his arms across his friend's shoulders, leading him gently back to the pew. Jacks found himself at the graveside watching the casket being lowered into the open ground by the bearers as Reverend Sinclair prayed with them all saying, "Amen," as he finished.

Maddie and his father were on either side of him with their arms locked in his. They felt him trembling and shaking before he went rigid. Maddie looked at her brother; his chin was jutting out below clenched teeth as the tears rolled freely down his cheeks.

Jacks was staring hard at something in the distance. It was the girl in the yellow dress who didn't exist, according to the hospital. Who the hell is she? he thought. Leanne's words came back to him, 'Find her killer, Jacks, she cannot rest until you do'.

Stumbling forward, nearly falling in the open grave, he was held firmly by Ron and Maddie. Jacks, slowly looking back up, couldn't see her, he looked all around the graveyard but she wasn't anywhere to be seen.

They managed to get him back to the car park, muttering incoherently to himself as he stared around wildly. He was bundled into Ron's car and driven back to the house where the wake was to be held. Only close friends had been invited.

Maddie, in spite of the just close friends ruling, didn't know most of those who had attended; all those who knew Jacks and Leanne came to pay their respects. Jacks retired to his room, not believing what he had seen at the graveside. What did Leanne want him to do?

Jacks went over to the door, and for the first time ever, he locked it. He didn't want to see or hear anyone. He went into the en-suite bathroom and sat down on the side of the roll top bath and put his head in his hands. He felt as if his temples were about to explode as a dark cloud went before his eyes. In the distance, he heard pleading voices and knocking on the door, but soon he banished them forever as he entered a very dark place.

Jacks must have fallen asleep. He woke up in the dark, lying on the bed. The house was quiet, very quiet. Feeling very uneasy again, he rose to see what the problem was, if there was one at all. He was alone as he went over to the bedroom window and looked out on to his drive below.

Jacks stepped back in horror as he noticed the girl in the yellow dress, standing under the street light opposite his drive. He watched, transfixed, as she looked up at his window and put out her hand to him, as if to invite him down to meet her.

Jacks retreated further but kept her in sight. Who was she? What did she want? Turning quickly, he rushed to the door. It wouldn't open and then he remembered he had locked it. He turned the key and rushed out, taking the stairs two at a time. His parents heard him from the lounge, the front door opened as he ran out and down the drive.

Jacks reached the street light. She was nowhere to be seen.

"What kind of game are you playing, you little cow?" he screamed out. "Where are you? Why don't you stop and talk to me?"

The neighbours were all looking out of their windows and coming to their front doors to see what the commotion was about. Jacks' father reached him, looking round to see what was bothering his son. He couldn't see any reason for the outburst.

"What is it, son? What is troubling you?"

"The girl at the hospital, she was here again, Dad, she was watching me at the funeral today as well." Jacks was searching the street, frantically looking for the girl in the yellow dress.

Lionel took him firmly by his arm and started to pull him back towards the house. "Come on, son, the whole neighbourhood is turning out," he urged. "Let's get back inside."

His mother had reached the other side of him and joined in, tugging her son toward the house. As they got Jacks back inside the house, some of the neighbours remained outside, discussing the latest happening in their street.

Lionel fixed him a stiff scotch, making sure he stayed in the lounge to drink it before going out into the hall and phoning the number on the pad.

"Doctor Edwards," the voice answered in a soft, educated Devonshire accent.

Lionel explained what had happened, and the doctor agreed to come out straightaway. Whilst he waited for him to arrive, he dialled a second number and waited for the call to be answered.

A very sleepy, very croaky voice barked into his ear. "Who is this?"

"This is Jacks' father, Sergeant King. Can you come over? I need to talk to you urgently."

The doctor arrived first, examined Jacks and told him he was suffering from stress and depression from his loss.

Great, thought Lionel, brilliant diagnosis. "Can you give him something, Doctor?" he asked.

"I can give him an injection now and I will drop by in the morning with some further medication."

Jacks was listening to all this as if it was happening to someone else. He didn't respond, even when the needle went in. Soon he was feeling very tired, relaxed and falling asleep.

Mike King arrived as the doctor was leaving. "Is there anything I should know about, Doctor? I'm his colleague and best friend," he asked.

"Mr Jacks, his father, can fill you in. They have my number. If anything else happens, call me."

Lionel filled Mike in on what had happened, including details about his son seeing this girl.

Mike was already aware of the internal hospital investigation. "I am not surprised, Lionel. I've never seen a couple so tuned in together, he must feel his heart's been ripped out. He's going to be depressed for some time and needs watching."

Mike had the good sense to bring an overnight bag with him, and settled into the third guest room. He slept with one eye open for the rest of the night, waiting for something else to happen.

Jacks awoke at six o'clock the next morning with a slight hangover. He showered, shaved, dressed and went down to the kitchen. His mother was sitting at the table, reading yesterday's paper, as he walked in.

"Morning, Mum," he said airily, as if nothing had happened the night before. "Are you doing breakfast?"

"Of course, what would you like, son?"

A tired Mike King entered the kitchen very sheepishly. "Morning, Jacks," he said, hopefully.

Jacks didn't bat an eyelid. "What are you doing here?" he asked flatly.

Mike thought quickly, even though he was trying to clear the cobwebs to do so. "I was near last night and needed a bed, you don't mind do you?"

"Good one, Mike. Have some breakfast and then you can be on your way." Jacks stared at him, letting him know he didn't need an answer. At this point his father walked in, saving them from any more awkward conversation.

"Yes please, Mother, I'll have breakfast too. It's nice to see everyone up so early."

When breakfast was over, Jacks told his parents he wanted to talk to them. Mike King diplomatically went out for the morning paper. As he pulled out of the drive, Jacks spoke to them. "Mum, Dad, I want to thank you for all your support, you've been great…"

Lionel interrupted him, "I feel a great big but in there, son."

"I want you both to go home, now. I have to learn to cope on my own and I can only do that by myself. You do see that, don't you?" He said it as if it was final, even though he asked the question.

His mum and dad were not convinced; it was too early, and how would he cope, etcetera, etcetera.

Jacks stuck to his guns, and by the time Mike got back with the papers his parents had packed their things and were ready to leave.

"Don't ask," Jacks said, as Mike came in, eyeing the suitcases in the hall. His parents left after kissing and embracing their son, and getting Mike to promise to phone them if they were needed.

After they had left, Jacks turned to Mike. "Your turn, pack and leave."

"Can't do that, Governor," he said formally. "I think there's something we need to talk about."

"Such as what?" Jacks asked sarcastically. "Payne and Child's trial is months away, and you and Bobby can finish the leg work. You don't need me yet."

"Don't sound so bloody naïve, Jacks. You know what I mean. This girl that you have been seeing, the one from the hospital and the graveside. Your father called me because he said you saw her again last night. That's what I'm talking about."

Jacks looked daggers at him; how dare he presume on their friendship. He clenched his fists and gritted his teeth as he rasped, "Keep a civil tongue in your head when you talk to me, King. Do you hear?"

"Oh, King, is it? I don't care what you think, we have to talk. We have to see if we can get to the bottom of this. If you don't, Jacks, they are going to cart you away to the looney bin."

Jacks, incensed, struggled to keep his temper. He didn't want to thump his friend and colleague, but he was fighting his feelings in order not to do so.

Mike picked up on the mood; he knew how dangerous Jacks was becoming. "Look, Governor, I'm not being facetious. I'm concerned, and I think I can help. Please let's just talk?"

Jacks remained staring at him with fire behind the deep brown eyes that seemed to turn dark black as they smouldered. He started to unclench his fist as the fire started to subside. His shoulders slumped in resignation as Mike walked towards him and took his elbow. They sat down at the kitchen table and talked.

It was five hours later when a very puzzled Mike left to go home before going on to the Yard. Jacks was on his own again. He went into the lounge, reached for a glass and the bottle of scotch and started to drink. It would be a couple of days before he was sober again.

EIGHT

Jacks was dreaming. Leanne was by his side, and they were walking hand in hand through a wooded area, admiring the array of bluebells covering the whole copse. They came to a shallow stream and used the stepping stones to cross. On the other side, he saw the girl, the pretty, fair haired-girl in the yellow dress.

"Hello, Chief Inspector," she said softly. "It's nice of you to come.

"What can I do for you? What is it you want?" he asked.

It was Leanne who turned to him, and answered, "This is Patsy, Jacks, the girl I mentioned to you, remember?"

"What do you want?" he asked again.

The girl remained looking at him, and again it was Leanne who spoke for her. "Find her killer, Jacks, she can't rest until you do."

All of a sudden the girl was gone, Leanne was gone, where were they? He became aware of a loud banging noise, what was it?

Jacks woke up. He was still in the lounge and had a blinding headache. There was further noise at the front door as Bobby McQueen kicked it in, came down the hall and looked in.

"He's in here," Bobby called out, as he reached Jacks. "Jesus Christ, Guv, you're in one hell of a state."

Mike King appeared, squeezing past the bulk of Bobby McQueen.

"Fuck off and leave me alone." Jacks was still drunk.

"Seal that door, Bobby. We don't want any prying eyes coming through."

Bobby went back to the front door that was hanging on one hinge, and forced it shut. The lock held it in place and he returned to the lounge.

"He must have been like this for the week," Mike said. "As soon as I left him."

"Let's get him up to the shower, Mike. We need to sober him up some." They both took an arm and literally half lifted and half dragged the protesting figure that was once their boss, down the hall, up the stairs and into the bedroom. They ran a cold shower, holding Jacks in it whilst he shook and shivered for about twenty minutes.

"You fucking bastards," Jacks muttered. "I'll sort you both out for this."

"Yes, Guv, but not today, eh?" Bobby retorted. "You're a sorry mess. You are a disgusting mess, and a disgrace to Leanne's memory."

Jacks was shocked and just stared, open-mouthed into space; was it true? Was he disgracing her memory?

He heard Mike King in the distance say, "Cool it, Bobby, that's a bit strong."

"No, Mike, he's right, I am a disgrace. I don't know what I think I am doing." Jacks looked up at Bobby with bloodshot, haunted eyes. "I'll get it together, don't you worry. I'll sort myself out."

The two of them fixed the door, opened all the windows and set about clearing the mess from the lounge and kitchen.

They fed Jacks copious amounts of coffee, Mike went out and got some food in, and a meal was cooked.

Jacks ate slowly as they both looked on, making sure he finished the lot.

Bobby McQueen went through the house, gathering up any alcohol he could find and tipping it away down the sink.

"Now we've cleaned you up, Jacks, I'm going to phone Maddie and ask her to come over for a while, okay?" Mike King was asking the question, but he knew it was going to happen no matter what he said, he just nodded.

Maddie turned up as requested, and the two of them decided it was time to leave. They had embarrassed their boss quite enough.

Before they left, they removed Jacks' car keys from the hall table. "He can have them back in a couple of days, if he stays sober," Mike informed Maddie. "Please make sure he doesn't have a spare set anywhere, Maddie, will you?"

She assured him she would look, and secure them when and if she could locate them.

It was a couple of hours later when Jacks discovered his keys were missing.

"The bastards," he said incredulously. "The cheeky bastards." He went to the bureau in the lounge watched by Maddie. He opened it. No keys!

"I'll kill the pair of them," he shouted.

"They're right," Maddie shouted back in frustration. "You shouldn't be driving; you will be way over the limit, let alone a danger to the public."

"I want to go to the graveyard," Jacks explained.

"I'll take you," said Maddie.

Jacks thought for a moment before realising it was a short walk to the bus stop; he could bus there. "I want to go alone, Maddie. I'll take a bus, if that's okay with everyone?" he said sarcastically. He grabbed his car coat from the hook in the hall and donned it as he went out the damaged front door.

"Don't worry, I'll be back without stopping off anywhere."

He waited at the bus stop for over half an hour, feeling cold and lonely. Pulling his collar up, he felt an icy gust suddenly hit him, making him feel the same as he did at the hospital. He stared around the road, watching people walk by; why did he feel this way?

He looked to his right and noticed the double decker bus coming round the bend through a patch of mist he hadn't noticed before. The number six bus pulled up at the stop. Jacks stepped up on to the platform and entered the bus. He chose a downstairs seat in the middle of the bus.

As it pulled away from the kerb, a conductor came down the aisle towards him. Stopping in front of Jacks, he looked down at him.

"Where to?" he asked.

Jacks looked up at the conductor and shivered with the cold. "St Mary's Church, please. I thought conductors went out with the ark?" he queried. "And to think of it, the bus is a bit ancient as well."

The conductor looked down at Jacks with a contemptuous sneer on his face. "I can smell the booze from here, mate, no wonder things look odd to you. That'll be fifty pence… please." He was short and sarcastic, no wonder they've done away with them on most routes, Jacks thought.

Jacks looked out of the window to see the swirling mist getting thicker. He hadn't seen the likes of this since his teens. Looking at the mist seemed to disorientate him, and he started to feel faint and light-headed. The conductor was right about the booze, he thought.

He tried to concentrate his attention on the passengers on the bus, but they were becoming fuzzy to the eye. Then he saw her; the girl in the yellow dress was back. She got up from her seat, turned and smiled at him before starting to the front of the bus.

Jacks struggled to his feet, reeling as he straightened. The bus came to a halt as he tried to make it down the aisle. A passenger got up just in front of him and slowed him down. He looked ahead to see another male passenger right behind the girl.

She turned to see who it was before looking at him with horror on her face. Jacks pushed forward, but the passenger was having none of it.

"You drunken bum," hissed the man blocking his way. "Who the hell do you think you're pushing?" He barred Jacks' way to the front.

Jacks stretched his neck round the passenger in time to see the conductor get in between the girl and the man following her. The conductor suddenly jumped back and stood between two seats allowing the man to pass, he was startled by something the man had said to him.

The bus stopped, and the girl and the man behind her got off together. She still had that look of horror on her face as she looked at the man.

Jacks tried to see his face but couldn't, but he did notice the series of stars tattooed on the man's right ear. The bus pulled away from the kerb, with Jacks looking helplessly out of the side window.

He eventually got passed the awkward passenger, and shouted for the bus to stop. "No stop here, mate," the ashen-faced conductor replied.

"If you don't stop I'm going to be sick all over the seats, you bastard," Jacks threatened.

The bus stopped instantly. He jumped out on to the pavement, running back up the road to where the last stop should have been, but it wasn't marked. He thought it was because of the mist, but then he noticed the mist had completely gone. The road, either way, was completely deserted.

Jacks turned round, mystified at this queer turn of events, and continued walking to St Mary's Church. He entered the churchyard by the lych-gate and made his way to the freshly covered grave of his beloved wife.

In spite of requesting no flowers, the grave was covered with bouquets and posies of all kinds. Jacks never knew her favourite flowers; whenever he brought them it was usually the biggest spray the florist could put together.

"You spoil me, Jacks," he heard her say.

He knelt down at the graveside and spoke to her. "Why… why… why? Why you, Leanne? Why not me? You were by far the better of the two of us."

No reply came as he waited expectantly for an answer. His shoulders shook and the sobs started as he pitched forward, prostrating himself over the flowers on the grave.

He was still in that position when Ron arrived and stood over this pathetic figure that he used to look up to with the utmost respect.

"Come on, Jacks, let's get you home. You've had enough for one day." He led him out of the churchyard, on to the road where his car was parked in the small layby. They were back at Jacks' place in just under twenty minutes.

As soon as Maddie and Ron left to go home, Jacks took a handful of sedatives prescribed by the doctor and went to bed. He just lay there, unable to sleep, asking himself over and over, mumbling, "Why, Leanne, why?"

He screamed out loud, shaking the walls of the bedroom. His neighbours next door just looked at one another, understanding his despair. Jacks slowly drifted into a fitful sleep and returned to that very dark place.

He was walking along the road through the mist as he came to a path that went across a field. Climbing over the stile he walked the path towards the woods on the other side. There wasn't a sound, no birds singing, no wind blowing through the grass or trees. He entered the woods keeping to the path and followed it until the mist parted revealing the babbling stream. The stepping stones that were there previously couldn't be seen.

"Hello, Jacks." Leanne was smiling at him from across the stream. She wasn't alone. Standing next to her, holding her hand, was Patsy, the girl in the yellow dress.

Jacks went to cross the stream, but Leanne stopped him. "You can't cross, Jacks."

"Why not? Why can't I join you and hold your hand?" he said to her. "Why do you want to hold her hand and not mine?"

He held his hand out, beseeching her to take it, to allow him to cross.

Leanne continued to smile at him. "Because you are alive, you silly man, we are dead. You have things to do, Jacks. You must find Patsy's killer… You must fine Patsy's killer… You must find…" Leanne's voice trailed off as she started to disappear, leaving Patsy standing on her own staring at him, before she, too, gradually faded and disappeared.

He was on the bus again, looking down the aisle. He noticed the conductor who had been so obnoxious, the passenger who had got in his way, and then he saw the back of the man with the three stars tattooed on his right ear.

Jacks couldn't move. Turn round, he urged, turn round, blast you.

The man took hold of the back of the seat to pull himself up. Jacks noticed a gold signet ring on the large finger of his right hand as he rose and started to move to the exit.

Jacks still couldn't move. The man got off the bus and walked along the path. Jacks was horrified to see the girl in the yellow dress walking in front of him.

"No, no, stop," he called out, and then woke up.

The sweat was pouring off his forehead, his top was soaked through. He raised himself up on his elbows, looked at the bedside clock radio, realised it was daylight and already seven thirty in the morning. He started to shiver with cold, lay back down and pulled the duvet up round his neck, whilst he tried to fathom out the dreams.

I'm going round the bend, he thought. An hour later he got out of bed, had a hot shower, went down into the kitchen and made a coffee, before pouring milk over two Weetabix sprinkled with currants and raisins. He devoured his breakfast hungrily, just finishing when the door bell sounded.

Jacks opened the front door, and there stood Mike King.

"Hello, Governor, you look terrible," he quipped. "You've got milk on your chin."

Jacks wiped his chin with the back of his hand. "It's what happens when people interrupt your breakfast, Mike," he retorted. "Come in." He collected his cutlery and bowl to take to the sink. As he did so he wobbled and staggered slightly before Mike sat him down again.

"Easy, Governor, you need to take it easy for a while." Mike was very concerned at his appearance, and watched his boss as his head started to shake from side to side. "I think you need to see someone, Jacks. The top brass are asking awkward questions about your health. We need to get you sorted."

"Piss the top brass," Jacks swore. "I don't give a toss what they think."

"Well I do, Jacks. You're the best governor I've ever had and by far the best detective the Yard has. Neither of us wants to lose you." Mike bent over him, trying to look into the eyes behind the black shadows. "Come on, Jacks, I know someone who can help without anyone else knowing."

"And who the hell is that miracle worker?" he sneered at Mike. "Is he going to bring Leanne back to me?"

Mike ignored the question. "A second cousin of mine, her name is Professor Suzanna Kaine." Jacks didn't reply, so Mike continued. "Suzanne is a brilliant psychiatrist…"

Jacks didn't give him time to finish before exploding in a typical diatribe.

"A shrink," he shouted out. "You want me to see a shrink? A fucking nut doctor? So you think I'm mad, do you? Well you can fuck off now."

Mike sat down opposite Jacks, ignoring the bad language so uncharacteristic of his boss. "I knew that would be your first reaction," he said in a quiet voice.

"And my bloody last one," Jacks scowled.

"Think, Guv, think long and hard. You don't do anybody any good acting like this, least of all Leanne's memory, or your parents." Mike leant back, away from the table, expecting the worst.

Jacks remained brooding silently and thinking of what Mike had just said.

Come on, get a bloody grip, he thought to himself, before saying, "Okay, Mike, I'll give anything a try, but I'll warn you now, if I think it's a waste of time I'll be out of there."

Mike King sighed with relief. "Good man, Guv, good man."

NINE

October 2013

Jacks related to Professor Suzanne Kaine exactly how the robbery and murder of Howard Jones went down, and filled her in on Leanne's death and his subsequent sightings of the young girl, and Leanne.

He eventually left her surgery in Harley Street after a session lasting over three hours. He had so dreaded the meeting, but after settling in found it to be therapeutic and mind-relaxing.

He got back to the Yard just after four in the afternoon, and was followed into his office by Mike King.

"How did it go, Guv?" he asked. "How did you find Suzanne?"

"Well, in both cases," Jacks replied. "And that's the last time I will discuss this with you, do you understand, Mike?"

"Got you loud and clear, Guv," Mike said with a grin. "Bobby and me need to go over our evidence with you in the cases of Payne and Childs. We've had to charge Payne with the manslaughter of one of the motorbike boys, and ABH for the second. We still haven't discovered the identity of the driver."

"Have we got it all sewn up with Payne?" Jacks asked. "Have we tied him in with the robberies and the murder of Jones and Treadwell?"

"He's pleading guilty to the robberies, Guv, but not to the murders of the jeweller and Treadwell. He says that Treadwell is responsible for the jeweller, and that Chalky killed him before he bled out."

"Does he really think he's going to get away with a cock and bull story like that?" Jacks asked, looking up at Mike. "In any case, we still have 'common purpose' in this case."

"What's he got to lose? He knows it's worth taking the risk with a jury. I've seen far stronger cases go to the wall."

Jacks smiled, remembering a few cases of his own. "You're right there, Mike, you are most certainly right there. Arrange for a meeting of all police witnesses, and make sure we have all statements and evidence listings for us to go through." Jacks went quiet, thinking to himself when Mike prompted him.

"Penny for 'em, Governor," he said, bringing Jacks out of his thoughts.

"Can you do me another favour? Can you see if you can find out if a girl was reported missing between twenty and twenty-five years ago in the Sunningdale, Twickenham areas?"

"Is this the girl your Leanne asked you to find, Jacks?" Mike referred to him by his name to keep it low key and unofficial.

"Yes." Jacks handed him a slip of paper with the girl's approximate age and a description of 'Patsy' as he could recall her. "I am going to check on the bus services running at that time."

That afternoon Jacks pulled up in the car park of the local bus depot, parked his Volvo next to a single decker bus, and headed for the offices. After flashing his warrant card he was ushered into the office of the area manager.

He sat down and waited, while they fetched the supervisor from the garage. On the walls were all kinds of pictures, time tables and past advertisements.

The door opened, and a small dapper man, aged about sixty, entered and made his way round to the business side of the desk.

"What can I do for you, Chief Inspector...?" he asked, as he gained his seat and settled in. The name on the desk plate read 'Depot Manager George Barton'.

"Jacks, Chief Inspector Jacks," he confirmed, showing his warrant card again. "I'm trying to find out about the bus services that ran in the Sunningdale and Twickenham areas about twenty-five years ago."

"Why, Chief Inspector? Why twenty-five years ago?" George Barton asked, puzzled at the request.

"I believe a young girl went missing round about that time, and have reason to believe she may have used a bus service in that area. What can you tell me about the service at that time that ran between Sunningdale and Twickenham?"

"Phew! Now you're asking something," he said, scratching his temple.

"If it helps, bus conductors were on that route," Jacks added.

"Then it has to be over twenty years ago. We stopped using them when we got rid of the old buses. I think, but I'll have to check, it was the number six that ran that route. If you give me a few moments I'll go and check."

Barton disappeared out of the door, leaving Jacks to sit and wait. He had been sitting there for about five minutes before a smiling George Barton re-appeared, holding a manila folder.

"Good news, Inspector," he beamed. "I've managed to trace the route, the bus and the time tables." George opened the folder and Jacks saw the photos of the Number six bus sitting on top of the papers inside.

"Is there anything else you can tell me about the service or the buses?" Jacks asked.

"Such as?" George asked, not knowing what was required of him.

"Such as the date this particular bus stopped running and, if possible, when this model started service on the route? Also, do you have any records of the male conductors who manned that bus service at the time?"

"Now that is a tall order, Chief Inspector. That will definitely take me some more time, if we have it at all. Can you give me a couple of days to see what I can find out?"

"I would really appreciate that, George." Jacks rose from his chair and offered his hand. As they shook, he added, "Give me a ring if, and when, you have anything. Here's my card, it has my direct line on it."

Jacks drove back to the Yard, feeling a little better than when he had arrived earlier in the day. As he parked, his mobile rang.

"Jacks," he answered.

"Where are you, Guv?" the voice of Mike King sounded in his ear.

"Just pulling into the car park, Mike. I take it you're here already."

"I'll be in your office," Mike confirmed.

Jacks entered his office to be greeted not only by Mike, but Bobby as well. "What have you got for me?" he asked neither of them in particular.

Mike got up from his chair. "Across London and the South East, we've had over seventy girls between the ages of twelve and sixteen go missing between 1989 and 1995. We have traced a few and accounted for some more, leaving an outstanding total of thirty-five girls."

Bobby butted in. "We have discounted those girls who have gone missing more than twice and whittled it down to just twelve, Guv."

"I take it you're up to speed on this then, Bobby?" Jacks enquired, looking accusingly at Mike King.

Mike jumped in immediately, not wanting there to be any misunderstandings over Jacks' meeting with his cousin. "Only where the girls are concerned, Guv," he assured him.

Bobby looked first at Mike and then at Jacks. What was that supposed to mean? he thought, but said nothing.

"I'll tell you later, Bobby," Jacks said, picking up instantly on Bobby's inquisitiveness as to why he should be left out.

"We have photos of all the girls, Governor. Perhaps these are going to help." He laid out the green folders on the desk, whilst giving Mike an accusing look, as if to say, 'I'll be having words with you later'.

Mike ignored the look, sat back down and started to open the folders. He took out the photographs of the first girl and showed it to Jacks. Not the one, so he shook his head.

Mike took out the next and the next, until he came to the eighth green folder. As he opened it, Jacks' eyes opened wide.

There on the top of the papers was 'Patsy', looking out at him with her bright blue eyes.

"That's the girl," he said simply. "That's her all right." He took hold of the photograph and examined it in minute detail, noticing the silver cross round her neck. For a moment, he was back in the hospital room, with the girl sitting in the corner. His mind raced on to see the girl at his beloved Leanne's graveside, then to seeing the bus when she had got off, followed by the man. Jacks felt weak and must have paled.

"You all right, Governor?" asked a concerned Mike, as he watched his boss's ashen face. He nearly said 'you look as if you've seen a ghost' but just stopped himself.

"It's her, Mike. What on earth is going on?" Jacks bit his knuckles, much to the surprise of Bobby, who watched as blood started to run down his hand to his wrist.

"Take it easy, Jacks." Bobby spoke softly. "We understand what you are going through." He didn't really, but wanted to re-assure his boss that he was on board with him.

Jacks couldn't take his eyes of the girl's, she seemed to penetrate his very soul, not accusing him, more with a pleading, baleful stare, asking for his help. He eventually moved the picture to one side and started to go through the file, watched by his two sergeants. It wasn't long before they were all involved, going over every detail of this missing girl.

Patricia 'Patsy' Josephine Kerridge was fifteen years of age at the time of her mysterious disappearance, some twenty-five years ago. Five feet, two inches tall, fair to blonde hair, depending if she had been out in the sun for long periods, trim athletic build, and quite a looker for her age. It appeared by the notes that she had gone missing after an evening athletics meeting at her school. There was talk that she had become involved with one of her teachers, and several of the men were questioned to no avail. Patsy was an only child and lived with her middle class parents at number eighty seven, Kirkbride Avenue in Twickenham. The daughter of an engineer, who played rugby for his county, and her teacher mother, who was a champion swimmer, it was almost inevitable that she would become an athlete, if she had lived.

"Other than the gossip about her teachers, it appears she was more into sport than the opposite sex," Bobby chipped in.

"Mike, go and get the car round. I think we'll pay her family a visit. Bobby, give the bus depot a ring and talk to George Barton with the dates she went missing. When you've done that, carry on sifting through the statements we have and see if anything comes to mind." Jacks knew he was clutching at straws but you never knew, a fresh pair of eyes sometimes did the trick.

***

Mike pulled up outside number eighty seven Kirkbride Avenue, parking just before the driveway so as not to block the entrance. Jacks got out of the passenger side and joined him, heading for the front door.

The property was a small, detached, three bedroom house with a pretty wisteria over the door, which ran the width of the house and disappeared, out of sight, round the corner of the building. Jacks noticed the neatness of the lawn and the raised flower beds on either side. The approach was decked out like a country-cottage type garden, rather than a house in the suburbs.

Jacks was not looking forward to this visit at all. He breathed in deeply as he eyed the smartly painted white front door, and watched his own hand move towards the knocker. He rapped three times and waited.

A few moments later they heard footsteps coming down a stone-floored hallway and the door opened.

An old, white-haired man, who looked about eighty years of age, was standing looking at them. He noticed their dark suits, ties round clean crisp shirt collars, and polished shoes.

"Yes? What can I do for you?" he asked. "I hold no truck with Jehovah Witnesses."

Jacks felt inside his pocket but before he could take out his warrant card, Mike had produced his.

"Detective Chief Inspector Jacks," Mike said, adding, "I'm Detective Sergeant King. We are looking for Mr Bertram Kerridge."

"I'm Bert Kerridge," the old man said. "What's this about? You sound like a comedy duo, Jacks and King." Realisation suddenly hit him as to who they were, and he stepped back.

"Is it about Patsy, have you found her?" he asked weakly.

"Can we come in please, Mr Kerridge? Its best we talk inside," Jacks urged gently.

The poor man started to age visibly as they followed him down the hallway to a small lounge. He invited them to sit.

Jacks looked round the room, noticing the pictures of Patsy and her parents on sideboards and on the walls.

"Is Mrs Kerridge at home?" he asked.

Jacks was met with a hurt stare, before Mr Kerridge answered, "My wife is dead, Chief Inspector. She died of a broken heart some ten years ago."

"I am very sorry, Mr Kerridge, you have my deepest sympathy." Jacks could never bring himself to say the new American condolence of, 'I'm sorry for your loss,' which sounded so heartless, cold and matter of fact, but now in use across the Force.

"Chief Inspector," he started, "is this about Patsy or not?"

Jacks looked him straight in the eye, seeing how painful this was for the man. "Yes, sir, I am afraid it is, not that we have found her, we haven't, but I wanted to go through a few things with you."

"After all this time, no one has been near us for years," he corrected himself straightaway, "me, for over ten years. Why now?"

"From time to time we have to undertake reviews of all unsolved cases, and this came up," he lied. "Have you heard from your daughter at all, Mr Kerridge? Have you ever had any inkling of what happened to her?"

"She's dead, Chief Inspector, she would never break her mother's heart in this way, or mine for that matter. I keep going only in case she does miraculously turn up, but I know in my heart of hearts, that is not to be."

Mike King cleared his throat, causing both Bert Kerridge and his boss to look at him. "Mr Kerridge, sir, do you remember the day Patsy went missing?"

"It's burnt on my memory. We feared the worst straightaway, Patsy would never go astray. There was talk about her involvement with a teacher, but it was just that, talk."

Mike King pressed on. "Do you recall her ever talking about anybody? Was she followed at any time, for instance?"

Jacks watched the tortured face, knowing the gut-wrenching turmoil that this man and his wife had gone through. He waited patiently for the man to turn his mind back twenty-five years.

"She did complain once that she was being pestered by a young man. She thought he was in the army because of his dress. You know, fatigues, combat boots, that sort of thing, as well as his short cropped hair."

"Was this followed up at the time?" Jacks asked.

"Yes, I think so, but at that time they were looking for a missing girl, a very pretty girl at that. They didn't come up with any leads, Chief Inspector, not one. It was as if she had been abducted by aliens, she just vanished." Bert Kerridge was becoming very emotional, with tears starting to fill his haunted eyes.

Jacks thought of his age and realised that the man was only in his sixties; Patsy, then his wife, had taken their toll.

"I'm sorry, gentlemen. I know it was so long ago but, when I think about it, when I am alone in the dark, it was yesterday. Until you lose someone so close, someone so dear, you couldn't possibly understand. I'll tell you one thing though, Patsy was a fighter. That's what hurts so much, I know she would have fought for all she was worth and probably suffered more because of it."

Mike looked at his boss, noticing the jaw set tight and his lips drawn across his teeth.

Bert Kerridge followed his eyes and saw Jacks. "You do know, Chief Inspector, you have been there, haven't you?"

Jacks stared ahead. He had to get out of there or he was going to lose it. The thought of Leanne was unbearable as he clenched and unclenched his hands, digging his nails into his palms. He breathed in heavily, turned to Bert Kerridge, looked him in the eyes and made a solemn promise.

"I will find her for you, Mr Kerridge. This isn't just an empty promise, I will find her," Jacks turned away and made for the door, leaving Mike King to say their farewells.

It was some five minutes later when Mike opened the driver's door and, without saying a word, fastened his seat belt and started the engine.

Bobby McQueen was still in the office when they got back to the Yard. Mike King filled him in briefly about their meeting in Twickenham.

"Have you managed to find anything from the files, Bobby?" Jacks asked, more in hope than anything.

"There isn't a great deal in here, Guv," he answered, flipping through the papers. "The normal house to house stuff. There was mention of some army type in fatigues, who they didn't trace to eliminate. Several male teachers and school kids were questioned, but that's it. She was popular at school and excelled at sport, by all accounts."

Jacks thought hard as they all sat round his desk. He eventually looked up at them both. "Tomorrow, we'll walk the route of the old number six bus and see if it turns up anything. Meanwhile, have an early night. Pick me up at home please, Mike."

***

Jacks stood at Leanne's graveside, hoping that she would appear to him again with Patsy; nothing.

He spoke softly to Leanne. "I miss you so much, love, I don't know if it's worth carrying on. What is there for me now? What is the point?"

He stood there, looking down at the mound of earth with the wilting flowers spread the length of it, and he started to go to that dark place once again, as tears rolled gently down his cheeks.

He reached home as it was getting dark, parked his car and went inside, knowing she wasn't there to meet him. Jacks made a sandwich from a tin of spam from the fridge, poured a large scotch and took it, with the bottle and sandwich, into the lounge. The curtains were still drawn tight from the night before. Or was it the night before that? He couldn't remember, and didn't care. He drank the scotch and poured himself another. After a couple more, he must have fallen asleep.

He woke up to the door bell ringing. He went and opened the door in a bit of a haze. Mike was standing on the doorstep. The smile on his face disappeared as he saw the state his boss was in.

"Oh, for Christ's sake, Jacks, not again." He followed Jacks back inside to the lounge, noticing the upended bottle of scotch and the untouched sandwich on the plate. "Go up and shower, Governor. I'll put the coffee on."

Jacks didn't argue. In the cold light of day he knew his sergeant was right. It was the blasted dark, the loneliness and the dark that got to him, he knew that. He mounted the stairs to his bedroom, undressed and showered. Half an hour later, he came downstairs to the aroma of freshly made coffee.

TEN

Jacks and King met Bobby in a roadside café just out of Twickenham.

Mike went to the counter and ordered a full English breakfast for all, which they ate, washing it down with large mugs of black coffee.

Jacks was starting to look human and alert again. Bobby watched him carefully as he took sideway glances at Mike to see what he was thinking of their boss.

"I'm fine, Bobby," Jacks said, as he noticed the furtive glances between them. "Don't you worry about me. Let's finish up here and hit the road. I want to start at Patsy Kerridge's school and make our way along the route," he explained.

"That's one hell of a walk, Governor," Mike chipped in. "We don't even know if she took the bus."

"She took the bus all right," Jacks replied. "I know that she took that bus. Anyway, the walk will do you good."

Mike and Bobby exchanged glances, both thinking to humour him and go along with this.

Ten minutes later, they parked the car near the school, making their way to the sports ground. The grounds were enclosed with wire mesh, but twenty-five years ago it was open, members of the public friends and relations of the pupils, had open access to it.

Jacks pictured Patsy running in her races, whilst people looked on. Where would he have stood? He tried to imagine the man with the tattooed ear standing watching her as she competed.

"We had better start walking, Guv. It's going to take us a little while," Mike suggested.

They walked the pathway beside the road, looking for anywhere that an abductor could take someone without being seen. For over three miles they walked, more if you counted the times they went off the road to explore driveways and paths that led from it.

They reached a point about a mile from the church where Leanne was buried. There was quite an expanse of open country behind a low hedge, and Jacks started to feel uneasy. He searched for pathways, hidden paths that would have grown over in the years that had passed. He couldn't see any, but he did notice a gap in the hedge, and as he looked over to the copse beyond, he noticed an unnatural gap between the trees.

Jacks pushed through, followed by Mike and Bobby. They made their way across the rough pasture land, making for the treeline about three hundred yards away.

"You okay, Guv?" Bobby asked, wondering why they had chosen to cross the field.

"I'm fine, Mr McQueen, thank you," Jacks answered, pressing on towards the trees. "Keep going, we'll see where this leads us."

"There seems to be an opening just ahead, Guv, or there was once," Mike said, as he moved ahead of them.

It had been a path at some stage, but was now overgrown with long reed grasses, which grew between silver birch trees that led ever deeper into the copse. The growth on either side of them became denser the further they entered. After two hundred yards the trees began to thin out until they came upon a small stream, straddled by weeping willow trees, intermingled with brambles and bracken.

"I should think it was a favourite for picnickers at one time," Bobby suggested, as he looked down at the slow flowing water making its way through the thick reed bed.

Jacks was standing still, rigidly looking across the stream; he had an awful sense of déjà vu. He was sure he had visited here before, immediately recalling his last dream of Leanne and Patsy.

Mike was watching closely and saw the change come over him.

"You, okay, Jacks?" he asked quietly. Jacks didn't reply, he just kept staring at a point opposite. "Can you see a way across?" Mike asked.

Bobby scanned upstream and thought he saw some movement on the opposite bank. "I think someone's on the bank opposite, Governor."

Jacks and Mike followed Bobby's pointing finger, and they too saw a figure standing in the trees on the bank. Jacks drew a deep breath as he felt his heart start to beat wildly.

"Let's see who it is, lads," he said, moving forward and keeping tight to the bank.

The figure saw them coming. As they neared, he put his hand up in welcome. In his other hand was a fishing rod. They had come across an angler.

"I wouldn't have thought there were any fish in this stream," Mike quipped.

"Fat lot you know about it, townie," Bobby answered, as they drew opposite the angler.

The man had come prepared, kitted out with waders and a catch net hanging in the water. There was movement in the net, lending the lie to the 'townies' comments earlier.

Jacks was disappointed in a way but, at the same time, relieved that it wasn't a ghost.

"Good morning to you," he ventured.

The man looked at his watch and then back at the three of them. "Still morning, well I never. Are you three out for a walk?"

Jacks ignored the question.

"Do you have fishing rights along the stream?" he asked.

"What's it to you? Who are you?" his tone suddenly changed with a hint of suspicion in it; they certainly didn't look like ramblers.

Jacks held up his warrant card. "Don't worry, I'm not here to enforce any fishing rights, I just want a little information on the area. Can you help?"

The angler placed his rod in the 'V' of a stick, stepped into the water and waded across the stream. Jacks noticed the depth as he came across, and estimated it to be about one and a half feet deep.

The man was about fifty-five years of age, well dressed under his bibbed waders, with a checked shirt and tartan tie. "My name is John Reynolds. I live about two miles away from here. If you ask me, have I got a licence, then I'm afraid the answer is no."

"Not a problem for us, John, if I may call you that? I wouldn't know what a licence looked like, anyway. I'm Chief Inspector Jacks, and these two gentlemen are Sergeants King and McQueen," he introduced them and continued. "Do you know the area well?"

"I should think so. I've been coming here since I was a boy. I've taken early retirement now so I'm able to come here a couple of times a week. Not what it used to be though."

"How do mean?" Jacks asked.

"It used to be faster flowing and wider, with a lot more water running through, especially after a good rainfall. Industry and the like have taken their toll on this stretch of water," John said with melancholy.

Jacks looked at him and asked, "Has there ever been a crossing, a bridge or something like that over the stream?"

John thought for a moment, before answering. "No, no, at least I can't remember any bridge. Hang on though, I think some lads laid some stones across at one point, but that was years ago."

"Some stones?" Jacks questioned. "Where is this?"

"It was years ago, Chief Inspector. They were removed when the stream started to lose its proper flow. All kinds of rubbish and debris were being caught up by them. It was affecting the river even more." John pointed downstream to where the three detectives had come from. "That's where they were. A path led from the main road. The stones took you across the stream and continued to what was the village, about a mile away."

"Can you give Sergeant King your details, sir? We may want to ask you some more questions about this area twenty-five years ago," Jacks asked pleasantly.

"Of course, Chief Inspector. Only too pleased to help." John turned to Mike, who already had his notebook out.

Jacks and Bobby had already turned, and were making their way back down the stream to the point of the old pathway. Jacks looked across the stream but couldn't see any way across.

"Oh, well," he said, as he started to undo his shoelaces and remove his shoes and socks. He stuffed the socks in the shoes, tied the laces together and draped them round his neck.

Mike caught up to them just as Jacks was about to enter the stream.

"Looks a bit bloody cold for a paddle, Guv," he laughed.

Jacks had rolled up his trousers to above the knees, didn't bother to test the water, put his foot straight in and started to cross.

"Not bad at all," he called over his shoulder.

Without any further hesitation, the two sergeants removed their footwear, copied their boss and strung them round their necks. They strode confidently to the water and, like Jacks, stepped straight in. They both howled as the cold hit them.

"You bastard, Jacks," shouted Mike, Bobby was gasping and couldn't say a word.

For the first time in a long while, Jacks allowed himself to laugh. He climbed the shallow bank the other side and watched the others cross the stream with pained looks on their faces. He held out his hands and pulled them both out as they reached the bank.

"What are we looking for, Guv?" Bobby asked his boss as he looked round at the trees and gorse bushes. "After twenty-five years I don't think we are going to see much, are we?"

"Probably not," Mike answered for his boss. "But now we're here, we might as well have a look round. Where do you think you saw her, Guv?"

Jacks was searching the ground as he moved forward. "I saw her just here, she was holding hands with Leanne."

Bobby and Mike looked at one another, and wondered deep down what to make of it. Jacks' face showed a determined look as he pushed his chin forward.

"Yes, I am probably mad, but I have to try." He had correctly guessed what they were thinking.

They searched the ground for any signs of a mound or a dip, anything to suggest that the earth had been disturbed. After an hour, they made their way back to the stream, crossed, dried their feet as best they could and donned their footwear.

They got back to the road across the field. "What now, Guv? Do we continue?" Mike asked his boss.

"Let's make our way back to the car. That'll do for today," Jacks said with a sigh, resigned to the lack of progress. "We'll get back to the office. We do have other cases to work on."

When they reached the office there was a message on Jacks' desk, reminding him of his appointment with Professor Kaine at ten o'clock the next day.

***

The Friday morning traffic into the city was horrendous, tail to tail from his home, right through to Harley Street. He eventually walked into Suzanne Kaine's office fifteen minutes late. The receptionist buzzed through to her, and Suzanne came out of her office to meet him.

"I'm so sorry, Professor, the traffic is very bad this morning. I did leave early but it is heavier than usual," Jacks apologised. He was surprised to see her smile as she held out her hand.

"Not a problem, Jacks, but please call me Suzanne." They shook hands and Suzanne led him back to her office. "How do you feel about hypnosis, Jacks?" she asked him bluntly, before he had time to settle in his chair.

"Hypnosis?" he repeated, as he sat down. "I don't really know, I've never given it much thought. Never had reason to. What does in entail? Will it affect my ability to function?"

"Good Heavens, no." Suzanne smiled encouragingly. "You will operate as normally as you do now, if you are normal that is. It just means that I can ask questions of you in a subconscious state, and without the normal inhibitions on giving straight answers." She watched him tense up, his face starting to show suspicion, and quickly added, "Not that you wouldn't give me straight answers, mind. It's just that people have a tendency to block things out, to involuntarily push things to the back of their minds."

Jacks relaxed. "If I do agree to it, perhaps you'll show me how to use it in my interrogations. I could do with an insight into peoples' minds, not that they aren't straight with me, mind." Jacks smiled back at her.

"Do you agree to hypnosis?" she asked bluntly.

"You don't hang about, do you, Professor?"

"Suzanne," she corrected. "I want to know if we can start a session today, Jacks, that's all." She looked him in his eyes, and added, "Well?"

He thought about it while she waited patiently for his answer; he had to admit, he did have his reservations about being 'put under', as most people referred to hypnosis.

Jacks eventually replied, "Okay, I'll give it a try, Suzanne, and I hope I don't regret it."

"You won't, have no fear on that," she assured him. "I would like you to go over to the couch, take off your shoes and tie, and lay down, please."

Smiling nervously, he sheepishly made his way over to the leather couch, kicked off his shoes without untying the laces, removed his tie, and lay down with it in his hand.

Suzanne moved over to his side and took his tie from him. She put it on the back of the chair by the side of the couch, before sitting down next to him.

"Relax, nothing's going to happen to you that you are not aware of. Nobody is going to eat you," she said, trying to relax him.

"I'm okay, Suzanne, really, I'm okay," he assured her.

"There are inevitably going to be some questions you will be uncomfortable with, and if I think you can't handle them I will stop, okay?"

"That's fine, let's get on with it, please, before I change my mind." Jacks lay there, looking up at the ceiling and started to relax.

"I am going to talk to you, and then ask you to count down from twenty to zero. Please close your eyes and relax, try to empty your mind of all your thoughts."

Jacks closed his eyes. Clearing the mind of thoughts wasn't as easy as it sounded, but he eventually relaxed and listened to Suzanne's soft, melodic voice. It didn't seem long before he was counting backwards from twenty, and couldn't remember how far down he'd got.

"Listen to my voice, Jacks," the voice instructed. "I want you to go back to the day Leanne was admitted to hospital." Suzanne was referring to her notes made at previous meetings, and continued. "You are in a side room with Leanne when you wake up. Something happens, can you tell me what?"

Jacks was back besides Leanne's bed. He didn't answer straightaway, and Suzanne was about to prompt him when he said, "She's woken up, her eyes are open… she is so cold, so very cold."

"Tell me, what is happening, Jacks?"

"She's speaking to me."

"What is she saying to you?" Suzanne asked quietly.

Jacks held his breath, before releasing it slowly through his lips. "Jacks, I love you. Find her killer, Jacks, she cannot rest until you do."

Suzanne wrote this down. "Is there anyone else in the room with you, Jacks?"

Jacks became uncomfortable and started to writhe on the couch, before he settled again and answered, "There is a girl sitting in the corner, but she won't answer me. She was there but now she's gone." Tears started to fall from his eyes as he carried on. "Leanne's asleep again, she's not breathing. Oh my God, she's so cold."

Suzanne moved quickly to take him away from the nightmare he was reliving. "Jacks, can you describe the girl to me?"

After a while he answered, "She is about fourteen to fifteen years of age, with blue eyes, long fair hair falling onto her shoulders, and dressed in a bright yellow dress."

"Do you know who she is?"

Jacks was now away from the hospital and became stiff, with his manner changing from a hurt individual to that of a policeman. "I do now, but I didn't know who she was when she disappeared. Her name is 'Patsy', Patricia 'Patsy' Josephine Kerridge. She disappeared over twenty-five years ago, believed to have been murdered. I saw her file and her picture."

"Did you see the file or a picture of Patsy before seeing her in your wife's room?" Suzanne asked.

"No," Jacks stated emphatically. "No, I did not."

"Have you seen Patsy since the hospital?" Suzanne wanted to keep the session moving, not allowing Jacks to dwell too long on his loss.

He went quiet for a short while, before saying, "I saw her at the graveside when I buried my poor Leanne. She was watching, but I couldn't get to her. The next time I saw her was in my dreams, when she was standing the other side of a stream, holding hands with Leanne. She wouldn't let me cross."

"Why wouldn't she let you cross?"

Jacks' tears were now running down his face, as he recalled the dream. "She called me a silly man, and I couldn't cross because I wasn't dead." He was becoming increasingly tense and started to become very agitated. "Why can't I cross? Why can't I hold your hand?" he pleaded. "For pity sake, why can't I join you? Don't go, please don't go." His voice was getting louder, and turning quite hysterical. "I need you, Leanne," he screamed.

"Jacks, listen to me, listen to me," the soft, melodic voice soothed. "Everything is fine, you feel well and rested. I will count back from twenty to zero, and on three you will start to wake up and become wide awake on zero. Twenty, nineteen, eighteen…"

On zero Jacks woke up refreshed and rested. He felt the wetness round his eyes, reached in his trouser pocket for his handkerchief and dabbed his eyes and cheeks.

"Was everything okay?" he asked, looking at a smiling Suzanne by his side. "I take it we have finished?"

"For today we have, and you were fine."

"What happens now?"

"I will book you in for a further session, and we will discuss what has been said today."

"Is that it? Can't you tell me anything today? Am I cracking up or not?" Jacks was puzzled; he expected answers.

"You are not cracking up, Jacks. Yes, you are under stress, but that is to be expected with your bereavement. You certainly believe the ghost of Patsy to be real, and as I said, we will discuss this at the next session."

***

After Jacks had left, Suzanne telephoned a familiar and often used number.

"Hello, Gramps, how are you?" she asked, as the phone was answered on the sixth ring.

"Suzanne, my lovely, how are you, dear girl?" Richard Kaine answered, the age of ninety-two years clearly telling in his voice.

After all these years, thought Suzanne, a little croaky but he still has that wonderful lilt in his voice.

Doctor Richard Kaine, retired, was an eminent psychiatrist, who championed post-traumatic stress disorders during and after the Second World War, becoming an advisor to a series of governments on matters concerning mental health.

Heaven knows, thought Suzanne, he had enough stress during his own life. He had fled his native Austria when it was threatened with annexation by the Nazis, who then killed his father when he stood against them. Gramps had fled to England with his English mother, where he set up practice as a psychiatrist after qualifying as a medical doctor.

"I have a case that may interest you, Gramps. You may be able to advise me on it." Suzanne waited for his reply.

"Well, Professor, I am surprised. The great Professor Kaine requires my advice. I don't know whether to be flattered or to cry," he laughed.

"Oh, stop it, Gramps, act your age," She chided.

"If I did, your grandmother will have me put in a home," he laughed even louder.

"Seriously, Gramps, can I pop and see you both this weekend? I'll do the cooking, tell Nanna."

"Since when did you need any invitation?" Gramps replied.

***

Saturday morning, Suzanne drove down the A3 in weak, early sunshine, turning off along the Hogs Back towards Fareham.

A small lane took her down towards the village, and she noticed the familiar church tower showing through the trees as she rounded a sharp bend in the lane.

Just off the bend and to the right, she turned into the drive of Firbanks, a detached cottage standing in its own grounds of about five acres. Firbanks, with its pretty, pale pink washed walls, decked with wisteria from gutter to ground, had been Richard and Marcia Kaine's home well before their retirement, some years ago.

Suzanne parked on the gravel drive in front of the open garage at the side of the house. Her grandmother entered the garage via an internal door from the cottage, and came out to greet her. Marcia Kaine was now eighty-six years of age, still relatively fit, and you could see that she had been very beautiful in her time.

"Suzanne, my child," she called, as she got out of her car. "How wonderful to see you."

"Hello, Nanna," Suzanne answered, smiling from ear to ear. "It's good to see you, too." They embraced and Suzanne just stayed there, holding her adorable grandmother.

Eventually, they parted. "Let's go in to see your grandfather, dear, he's in his study."

Suzanne took her grandmother's elbow and was turning to go in through the garage, when she spotted her grandfather waving at her from his library window that over-looked the entrance to the drive. Suzanne waved back and entered the house from the garage, and they made their way to the library.

Grandfather was in his wheelchair with a light brown car rug over his knees. He wheeled round, using his right hand as a brake against one wheel, whilst at the same time propelling the other until he faced his granddaughter.

"Hello, my lovely," he said, smiling happily.

Suzanne went over to him, throwing her arms round his frail shoulders and kissing him on his forehead, his eyes, and lastly on his lips. "Hello, Gramps, how are you?"

"You certainly know how to get an old man going. You look absolutely wonderful." He pretended to look past her and added, "No husband following you then? So you managed to get rid of the bent solicitor?"

"Stop it, Richard, behave," Nanna chipped in. "Don't embarrass her. Don't take any notice of him, Suzanne."

"He never gives up, Nanna, does he?" Suzanne feigned hurt, before kissing her grandfather again. The bond between these two was obvious to see.

Suzanne straightened up. "I'll get my bags from the car and be with you again in a moment. Same room, Nanna?" she asked.

"Of course, my dear, it will always be your room, even after we both die, if you decide to keep the house that is."

Suzanne stood to inherit everything they had, with just tokens and keepsakes going to her engineering father, who lived in Australia. Her father had made it quite clear after her mother's death that he wanted a clean break, and that everything should go to his daughter.

"And where else would I go?" Suzanne said over her shoulder, as she went back out into the garage to collect her bags. The grandparents looked at each other and smiled.

After supper, they all retired to the sitting room. Suzanne was sitting facing Richard, who was still seated in his wheelchair, with her grandmother sitting by his side in an upright Queen Anne chair.

"Right, Suzanne, you have come down for a specific reason, so why don't you start?" Richard suggested.

"All right, Gramps, I'll tell you a little about an existing and ongoing case that I have." Suzanne told her grandfather all about Chief Inspector Jacks, the death of his wife and the ghost of a girl he believed was murdered some twenty-five years ago. "And that really brings you up to date," she finished.

Richard Kaine had sat all the way through her story without making any comment, with his eyes often closed until Suzanne stopped talking, thinking he was asleep, only for him to open them and stare at her. Her grandmother smiled at her with encouragement each time this happened.

"You say that this chief inspector told the same story, even though under hypnosis?" he enquired thoughtfully.

"Yes, Gramps, he told it as if it was happening and he was still there, observing it. He was under, completely under, I'm pretty sure of that."

Richard closed his eyes and pondered for a moment. Suzanne thought he had really gone to sleep this time, only to see her grandmother hold her hands up, indicating for her to wait.

He opened his eyes again and looked at Suzanne. "If he relayed that to you, then he firmly believes what he was saying, but this does not necessarily mean it is actual fact."

"I know, Gramps, but it led him to make enquiries amongst old missing persons' files, and he came up with what he said was the girl. He swears it was the girl he saw in the hospital, the same girl by his wife's grave and the same girl in successive dreams, holding his wife's hand."

"What do you make of it all, Suzanne? What do you think is going on in the young man's mind?" Richard was well alert by now, and remembering a case he had during the last war. Even the numbness in his legs didn't stop the tingling in his feet, as he remembered the haunting of Jack Kent.

"The man is honest, straight forward and a pragmatist. He's no fantasist, Gramps. He's a warm, caring individual who wants to make a difference. He wants to find this girl and track down her killer."

Richard eyed his granddaughter with a smile behind his grey blue eyes. "Sounds as if you like this young policeman, Suzanne. Anything we should know about?"

"Oh, Gramps, for goodness sake," Suzanne protested as her face started to redden. She hadn't really thought about it, had she? She did like Jacks from the moment she laid eyes on him but she put that down to the vulnerability she had spotted when he first stood by reception.

"You know your Gramps, Suzanne, he can't help but make mischief," her grandmother chided, as she looked at her husband sitting innocently in his wheelchair.

"I don't know what you are talking about, Marcia." He acted hurt. "But I do think the lady protests too much." He looked at Suzanne, who had gone even redder, and smiled "With your grandmother's permission, I am going to tell you a story."

Suzanne looked across at her grandmother, who was looking at Richard and seemed to know what was coming.

151

"Why should you need Nanna's permission?" she asked.

Richard ignored the question and continued. "During the last war, as you know, I treated quite a few service personnel for post-traumatic stress disorders, as well as my civilian work. Harry Hammond, your great uncle, was the commander of a bomber base up north." Richard stopped as Suzanne held her hand up and interrupted.

"But it was one of his nephews who sent me this case, Mike King. He's a detective in the Metropolitan Police, and on the same murder squad headed by Jacks." Suzanne was puzzled, what had all this to do with a case some sixty years ago?

"You never told me that," her grandfather stated.

"Why should I? They can't be connected, can they?" Suzanne queried, doubting herself.

"I'm sure it's a coincidence, my dear, but I'll continue. One of his young airman, a bomb aimer and gunner on a Lancaster, was seeing apparitions and ghosts round his base in Norfolk. He'd been on over thirty-odd missions, and so it was put down to stress. Over fifty-five thousand aircrew died on these missions, life expectancy only stretched to an average six missions, so it was no wonder young boys cracked up. But," Richard paused remembering Jack Kent all those years ago, "this man was as cool as a cucumber over the target and in combat, until one day, returning from a mission over Germany, he brought down a night fighter that no one else had seen until it exploded. He went to pieces, saying he had slaughtered the face that had plagued him over the past months, despite his crew telling him it was a German fighter. He came into my care and I thought I had made him better, well me, and your grandmother, that is."

Suzanne looked more puzzled and gazed questioningly at her grandmother, but before she could ask the question, her grandfather continued.

"He returned to civilian life and took up where he had left off before the war, and finished his studies to become an architect. He became damn good as well, his company eventually being taken over by an American senator, whose son had served with him aboard a Lancaster during the war until his breakdown. This was unfortunate for the young man, because he started to relapse and see things again. Anyway, he was taken over to Germany to open a new town that he and his partners had designed. Part of the opening ceremony was the blowing up of an old concrete water reservoir, which was used to service the factories that turned out tanks during the war. It turned out that the Lancaster crew had dropped bombs on and around the area, and on one occasion had difficulty dropping their bombs because they received a lot of damage to their aircraft. The bombs went astray and hit the town taking out the centre, but, evidently, not all the bombs went off, two buried themselves under the square. The blowing up of the concrete water tank was enough to set these bombs off, with the result of many deaths, including the senator, his son and the English architect."

Looking first at her grandmother, then at her grandfather, she said, rather puzzled, "I'm sorry, I don't see the connection, Gramps."

"This young airman had seen and described the figures in the square to me and your grandmother over twenty years before. I knew then he had seen them, had predicted the outcome, although he didn't know it. He also gave the same story under hypnosis, which transpired to be true. We know this to be fact." He looked at his wife, and then added, "The young man was named Richard Kent. He was your grandmother's first husband. We had your father after your two uncles."

"The picture hanging in my office," she said, realising the significance. "The one of the Lancaster bomber. That was by Jack Kent, wasn't it? He was the airman, wasn't he?" Suzanne exclaimed incredulously.

Her grandmother crossed to a bureau and opened the top. She turned over some papers and took out a buff coloured file. Marcia went over to her husband and handed it to him, without saying a word. Richard opened the file, took out a copy of a newspaper and handed it to Suzanne.

She opened the paper and saw the headlines: 'SENATOR AND SON DIE IN WW2 BOMB EXPLOSION.' The article went on to mention the death of the architect, Jack Kent, along with thirty-six other people.

Before she could say anything, her grandfather spoke, "Who knows what is in the human mind? Who knows what it is capable of or what it is able to see and perceive? I have always maintained that it is so complicated we will probably never understand the brain completely."

"We have to try, Gramps, we can't just walk away from these issues," Suzanne suggested naively.

"That is not what your grandfather meant, Suzanne," her Nanna interceded, almost scolding. "What he does mean is that the brain is so complicated and so individual, who knows what makes one person see something another cannot?"

"I'm sorry, Gramps, I didn't mean to belittle your statement, it's just that I am at a loss on how I deal with this." Suzanne went over to her grandfather, put her arms round his frail shoulders and kissed him.

"I have the skin of a pachyderm, my dear, I know what you are trying to put over, so don't worry about hurting my feelings." Richard took hold of his granddaughter's hand and squeezed it in reassurance. "You must carry on seeing your young policeman, Suzanne. I know you want to help him, but don't be too hopeful that you can find all the answers."

***

Two months later, Suzanne was back at Firbanks for Christmas. Jacks was not going anywhere, or seeing anybody but his close family, and even then he was very reclusive. He either stayed in his bedroom whilst at home, or the bedroom he once occupied as a single man at his parents.

The Christmas of 2014 came and went, largely unmarked. Suzanne was quite distant at Firbanks, and her grandparents put it down to the split with her solicitor who was on the scene the previous Christmas; they didn't think for one minute that her mind would be so occupied with her chief inspector at the Yard.

Suzanne was troubled, was it the weird case surrounding Jacks, or simply Jacks himself?

ELEVEN

January 2015

Jacks heard a ringing in the distance, before he became fully alert and realised it was the front door bell. How long had he been sitting there? What had he been thinking? He couldn't remember anything; he knew he had not had a drink so it wasn't a drunken stupor.

Realising he was in the lounge he got up and went down the hall to the front door. He opened it to see a smiling Mike King looking up at him. The smile soon died on his face as he eyed his boss.

"You okay, Governor?" Mike asked with concern, as he looked at Jacks' drawn, haunted face.

Jacks didn't answer and walked back inside, to be followed by Mike as he closed the door behind him.

"We've been trying to raise you for over four hours, Guv," Mike explained. "We rang both your landline and mobile, they both just rang out."

"I'm sorry, Mike. It appears I've been out of it and I don't know for how long." Jacks turned to look at him. "I heard your ringing on the bell, but I can't remember even getting home let alone how long I've been sitting here."

"Have you had a drink, sir?" Mike ventured to ask.

"No, I bloody well haven't, Sergeant, and if you want to keep those stripes you'll mind what you say to me." Jacks was seething, but his manner was icy cold.

"I'm sorry, Guv," Mike added quickly. "I won't bring it up again, it's just that…"

Jacks stared at his close friend and colleague realising he was being far too sensitive. "It's all right, Mike. Going on past performances you had every right to jump to that conclusion. What brings you here, anyway?"

"We had a call from your bus manager, George Barton, at the depot. He managed to track down the work records for the number six bus, and he found the conductor and driver who were normally on the route to Sunningdale at the time in question."

"That's good news. We had better go and see them both." Jacks was pleased with this small bit of progress, even though it probably wouldn't lead anywhere.

"Bobby went to see both of them. The driver couldn't help. He's now quite old and forgetful, and doubted whether he would have noticed anything anyway. The conductor, on the other hand, remembered a little more. He remembered a very pretty girl in a yellow dress using his bus after athletics at her school. He remembered because every so often she wanted to get off the bus where a path used to cross open fields. She used to walk to the village through the woods."

Jacks was dumbfounded at this piece of news. "There's no mention of this in the file. Why the hell didn't he come forward at the time?" he spat out coldly.

"Bobby did ask that question, Guv. Evidently he went to Australia to visit family for a month just after Patsy's disappearance, which, added to the fact that it was treated as just a missing person case, he missed it. Bobby's checked with Barton, who confirms his absence from work at that time."

"Okay, he may have gone to Australia after she disappeared, but he was here at the time of her disappearance. I want him ruled in or out of any involvement before I let this go, is that understood?"

Mike looked at his boss and answered, "That's why I have arranged for him to come in tomorrow for a formal interview with you, Guv."

Jacks smiled. "I should have known better. Well done. I'll be there first thing in the morning."

Instead of leaving, Mike stood his ground. "There is one other thing, Jacks. Suzanne has also been trying to contact you with regards to coming in for another meeting."

"I'll ring her tomorrow," Jacks promised. "After I have dealt with the conductor, what's his name?"

"David Trent," Mike answered.

***

Jacks arrived at his office early. He busied himself making phone calls in an endeavour to track down the officers who dealt with Patsy's disappearance. It was no surprise that they had all retired, and he had to ask for their personnel files along with any up to date information be forwarded to him.

He looked out of the glass partition separating his office from that of the rest of the squad, and saw the man being led to Mike's desk by a uniformed constable.

Jacks watched, mesmerised at the figure he had first seen on the bus, a lot older, a lot heavier, balder and grey, but no mistake it was him. He noticed Mike pick up the phone and dial. As the phone rang, he picked up the handset straightaway.

"It's Mr Trent, Guv," he said into the phone, as he recognised that Jacks had seen him. He replaced the handset, got up from his desk and showed Mr Trent into his office, followed by Bobby McQueen.

"Mr Trent," Jacks opened, offering his hand. "I'm Chief Inspector Jacks. Thank you for coming in, I do appreciate it. Please take a seat." How surreal is this? he thought, as he eyed the once belligerent conductor of some twenty-five years ago.

Mr Trent sat down in the chair opposite Jacks, which had been drawn back by Bobby who sat down next to him. Mike made himself comfortable in a chair at the end of the desk.

"I saw you on the telly, Chief Inspector, after that murder at the jewellers. I'm not in any trouble, am I?" he asked, as he eyed Bobby on one side and Mike at the end.

"That depends, Mr Trent, or may I call you David?" Jacks smiled cordially. "Do we know one another?" he asked.

"No, please do," he answered nervously. "And I don't think so, not until I saw you on the box."

Jacks let it go and continued to smile warmly at him. "David, I appreciate you have already spoken to Detective Sergeant McQueen, but I must ask you a few more questions to see if I can jog your memory further."

"It was a long time ago," he said defensively, just in case something else came up.

"Yes, I do understand that, David, but I am going to ask you to do your best. Are you happy with that?" Jacks couldn't have been nicer. "Now, you told DS McQueen that you remember Patsy, and that she was a regular on your bus. Why do you remember her?"

David Trent felt uncomfortable and started to fidget in his seat. "She was very nice, always polite and passed the time of day, if the bus was not busy that is."

"Go on," Jacks urged gently.

"She used to travel home from athletics meetings after school. She was very pretty, used to wear nice bright clothes. That's what I remembered when Sergeant McQueen mentioned it to me." He waited for Jacks, who he thought was going to speak before continuing, "The yellow dress, it was very bright. With her fair hair and blue eyes she was quite startling, for a school girl," he added quickly.

"For a school girl," repeated Jacks. "Did you think she looked older than her years, David?"

"No, no, not like that. I thought she was pretty. I'm married, I mean I was married then, I still am," David Trent started to bluster.

"Yes, but did you think she looked older than her years? There's nothing wrong in that, David, I'm not trying to trap you."

"Well, yes, she did look older, perhaps eighteen or nineteen, if it wasn't for her white ankle socks, that is." David looked nervously at Jacks, not sure if he was telling him what he wanted to hear.

"That's okay, David, so you even noticed her white ankle socks, did you?" Jacks asked as if he meant something differently.

"Only because they were in conflict with the rest of her, Chief Inspector. I didn't mean that I lusted after her." David was becoming desperate, thinking he was being misunderstood.

"Did you lust after her?" Jacks might as well have slapped him as he recoiled away from the desk.

"I told you, I'm married, was married then. No way would I have gone with anyone else, no matter how attractive they were." David was now beside himself, what would his wife think if she found out?

"Okay, David, calm down. No one is accusing you of anything, but we have to clear some things up. I know you went to Australia at the time, but it was after the girl's disappearance. You were still here, and on that bus route the day she disappeared."

"That's right," a triumphant David Trent conceded. "I was on the bus, completed my shift and then I went to a party to celebrate going to Australia for a long holiday the day after." David sat back, feeling a lot easier in his seat.

Jacks turned the interview. "David, you have completely misunderstood my intentions," he protested. "I merely want to establish what Patsy was like. I also have to rule you out to move forward with this. Now, what can you tell me? What do you remember about the day Patsy wore that yellow dress?" Jacks sat back in his chair, his body language indicating he was relaxed with David's interview.

David was now more relaxed, he was here to help. "Sometimes, instead of going all the way to Sunningdale, Patsy would ask to be let off the bus, opposite the woods leading to Brackenbridge Village. As far as I can remember, the evening she wore the yellow dress she got off there. I can only think it was to go to the village."

"What else do you recall about that evening, David?" Jacks encouraged.

David tried to think. "There was a fog that evening. The land around Brackenbridge is quite swampy, very wet. I think there is a river running through the copse, or a lake. Sometimes it causes a hell of a mist to roll out over the road."

"Can you remember anyone else on the bus that evening?" Bobby chipped in.

"For Christ's sake," David responded. "It was twenty-five years ago, I'm not Mr Miracle Man."

"That's all right, David, try and think back, was there a man that didn't look right, looked odd, that sort of thing?" Jacks cajoled.

David thought hard. They all waited with bated breath for his reply before he finally spoke. "There was a man, come to think of it. He was strange, always staring, especially at the females. I thought he was in the army, short haircut, black boots and denim-type trousers, you know the sort."

"Can you remember anything else about him? Tattoos, scars, colour of hair and skin?" Bobby chipped in again.

Again, David thought hard. "There was something, I can't quite put my finger on it though."

Jacks wanted to ask about the man in his dreams, the man he had seen on the bus, but he didn't want to put ideas into the man's head. "Try and think, did he have any distinguishing marks at all, on his arms, or his face, or his neck? Anywhere at all?"

David's eyes suddenly lit up. "Yes, yes he did," he said loudly. "He had a tattoo, not a normal tattoo, one on his ear. In actual fact, he had a series of them, little stars on the top part of his ear. You could also see a small hole in the lobe below the ear that probably used to have a stud in." David was elated at having remembered the details of the man.

"Do you remember anything else about the man, his voice for example?" Jacks wanted every little detail he could glean from this man, and suddenly remembered the conductor recoiling on the bus from something the man had said to him. "What did he say to you that made you jump backwards as he was leaving, David?"

David looked firstly at Jacks, and then at Bobby next to him, before looking along the desk at Mike. Bobby and Mike were as amazed at this statement as Trent and wondered where it had come from.

Trent remembered the ugly incident that had disturbed him, keeping him awake for a few nights afterwards; such was the menace in the voice and eyes of the man.

"How do you know he said anything?" he asked, dumfounded and bewildered. He looked at Jacks, how old was he, for God's sake? He must have been a child at the time.

"Well, did he? Did he say anything?" Jacks pressed.

David relived his fear that he had forced to the back of his mind for all these years. "Yes, he bloody well did, the prick," he said, with false bravado. "He said, 'if you don't get out of my way, you bastard, it will be like a bullet in the brain', and he meant it."

"Now, do you remember anything else about this man who made you jump out of his way?" Jacks sat back triumphantly, feeling he was getting somewhere.

"His eyes, Chief Inspector, his cold, black, murderous eyes." He thought for a minute, before adding, "A bit like yours."

Jacks smiled at this and looked on with satisfaction as he eyed Bobby and Mike either side of David. "Right, David, as you know we have taped this interview, but I would like you to go with Sergeant McQueen and make a statement, outlining what we have spoken about today. Will you do that for me, please? Bobby," he turned to DS McQueen, "when you have done that, will you run Mr Trent home, please?"

When David left with Bobby, Jacks turned to Mike. "We need to go back and see Patsy's father again, and we need to find out why she was bunking off to Brackenbridge Village of an evening. We'll go later this afternoon, so have an early lunch."

Mike looked at his boss and couldn't help but ask the question. "Where did that come from, Jacks? I've not heard you mention it before?"

"Long story. I'll tell you some other time."

"Have you got plans for the rest of the morning, Guv?" Mike asked.

"Yes, I am going to visit the gym. I need to harden up a little."

***

Jacks entered the gym, smelling the sweat and liniment in the air. He went to the changing room, stripped and put on his shorts and vest before entering the gym proper.

"Well I never," the voice spoke from under the towel covering the man's head. "Jacks, if I live and breathe."

Jacks recognised the man as the towel was removed. "Hello, Denny, yeah it's been sometime."

Dennis 'Denny' Andrews got up from the bench he had been sitting on, and shook hands. "I should think you are well rusty, old son," he laughed. Denny used to train Jacks for the amateur boxing championships, and was proud to be in his corner when he inevitably won, mainly by way of knockouts.

"I need you to put me through my paces, Denny, how about it?"

"If this is your first time back, we are going to go easy," Denny lied.

Thirty minutes later, Jacks was sweating like a pig over a spit roast, and just as red. "Three rounds in the ring should finish this session off, if it doesn't finish you first," Denny grinned, as he put on a pair of gloves.

"You may be right there, mate," Jacks retorted as he donned a pair of training gloves and climbed through the ropes into the ring.

"You ready, Jacks?"

"As I ever will be, do your worst."

Denny didn't hold back and came at him with both hands. He knew all of Jacks' counter moves, skipping easily away from any retaliatory action from him.

Jacks pretended to be hurt by a right cross that he rode, it was just enough to open up Denny's guard as he brought up a left uppercut, which sent Denny's head back, forcing him against the ropes. He came off the ropes and held on tightly.

"Okay, big boy, that'll do for now." He let go of Jacks and stood back, grinning. "I suppose I deserved that, didn't I?"

Jacks winked at him. "I'm unfit, yes, but I've still got me marbles."

"Can I suggest you make this a regular occurrence then, Jacks?" a more serious Denny asked.

"You've got it. I need to tone up quite a bit."

***

Bert Kerridge was out when a bruised and aching Jacks knocked his door. A neighbour stuck her head out of a side window and shouted, "He only walked to the shops, he'll be back in a mo."

Jacks waved at her, acknowledging he had heard and understood. They went back to wait in the car as Bert Kerridge came down the road.

"Here he is now, Guv," Mike said, as Bert waved in recognition and increased his pace.

"Good day, Mr Jacks, any news?" he asked with a frown.

"I wonder if we can have a few minutes, please, Mr Kerridge?" Jacks enquired pleasantly.

"Come on in, gentlemen," Bert invited, as he led the way and opened his front door. "How can I help you further?" Bert invited them to sit at the scrubbed pine table in the kitchen.

Mike asked the first question. "Did Patsy know anyone who lived in Brackenbridge village? Anyone at all? School friend, teacher, parent, relative, or anybody?"

Bert thought for a moment. "I don't think so, she never mentioned anyone. Her mother would have known more than me, though."

Jacks was about to wrap it up and leave when Bert had a rethink. "Just a minute, I think one of her teachers lived in that area. Give me a minute and I'll see if I can find a photograph." He left the room as Mike and Jacks exchanged hopeful smiles, returning about three minutes later.

"Yes, here it is, her sports teacher with Patsy on the annual sports day, when she won quite a few medals and cups." Bert handed Jacks the photo, which showed a smiling Patsy in shorts and vest, holding a javelin across her chest. Standing alongside her was a smiling, handsome, bronzed male, aged about twenty-five years, dressed in white trousers and a blue sports vest.

"What's his name?" Jacks asked.

"I usually write them on the back, but there's nothing on this one and I can't recall it. I know I took the photo though. It was one of those rare occasions I could make it to a school event," Bert said, with nostalgia and regret.

"We need to take the photo, Mr Kerridge," Jacks said handing it to Mike. "We will make sure you get it back. If you can remember the name, please give me a ring at the yard. You've got my number."

"Was it him? Did he have anything to do with Patsy's disappearance?" Bert Kerridge looked pleadingly into Jacks' eyes, wanting an answer.

"Bert," Jacks softened, "we can't say what involvement he had at this stage, if any at all. What I can tell you is we will pursue it until we have eliminated him from our enquiries, and that is as far as I can go."

Bert Kerridge held out his hand. "I know you will, Chief Inspector. I believe you'll not rest until this is finished." They shook hands and the detectives left.

Back in the car, Jacks turned to Mike, who was sitting thoughtfully in the passenger's seat. "No time like the present, let's make for the school."

"Do you reckon he'll still be there, Guv?" Mike ventured.

"Probably not, but the school records will show where he's gone, and we can check with the education authorities to track him down if he's moved on even further."

They entered the school gates and followed the signs for 'Staff Parking Only'.

"Here's one, Guv, a nice JSH," Mike quipped, as he spotted one of the larger bays.

"JSH? What's that when it's at home?" Jacks asked, still not used to his sergeant's humour. "Oh, I get it," he looked at Mike. "Jacks' Size Hole, very funny." He parked up.

They went through the entrance to the main school just as the pupils were piling out, having finished their school day. Jacks and King hugged the wall as they moved against the flow of this unruly rabble that called themselves pupils. They made it safely to reception and tapped the glass screen.

"Hello," Jacks called out.

"Hello, yourself," the reply came from behind, as a figure got up from below the counter with a stack of papers in her hand. "What can I do for you, gentlemen?" she asked, spreading the papers over the counter and eyeing them with suspicion. The woman was about forty years of age, and had decided that her appearance didn't matter too much anymore.

Jacks showed his warrant card. "Chief Inspector Jacks, and Sergeant King," he answered. "I would like to talk to someone about a member of staff who was here twenty-five years ago."

"Well, quite obviously I wasn't here then, Chief Inspector, so I can't help. You will need to speak to the headmaster, although he wasn't here at that time, either."

"Do you have any member of staff that would have been here that long ago?" Jacks asked patiently.

The dowdy receptionist searched her memory and Jacks saw the light enter her eyes. "Yes," she said triumphantly. "Mr Jenkins, the caretaker, he's been here since the year dot. I'll page him for you."

A few minutes later, an elderly Mr Jenkins entered reception and was introduced to Jacks and King. Mr Jenkins showed them to a side office where they could talk away from the howling youngsters as they left the building. He was about sixty-five years of age, and seemed to be well past retirement.

"What can I do for you, gentlemen?" he asked in a Geordie accent.

"Were you at this school twenty five years ago, Mr Jenkins?" Mike enquired.

"I was here forty years ago, young man." Jenkins puffed out his chest. "Right after I finished in the army, man and boy, so to speak."

Mike took out the photograph and showed it to him. Jacks watched the man for his reaction. "Do you know who this is?"

Jenkins looked hard and long at the photograph. He started to tap it with his finger. "I remember him, and I also remember her. She was the girl who went missing after school. He was the sports teacher at the time, very popular he was, especially with the girls." Jenkins was searching for a name and eventually looked up at Jacks and King in turn. "Blandford, Derek Blandford," he said with satisfaction. "I remember him being questioned at the time but you guys ruled him out, or so you said."

"Did he live at Brackenbridge?" Jacks asked.

"I'm not sure, but I know he didn't live round here, had to travel in. He had a little yellow sports car if I remember correctly."

"What happened to him, where did he go from here?" Mike asked, holding his notebook in front of him.

Jenkins shook his head slowly. "I'm not sure, but he will be on school records, the school keeps pretty good records of all past teachers. You'll have to ask her in the office."

"Us again," Jacks said through the window of reception. "I wonder if you can help me further?"

The dowdy woman was put out, it was getting very near time to pack up and she still had a pile of paperwork to do.

"Can it not wait until tomorrow, Inspector?" she snapped irritably.

"Chief Inspector," Jacks corrected her; he was getting annoyed. "No, I'm afraid it bloody well can't. The information I need is of paramount importance to an investigation and I need it now."

She looked at him with her mouth and eyes open wide, not used to being spoken to in this way. She looked into the fierce eyes of Jacks and realised she was going to have to comply.

A very contrite receptionist answered, "I'm sorry, Chief Inspector, what do you need?"

"A sports teacher by the name of Derek Blandford was at this school twenty-five years ago. I want to know where he went from here."

"That's easy, Chief Inspector," she conceded. "We have all records on computer, I'll just tap the name in on the staff files. I won't be a minute." She moved over to the computer and typed in the information. "Yes, here he is. I will just print his record off for you."

A few minutes later, Jacks and King left the school with the information to track down Derek Blandford.

TWELVE

"I'm not having it. No. How long have you been at this, Jacks?" AC Carstairs was livid. "You've been chasing ghosts, for Christ sake, and using key staff in the process. I know you have not been well, man, but..." Carstairs trailed off, lost for further words.

"The girl is real, was real, sir. I have located her file, she was very real, not just a ghost at all. She went missing in suspicious circumstances over twenty-five years ago, and nothing has been heard of her since. We owe it to her father to do something about it," a desperate Jacks pleaded angrily.

"It's not enough to go charging across the world to interview a man when there is no evidence to prove her disappearance had anything to do with him. We also have budgetary constraints to consider." Carstairs was not giving one inch.

"Look, sir, the girl used to slide off over to Brackenbridge village after athletics meetings. The sports master is the only person she knew living in Brackenbridge. He was interviewed at the time, but the enquiry was still regarded as a missing person, even though it was way out of her character to go missing, even for a day. Derek Blandford now works and lives on the army base in Cyprus. He moved on from the school and joined the army and is now a civilian instructor on the permanent staff at the base." Jacks was starting to lose his temper, his voice was gaining in decibels at each sentence.

"Keep your voice down, Chief Inspector, and a civil tongue in your head. There's only so much I will take, even from you." Carstairs sat down, gesticulating to Jacks to do the same. "Now, here is how this goes down. You have a missing person, a missing person under suspicious circumstances and you believe you know the area in which she went missing. Sooner or later we would have to mount a search for her, if it is proved that your man in Cyprus had anything to do with her disappearance, so what I propose–"

Jacks went to but in, to tell him that Derek Blandford could tell them where she was, but Carstairs held his hands up to stop any interruption.

"What I propose is, I sanction a small party of uniform men to assist you and your team for one week. One week, and that is all you get to come up with the girl's remains or what has happened to her. After that, I don't want to hear another word about it, is that clear?"

Jacks just stared at him.

Carstairs thumped the table and shouted, "Is that clear, Chief Inspector Jacks?"

***

Mike and Bobby were waiting in his office when Jacks returned, red-faced and still very angry.

Mike was the brave one who asked, "What happened, Guv, you look a tad angry?"

"One week, one bloody lousy week. He'll give us a team to search for just one week, and don't bother to pack your bags because we ain't going to Cyprus." Jacks went behind his desk and slumped down in his chair.

"Well it's something, Guv. We weren't even expecting that. Bobby and me thought he would have thrown you out of his office without even a hearing."

"Did you now?" Jacks added sarcastically. "One bloody week," he repeated.

"If he said the whole team plus uniform, Guv, at least we can try. We can put out ten of us, and with twenty uniforms we could give it a bloody good try," Bobby assured him, with a very determined look on his face.

Jacks lapsed into silence whilst the two of them waited anxiously, knowing just how important this was to him. He looked at their expectant faces and eventually broke his silence.

"Okay, you two, we work round the clock for a week and give it our best shot. We organise a search of the path leading from the main road, through the woods, down to Brackenbridge and see what that reveals, before we apply to dig up Blandford's old garden. We start the day after tomorrow, so let's get cracking."

Jacks got home that night at ten-thirty, took two sleeping pills, showered and went to bed.

It was no good, he couldn't sleep; it was always the dark that got to him when he was alone. He set the alarm clock for six thirty the next morning, heaven knows why, he couldn't get to sleep. Thinking of his beautiful Leanne, tears filled his eyes and then ran down the side of his face, wetting his pillow, praying for sleep, praying for the silence to end.

He was aware of the temperature dropping in the room and looked over to the bay windows. It was a clear, moonlit night but he thought he saw a mist drift over the window.

Jacks got up, sensing something was wrong. The hairs on the back of his neck started to rise as he made his way over to the window.

Looking down at the lamp post opposite the drive, he caught his breath. There in the swirling mist, directly under the lamp, was Patsy in her yellow dress. She looked at him accusingly as she held her arms out in front beseeching him to help her. Jacks couldn't move, he remained transfixed and rooted to the spot.

Patsy started to levitate until she was level with the lamp at the top of the post, Jacks could see her piercing blue eyes staring directly at him as she started to float forward, towards the house, towards him, still with her arms outstretched.

As she neared the window, Jacks backed away, he didn't know what to expect. The cold was creeping up his legs and running up his back as she came through the closed windows, levitating right in front of him.

Jacks fell, seated on his bed as she stayed just in front of him. Her mouth opened, she was trying to speak, and then Jacks heard Leanne's voice.

"Find her killer, Jacks, find her killer." It was Leanne's voice coming out of Patsy's mouth. Not for the first time, Jacks bit his knuckles until they bled.

"I can't find your killer until I find you, Patsy," he pleaded. "For God's sake why can't you and Leanne help me?"

"Take my hand," Leanne said through Patsy's mouth. "Come with me, Jacks. We will do it together."

Jacks reluctantly held out his hand and took the small ice-cold hand that was offered to him. It was like taking hold of dry ice, almost burning him.

They went out through the closed bay windows, over the street, and followed the bus route to the path leading off the main road to the copse.

He had no trouble going over the stream this time, and found himself just a few yards inside the copse on the left hand side.

Jacks was now standing on the grass and looking down. He couldn't see anything of significance, other than a small shrub, and he looked up. Patsy was standing, watching him with her piercing blue eyes and pointing down.

"I can't help you any further, Jacks. Find her, find her killer." Patsy was disappearing before his eyes, and he started to panic; how was he going to get back?

"Leanne," he called out pitifully. "Leanne, please don't leave me, please..."

Jacks woke up with a start as the alarm went off, sobbing uncontrollably, confused as to what had really happened. He was saturated with sweat, which had even soaked the sheets through to the mattress cover below.

Jacks got up and stripped the bed, leaving the mattress bare. Gathering the bed clothes, he placed them on the already over-flowing laundry basket in the bathroom.

Jacks showered, shaved and dressed before picking up the laundry basket and going down to the kitchen. He put the basket with its overflowing contents into the utility room and closed the door.

He dropped two Weetabix into a bowl and poured the milk. He took one mouthful before feeling sick, and settled on a strong cup of black coffee instead.

At eight o'clock, he took out Suzanne's card and rang her private number. She answered on the second ring.

"Good morning, Suzanne. I wonder if you can find me some time today? I've had a particularly bad night and I think I could do with your help."

Suzanne, listening to his voice, could hear the pain, the longing and the desperation. "If you're as bad as you sound, Jacks, you had better make your way in now, or do you want me to come to you?"

Jacks took one look around his once proud home, before saying, "No, I'll make it in to see you."

At nine o'clock, Jacks walked in to Suzanne's surgery to be met by Isabelle, the smiling receptionist.

"Go straight in, Chief Inspector, the professor is waiting for you."

Jacks tapped lightly on the door and walked in. Suzanne looked up from behind her desk, smiled as she rose on seeing him, and gesticulated to the chair by the side of her. "Come and sit down, Jacks, would you like a coffee?"

After half an hour, Jacks finished relating things to Suzanne, who had listened in silence. He didn't know what to expect, whether she was going to have him committed, or suggest he stay away from work, but what he didn't expect is what came next.

"I want to tell you a story, Jacks, a story of a case my grandfather was involved with during and after the last World War." She looked up and pointed to the painting of the

Lancaster bomber. "It involves the man who painted that picture. He gave it to my grandfather as a present for treating him. As it turned out, my grandfather says he didn't deserve it but he kept it as a reminder of just how complicated the human mind can be."

Suzanne paused before going to the door and asking Isabelle to arrange more coffees for them. As they waited, she continued with her story. "Jack Kent was a young bomb aimer forward gunner on a Lancaster bomber, who had completed well over thirty missions across enemy territory, when he started to see apparitions, ghosts, spirits, call them what you will. Do you know what post-traumatic stress is, Jacks?"

Jacks, looking up at the bomber answered, "Of course I do. It's a condition brought on by over exposure to danger causing the nerves to fray, that sort of thing."

Suzanne was about to carry on when Joy, her secretary, came in with the coffees. After she left, Suzanne continued.

"Well, stress was one of many things they lived with. Each airman was only expected to survive just six missions, so it was no wonder a lot of them cracked up in one way or another. But not Jack Kent. Although he was seeing things, he was still cool under combat conditions, even saving his crew from a German night fighter on their return flight to England, and earning the distinguished flying cross for valour. But it did not stop the visions that were becoming increasingly more violent towards him. He eventually succumbed and was taken into the care of my grandfather who, although quite young, was already famous for his treatment of these cases.

"After the war, my grandfather thought he had him cured. Jack Kent even married my grandmother, who was grandfather's secretary at that time.

"He was fine for a while, but he had to go to Germany for his company, which was now owned by an American senator and his son. Jack had served aboard the Lancaster with the son during the war, when they had dropped bombs on the small town of Lechen by mistake when bombing a munitions factory. Anyway, they had been commissioned to design a new town and went over to open it. Part of the opening ceremony was the blowing up of an old water tower that had served the munitions factory during the war.

"The vibrations of the explosions awakened two of the very bombs they had dropped, and were still buried under the town's square. These exploded, killing Jack Kent, the senator, the senator's son and scores of others. When my grandfather saw the pictures of the crowds before the explosions, he realised that they had been described to him in detail by Jack Kent during his treatment of him. These were the very same demons that had been haunting him during his service and tours of duty." Suzanne finished her coffee.

"Are you telling me that he foresaw his own death?" Jacks asked incredulously.

"No, I am not. I am saying that sometimes the human mind sees things that the rest of us cannot perceive. It is easy for us to dismiss or to find a rational reason for them, anything other than to understand, even if that were possible in the first place, of course."

"So what am I to make of it? What am I to make of Patsy, of Leanne talking through her? For God's sake, tell me," he pleaded.

Suzanne moved closer and took his hand. "Jacks, sometimes even our profession can't understand certain things that happen to the mind. As a policeman dealing in facts, it must be even harder for you. I do understand that."

"Then what the hell am I to do?" he asked, with his head in his hands.

"You must run with it, Jacks, don't fight it. We will run with it," Suzanne answered. He picked up on the 'we' as he raised his head and looked at her.

"Yes, Jacks, we, I, will be with you all of the way."

THIRTEEN

The murder squad team, with two uniformed police sergeants, were assembled when Jacks came out of his office to address them. It was seven thirty on a Tuesday morning.

"Right, listen up," he started. "We are restricted on time over this so I want you all to look at the board behind me." Jacks turned to look at a large map of Brackenbridge Copse, showing a red line from the main road through the copse to Brackenbridge the other side. "We believe a young girl went missing along this route, possibly abducted and murdered. The problem we have is, it was twenty-five years ago." Jacks paused as a uniformed sergeant held his hand up. "You don't have to hold your hand up here, Sergeant…" Jacks waited for his surname.

"Baines, sir, Sergeant Baines," he answered.

"Just pitch, Sergeant Baines, don't wait for permission," Jacks invited.

"Yes, sir, thank you, sir. Why has it taken twenty-five years for this to happen? If she is still missing, why hasn't she been declared dead and an investigation started before now?"

"That's a very good point, Skipper, why indeed? From looking at the files, she was quite a good looking girl, and although only fifteen looked a lot older. There was talk about her having a fling with a teacher, or some other older man, but nothing came to light. Anyway, it was treated simply as a missing person and, unfortunately over the years, has become forgotten. We have gone through the statements of the officers involved, which were pretty sketchy to say the least, and no surprises, they are all retired now." Jacks turned back to face the map, but Sergeant Baines hadn't finished.

"Do you have any further information to help locate the girl, sir, like a particular area of these woods, or are we searching the whole lot?" Sergeant Baines was looking at the size of the area covered by the map on the board.

"We are going to be systematic with the search, starting with the path and gradually spreading out through the woods," Jacks started to explain, glancing round the room before turning back to Baines. "You and the other sergeant will be responsible for two teams, and will systematically search using the gridded maps you will have."

Mike King handed the two sergeants the gridded maps as Jacks continued. "You will mark off in turn as each area is covered. Any questions?"

It was the turn of the other sergeant to speak out. "Sergeant Simms, sir. What exactly are we looking for?"

"Okay, Sergeant Simms, what we are looking for is any unnatural mounds, any unnatural and out-of-place depressions in the ground. Anything that could hide a body. You are not a novice in this type of search, Sergeant, that's why you and Baines were selected for this. Any other questions?" he asked the whole room.

***

Two Ford Transit vans with police markings pulled up alongside the road where the path went over the field and entered the wood. Three other unmarked cars pulled up behind them with the murder squad. Jacks, King and McQueen were in the lead car. Men and women were piling out of the vehicles, donning overalls and wellington boots. They were all equipped with long thin metal rods for testing any area they found suspicious. The two teams of uniformed men started out across the field, with one team taking the left and the other the right. The search had begun. Jacks led his squad along the path until they reached the stream.

"I want five either side of the path as we get to the other bank. We keep to our grids that are marked, staying abreast of one another and the same on the way back. We stay close and in touch at all times. We do not miss a thing. If you see anything suspicious, shout out and everyone will stop. Is that clear?" said Jacks, demanding a response.

"Yes, Guv," they all answered together, as they began to wade across the stream to the other side.

Jacks was positioned two in on the left hand side of the path. He was trying to remember the area he had been taken to by Patsy in his nightmare.

They searched and searched. Jacks heard the occasional shout from one of his team and they all stopped, waiting for it to be cleared by Bobby or Mike before setting off again. It was a slow, laborious, most boring and gutty job, but Jacks felt no guilt for putting his men through it. He heard shouts now and again in the distance from the uniformed teams, as they systematically ruled out depression after mound as they went through their grids.

At four o'clock in the afternoon, the sky darkened as rain clouds started to drift across the woods, drawing in the evening much earlier than usual.

Jacks radioed Sergeants Baines and Simms to call the search off for the day. He was disappointed and it showed, as Bobby and Mike walked back to the vehicles alongside him.

"We'll do it all again tomorrow, Guv," Mike encouraged. "Another day might show something up."

Jacks carried on walking as if he hadn't heard him.

It was Bobby's turn to be encouraging. "You didn't expect anything on the first day, did you, Guv? It was never going to be that easy."

Jacks stopped in his tracks as they feared the worst and prepared themselves for a tirade of abuse. "I must admit I did think we would find her in our grids, I really did." To their surprise, Jacks spoke quietly, almost to himself.

He phoned Suzanne when he got home that evening and filled her in on the day's unfruitful events.

"Are you back there tomorrow, Jacks?" she asked with concern, hearing the despondency in his voice.

"I'll be back there all week if I have to," he asserted strongly. "I must find her."

"You will, I am certain of that. You will find her."

Jacks had a very fitful night, hardly sleeping at all. How he wished he had some alcohol in the house; the sleeping pills were not working at all. His mind, as usual, was filled with thoughts of Leanne. His pain and longing just would not desist or subside. How long was he going to suffer this agony; what was it all for?

Rising early in the morning, he spent a considerable time standing in the shower, trying to get some life back into himself. Forcing a bowl of Weetabix down, Jacks drank cup after cup of strong black coffee before setting out for Brackenbridge Copse. Instead of stopping when he saw the police vehicles parked at the side of the road, he went straight on.

Mike saw him go past and nudged Bobby. They both stared after him, wondering where he was going.

"I don't know where he's off to, Bobby, but we had better get started." Mike and his team moved off with their long metal sticks.

Jacks drove on for another three miles, ignoring his radio that had started to chatter, repeating his call sign. He turned off the main road and followed the signs directing him to Brackenbridge. Jacks pulled up on the other side of the woods, got out of his car, locked it, and entered the woods by a path that went between two gardens and followed it, heading towards the stream. He started to feel cold as a mist began to swirl through the trees and scrub either side of the path, it was getting colder, and the mist was getting thicker as he got closer and closer to the stream.

Jacks was getting the feeling of déjà vu, surely he had been this way before, in these conditions, he just couldn't remember when. He reached the stream and looked over to the bank the other side.

Suddenly it dawned on him.

"You bloody fool, Jacks," he said out loud. "You bloody stupid moronic fool. You've been looking at it from the wrong side."

Just at that moment, Mike appeared on the opposite bank, radio in his hand. He called over to Jacks. "We've been trying to raise you, Guv, I wondered where you had got to."

"Stay where you are, Mike, I'm coming to you." Jacks waded across the stream, forgetting he hadn't put his wellington boots on. Mike looked on, amazed as he watched him wade through the water, immersed almost to his knees.

Jacks climbed the bank, assisted by a helpful Mike.

"I'm a bloody fool, Mike, that's what I am," he stated assuredly. "She's here, this side and to the left over here. Get the team here, I want them to start from here and work back towards the road on this side."

Mike didn't argue or ask why; he got on his radio and called all Jacks' team to meet them at this point. Diane Plant was the first to arrive, and looked down at Jacks' sodden trousers.

"Forget your boots, Guv?" she enquired cheekily.

Jacks realised for the first time what he had done as he answered her. "If I'm right, I shall dive in fully clothed."

"I'll hold you to that, Guv," Diane laughed.

Ten detectives spread out along the bank and started to inch their way forward.

They got just fifteen yards into the woods when Detective Constable Len Baines shouted, "Over here, Guv."

Jacks reached him and looked down at the metal spike, which had been pushed about a foot into the ground in front of a small shrub. He knew in his heart he had found her. He couldn't move as they all watched him standing there, open mouthed.

Mike rushed to his side, taking his arm. "What do you reckon, Guv, is this it?"

"I bloody think so, Mike. I bloody well hope so."

Bobby was the first to react positively to what was happening. "Remember, everybody, this is a potential crime scene, so let's go carefully."

"Well done, Bobby," Jacks congratulated him. "Get some spades and forks then let's canvas the area. Anything taken out is to go through sieves, and we preserve the earth as well. Let's get to it."

Jacks watched as Bobby and Len Baines dug up the earth, starting with the shrub. As the soil was removed it was carefully placed on a canvas sheet, which was spread out on the ground alongside the digging area.

"Stop as soon as you find something, Bobby," a confident Jacks ordered.

Bobby just nodded and got on with his excavation, helped by Baines.

A few minutes later, Len Baines struck something, and it wasn't a stone. He stopped immediately and got out of the shallow grave, followed by Bobby.

Jacks nodded to Diane who stepped carefully down into the loose soil and started to scrape away with a trowel. Jacks, alongside the rest of the gathered team, held his breath and waited. Diane worked the earth around the obstruction until she started to uncover a bone.

"Eureka!" she exclaimed. "Let's hope it's not an animal."

"Out you get, Diane," Jacks ordered. "This is now a murder scene everybody. Mike, radio forensics and the scene of crime bods, get them down here, pronto." Jacks thought for a moment, and added, "Oh, you had better let Carstairs know straightaway."

Within the hour, the woods and surrounding area were cordoned off, and a canvas structure covered the shallow grave area, which was the resting place for the past twenty-five years of young Patsy Kerridge. Thanks to Jacks and his team, it was not to be her last.

Jacks was satisfied that he could do nothing further until the forensic team had done their job, but he was relieved that he had at least found Patsy, if not, her killer. He walked back the way he had come as Diane and the team watched him wade uncaringly through the stream, with the water up to his shins, and climb the bank on the other side.

Mike was about to go after him when Bobby took his arm. "Leave him, let him be for a while. He deserves a bit of space before the circus starts. I'll stay with the remains to ensure continuity back to the lab, and make sure any evidence is bagged and labelled."

Diane Plant watched him disappear into the copse and head for Brackenbridge.

"I thought he was going to throw himself in if we found her," she said disappointedly.

"We'll let you take that up with him, Diane," Bobby quipped. "If you dare that is. I don't fancy you keeping your job, though."

Jacks was either unaware of his soaking feet or he just didn't care, as he drove away from Brackenbridge and headed for the church. He parked his Volvo in the layby and made his way through the lych-gate, to the grave of Leanne.

As he stood over the graveside, now decked out with a brand new headstone, he expected to see Leanne or Patsy appear.

"I found her, love. I found Patsy for you, and I will find her killer too," he vowed. "I love you and miss you like hell, Leanne. It's hard to cope without you. I can't even operate the blasted washing machine." Jacks tried to control himself, tried not to cry, but the tears just kept coming and coming.

That evening he was sitting in the lounge, looking at the wall opposite, not fully conscious of his surroundings, when his mobile phone buzzed in his pocket. He opened the phone and read the text message from Mike King.

"Turn on the news, now!"

Jacks picked up the remote and pressed channel one for the BBC news. Pictures on the screen were showing their activity of the day, even getting a picture of the canvas screens erected round the site.

The female reporter was speaking into a hand held microphone, as she walked the main road leading to the site. "The remains found earlier today are believed to be those of a young girl who went missing over twenty-five years ago. The police are not releasing any more information until the next of kin have been contacted."

Jacks cursed. "How the hell did they get that information so soon?" he asked himself. He rang a number on speed dial. Mike answered. "Meet me at Bert Kerridge's straightaway."

***

Jacks wasn't the only one taking an interest in the news that evening. A man watched the screen with keen interest. His hands were shaking as he lent across to turn the sound up. On his right ear were three faded small tattoos in the shape of stars.

***

Half an hour later, Jacks parked his Volvo outside number eighty-seven Kirkbride Avenue. He noticed the pretty wisteria he had seen on his last visit had now finished flowering.

Jacks hated this bit, it was never easy or the same each time he had to break the news. Looking into his rear-view mirror he watched Mike park behind him, almost touching his bumper.

They got out together, locked their cars and went up the neat little path to the front door. Bert Kerridge was at the open door to greet them.

Jacks looked at the old man and felt his pain, the look on his ashen gaunt face screamed volumes.

Bert Kerridge held his hand out. "Come in, Chief Inspector, won't you?" Jacks and Mike shook hands with him in turn and followed him into the house.

Sitting in the lounge, Jacks noticing the pictures of Patsy with her mother and father on the sideboard.

"I saw the news, Chief Inspector," Bert said, as he picked up a picture of Patsy. "I take it that there is no doubt it is Patsy then?"

"I am most terribly sorry, Mr Kerridge, I don't know how the news people got hold of this. We still need to complete forensics and other enquiries, but it is not looking good." Jacks was hurting as much as he was. "As soon as we have something positive I will make sure you know. I would like to have a forensics officer come and see you, to see what we can get from Patsy's room and her possessions, if that's okay? And to take a DNA sample from yourself."

Bert Kerridge nodded his consent. "Her room is as she left it the day she disappeared, Chief Inspector. I believe there is still a lock of her hair and her mother's in one of the drawers in her room."

"If you can leave things exactly as they are, sir, our forensic officer will deal with it," Mike added.

"What happens next?" Bert asked.

"There will be a post mortem followed by an inquest," Jacks said gently. "Once the cause of death and the identity is established, we will take it from there. I am going to ask you to be patient a little while longer."

Bert held out his hand and grasped Jacks' firmly. "I have waited twenty-five years for news, Mr Jacks, a few more days I can take. If she was killed, do you have anyone in mind?"

Mike was about to say something when Jacks held up his hand. "It is early days, Bert. We have to be careful not to jeopardise any outcome to this. You have my word that I will pursue this until I get a result for you."

Bert looked into Jacks' deep brown eyes, seeing the sincerity and determination. "I have no doubt about that at all, Mr Jacks, none whatsoever."

***

At the same time as Jacks and Mike were taking their leave from a baleful Bert Kerridge, the figure with the three small tattoos shivered involuntarily as he felt someone walk over his grave.

FOURTEEN

Jacks was looking out of the glass partition that separated his office from the main murder squad room. He watched the team as they went about their business of tracking down leads, including potential witnesses and retired police officers.

Mike got off the phone and made his way to the office. He tapped the door, didn't wait for an invite, and entered.

"Come in, Mike, sit down. You've got something for me?" Jacks asked.

"Doctor Gregory will be ready for us at ten thirty this morning, Guv. He says there are quite a few interesting items that will prove the identity beyond any reasonable doubt."

Jacks was about to respond when he spotted Assistant Commissioner Carstairs enter the main office and make towards his door. "I'll speak with you later, look who's coming."

Mike turned round and saw AC Carstairs advance on the door. "I'll make myself scarce, Governor."

"No need to scuttle off on my account, Sergeant King, what I have to say includes you as well." Carstairs was smiling as he entered the office. Jacks started to rise, when Carstairs stopped him. "No need to stand, Chief Inspector, sit down."

Jacks smiled at Mike. "Thank you, sir," he said politely, as Carstairs sat down in front of him.

Mike left the room on the pretext of having to make some urgent enquiries.

"Well I don't know how you do it, Jacks," he said when they were alone. "I must admit I didn't think there was anything in it. I thought you had gone over the top. How you pull things off is beyond me, even when you are at rock bottom, and I know you've been there, you seem to get the most amazing results. I sometimes think you must be in league with the devil, you seem to get his luck."

"Thank you, sir," Jacks responded, feeling a little uncomfortable at the praise he was suddenly getting. A lot different to what he got just a few days ago, he thought. "But I think an apology should go to the devil. We must remember we have only heard one side of the case. God has written all the books."

Carstairs shook his head. "I don't know where you get them from, Jacks. Is it the girl you… saw at the…? I don't quite know how to put this." Carstairs faltered, shaking his head.

"Is it my ghost, sir? Yes, it is. Is it the girl I saw at the hospital? Yes, it is. I don't know how or why, and quite frankly I don't care, as long as I get her killer."

"So what's you next move? Do you want to go to Cyprus?" Carstairs asked.

"Not just yet, sir, I have a meeting with the pathologist and forensics at ten thirty this morning. Depending on what I have then, I will need to see Mr Kerridge before another leak to the papers gets out. Derek Blandford is in the frame, but I don't intend to put all my eggs in one basket. Other lines of enquiry must be pressed home."

"Needless to say, Jacks, you get what you want on this one. To clear up a twenty-five-year-old murder is quite something." Carstairs got up from his seat and went to the door. Before going out he turned to Jacks, "I want no mention of any ghosts, or of any supernatural beings of any kind. Good old common police work from you got you this far, is that quite clear? Keep me informed," he ordered, as he left.

He smiled to himself as the door closed. He watched the back of AC Carstairs as he strode happily across the main office, nodding to all and sundry as he went.

"Good old common police work, no help at all," he muttered, grinning to himself.

***

At ten thirty, Jacks, Mike and Bobby entered the pathologist's laboratory, where the skeletal remains were laid out on a white table. Jacks noticed some other items on a table by the side of the body.

"Good morning, Chief Inspector," Doctor Adam Gregory addressed Jacks as if the other two weren't there. He made a science of ignoring or putting down those he believed to be inferior to him.

"Morning, Adam," Jacks replied pleasantly. "I understand that you have some positive results for me."

Adam Gregory had been the local pathologist way before Jacks' time in the Met. He was slightly overweight, which wasn't surprising the way he enjoyed his food and fine wine, and was getting very near his time to retire. His bald head reflected the overhead lights as he bent over the skeleton spread out below him. He had the greatest respect for Jacks' reputation, but was always rather rude and abrupt to others.

"The remains are that of a female, aged between twelve and twenty one. She was five feet two inches tall, and in good health at the time of her death. Her hair was blonde to fair and, as far as I can ascertain from her DNA, she had blue eyes. The DNA that was extracted matched the DNA of a sample of hair taken from the girl's home. DNA analysis of the mitochondrial DNA matched that of a sample of hair that belonged to the mother, and the Y chromosome analysis matched that of the sample taken from the father. There is no doubt that these are the remains of one Patricia Josephine Kerridge." Doctor Gregory looked up at Jacks and smiled in triumph.

"How did she die?" Jacks asked simply.

"Straight for the jugular, Jacks, how typical," Gregory retorted. "Okay, let's get on with it. She died of a broken neck, has a broken jaw and cheek bones, but by the look of the bones on her right knuckles, she fought back. Can you see the bones are broken, as if she had punched something hard? Also, her front teeth have been smashed. She had been beaten pretty badly." Gregory moved over to the smaller table, but Jacks remained staring at the skull. He imagined the fear and pain that poor, pretty Patsy had gone through.

They waited patiently for Jacks to join them. When he eventually moved away from the skeletal remains and joined them at the table, he noticed a small crucifix and a gold signet ring, along with some pieces of rotted clothing.

"The father identified the crucifix to your sergeant, I understand, but the ring remains a mystery."

"Where was the ring found?" Jacks asked bitterly.

Doctor Gregory reached for one of the photographs of the grave and showed it to Jacks. The ring was clearly seen at the bottom of the grave and had been marked before the photograph was taken. It could only have been left by the girl, or her killer.

"Her father did not recognise the signet ring at all," he said, as he pointed to it.

"So the only way that ring could have got under the remains is at the time of her death," Mike interjected.

"Quite so, Sergeant King." Gregory at last recognised him. "Quite so. The ring is also marked inside with the letters BB and an M marked on the signet face.

Jacks took hold of the ring and examined it carefully. "Thanks, Adam, good work," he praised him.

"Praise indeed coming from you, Jacks. I'll settle for a bottle of my favourite wine, though," Gregory laughed, as he handed Jacks the pictures of the ring and crucifix. "One other thing, Chief Inspector, there was a clump of hair that did not belong to the girl in the grave. My guess is that it belonged to her killer, and that is why she was beaten so badly."

"Why the blasted hell did you not start with that, man? You are so infuriating," Jacks exploded. "Have checks been made on it?"

Doctor Gregory looked into the seething, angry eyes of Jacks and realised he had made a grave error of judgement in trying to be clever and keeping this until last.

"The sample is very poor, and has been sent to our laboratory in Holborn. It is not so easy to analyse as the girl's, and we do not have a sample to compare it with anyway," he added sheepishly.

"You bloody stupid moron," Jacks shouted. "We have a whole database to compare it to. Get me those results, pronto, do you hear?"

"Now look here, Chief Inspector," he started to say but was not allowed to finish before Jacks was in his face.

"You bloody well look here, Gregory, I've had enough of your high handed attitude towards my men, and this is one step too far. Get me those results."

Gregory didn't dare say another word as Mike looked on, slightly embarrassed but pleased at the put down.

**

AC Carstairs joined Jacks in his office to discuss their next move on this twenty-five-year-old murder. Jacks had laid out the evidence on his desk in front of him, minus the hair sample sent off to Holborn.

"Do you have any evidence to link Blandford to the girl's murder, Jacks?" he asked.

"No, I do not," he answered honestly. "But we do need to eliminate him from our inquiries, and until we do he remains our only suspect. If it's the expense for going out there, sir, I'll foot the bill for this one," Jacks offered.

"Don't be so absurd, you are bordering on insolence," Carstairs warned him.

"That is not my intention, sir, but I do mean to see him, one way or another."

Carstairs stared at him, a smile gradually filling his face. "Okay, Jacks, just you and King… and you go economy."

"Thank you, sir. We won't need accommodation, we will be staying in our house," Jacks checked himself. "The house Leanne and I bought with the money from her inheritance some years ago."

"Whatever, Jacks, stay in a hotel if you wish. I know how painful this time has been for you. How are you getting on with Professor Kaine, are you making progress?"

Jacks was uncomfortable; he knew the man meant well and he had been very good over this not appearing on his record, but it was a very personal and private matter and he wanted it to stay that way.

Carstairs could see his discomfort, and quickly added, "Don't answer that, Jacks, that's between you and the Professor. I'm sorry I asked."

***

Before going out to Cyprus, Jacks had a meeting with his murder squad in the main operations room. The man with the three star tattoos on his right ear was upper-most in his mind. They needed to track this man down; as far as Jacks was concerned he was a very strong suspect and, if they eliminated Blandford in Cyprus, he would be the only one. Jacks also wanted all the witnesses interviewed again and their stories checked, especially the police officers who dealt with the enquiry and the staff who were at the school at the time. After the meeting and setting the team their tasks, Jacks saw Bobby in his office, together with Mike.

"Whilst I'm away, Bobby, I want you to take this by the scruff of the neck and keep this lot working. Every police officer and civilian who had worked on this case as a missing person is to be interviewed, together with all the teachers. I want you to personally interview the bus driver, as well as the conductor. Use Diane and Len as your wing men. Make sure they check all statements coming in. You answer only to AC Carstairs and only then after keeping me informed, is that clear?"

"Goes without saying, Governor," Bobby assured him. "Don't worry, I'll keep on top of things. When are you off?"

"Our flights are booked with British Airways the day after tomorrow," Mike chipped in. "Not only economy but the red eye out at ten thirty at night."

"Would you like to swap with Bobby, Mike?" Jacks asked, as Bobby put his hands out to be quickly disappointed.

"Not bloody likely, Guv, someone has to look after you," Mike quickly responded. "What are the temperatures likely to be?"

"Pack your trunks, and your short sleeve gear. It will be about thirty plus degrees out there this time of year." Jacks remembered late September was his and Leanne's favourite time to visit their little house and the many friends they had made over the years.

Jacks had a call to make before swanning off to Cyprus. "Hello Suzanne," he said on being put through by Isabelle. "I have to fly out to Cyprus for a few days, and wondered if I could see you before I go?"

"Lucky, lucky you, Jacks. I take it's for work?" Suzanne responded, and continued without waiting for his answer. "I am fully committed all day today at the Drop-in-Centre in

Hammersmith, and fully booked here tomorrow with appointments. I could meet you this evening, say over dinner?"

"Is that permitted, Professor?" Jacks asked. "I thought you couldn't mix socially with a patient."

"Dinner, Jacks, a working dinner if you like. I'm not trying to get into your pants, dear man," she laughed.

Jacks sighed, "Great pity," he said, "Ah well, where do you want to meet? I could pick you up if you like."

"Can you pick me up in Belgravia, say at eight tonight? I'll text you the address."

"Consider it done. Where do you want to eat?"

"Your choice, Jacks, surprise me," and with that, she hung up.

***

He got home at four o'clock in the afternoon, and set about reading the instructions for the washing machine, he couldn't keep on relying on his mother and Maddie to come round and do his laundry for him. After a great deal of deliberation he determinedly set about the enormous task of programming the damn thing. Jacks eventually settled for a short wash, separated out the whites and colours as instructed by the manual, threw in a detergent capsule, closed the front loading door and pressed the button. He was amazed that it actually worked, and stood in front of the machine, mesmerised at its perpetual rotation.

Taking the time it would take the machine to complete its cycle, Jacks showered, brushed his teeth and shaved in that order. By the time he had made a pot of tea, the washing machine had come to an abrupt halt. Locating the ironing board under the stairs, he went to the washing machine and took the clothes out, selecting a white shirt for ironing. The blasted thing was still wet, too wet to iron dry, that was sure.

"Oh, bloody Christ!" he exclaimed. Jacks panicked, not having a clean shirt to wear, he'd gone through the lot.

Sitting down with a second cup of tea he thought, before picking up his phone and dialling.

"What's up, Guv?" Mike answered.

"Nothing, but I do need a clean shirt for the tonight. What size do you take?"

Mike was surprised by the request. "Shirt, Guv? Not done your laundry lately, eh?"

"Size, Mike?" Jacks hissed.

"Seventeen neck, Guv."

"That'll have to do, I'll leave it open without a tie. Can you get one round to me straightaway? I need it for tonight." Jacks was a seventeen and half neck so it would be a little tight, but it would do. "Make sure it's a plain white one, Mike, please."

Jacks got dressed and waited bare-chested until Mike arrived, carrying the precious shirt.

"Going somewhere nice, Jacks?" Mike had a big grin on his face, as he looked out of the kitchen window to see the washing line full of fresh laundry. "My, you have been busy, dear."

"Mind your mouth, Sergeant, none of your bloody business, but thanks for the shirt," Jacks said, as he put on and buttoned up the crisp, white shirt, doing up the cuffs with a set of gold cufflinks. "I'll see you in the morning."

***

Jacks arrived outside one of the smartest houses in Belgravia at exactly eight o'clock. He went through a set of black painted, wrought iron railings, flanking the white stone steps leading up to the immaculately painted, deep-burgundy-coloured door. Just as he was about to use the gleaming brass knocker the door opened to reveal Suzanne dressed in a deep blue dress covered by a cream, waist-length jacket. She looked lovely, quite stunning, and Jacks felt a little disconcerted as he thought what to say.

"Are you a net curtain twitcher?" he asked with a broad grin.

"You look great as well, Jacks," she responded. "Closed circuit television in case of unwanted callers," she explained.

"I'm sorry, you look stunning, Suzanne," he added as a belated compliment. "Simply love the outfit," he added awkwardly.

"Don't overdo it. Where are you taking me?"

Jacks stepped back to allow her to come down the steps. "I know a little Italian restaurant just off Leicester Square. Thought you might like to try it."

"No Greek restaurants?" Suzanne queried. "I thought you might be into Greek food, seeing as you're off to Cyprus."

"Greek food's fine but I rather like the sauces that you get with Italian," Jacks explained.

***

Antonio's was busy. The head waiter saw Jacks and Suzanne arrive and called his boss, who came out from the kitchen to greet them.

"Chief Inspector Jacks, how nice to see you. It has been too long." Antonio had known Leanne and, like everybody that knew her, was saddened by her premature death. He was careful not to mention her as he shook hands with Jacks, and was introduced to Suzanne.

"This is Suzanne Kaine, Antonio, a friend of mine. Do you have table? I can see you are quite busy." Jacks looked round and wondered if they would have to move on.

"I always have a table for you, Mr Jacks. If you and Madame would like to come this way, please." Antonio led them to a table he always kept clear in case an important person turned up unexpectedly. He settled them in as a waiter appeared with the menus.

After ordering, Suzanne looked up at Jacks over her wine glass. "So what is so important that it can't wait until you get back?" she asked tentatively.

Jacks looked at her, it was hard to think of her as his analyst sitting in these surroundings. "Several things actually," he replied. "I'm going over there to question a suspect about Patsy's murder. He was her sports teacher and may have been having an affair with her."

"She was a bit young for that, wasn't she?" Suzanne queried.

"Oh, come on, Suzanne. I bet you had a crush on a teacher when you were younger. Girls do it all the time these days, but it is only some foolish teachers who take advantage." Jacks couldn't believe how naïve she was.

"I know, you're right, but it still sounds wrong, and anyway, I did have a crush on a teacher when I was young. Her name was Lilian Marshall and she was my music teacher."

Jacks couldn't believe what he was hearing, he had no idea. This came out of the blue, he'd landed himself a gay analyst. He just stared at her as his wine missed his mouth and spilt onto the tablecloth.

"Don't look at me like that, Jacks. No, I'm not a lesbian. A lot of girls have crushes on their female teachers when they are at school, it's not uncommon. I can't believe how naïve you are in some things."

Touché, thought Jacks, *who is naïve now?*

"I didn't think that for a moment," he blustered, as she smiled at him. "Anyway, he works for the military out there and I must eliminate him from our enquiries, if nothing else."

"So what's the problem?" she pressed.

"I have a house there. Leanne and me, we bought it with her inheritance when her parents died in a road crash." Jacks looked down into his wine glass morosely, remembering the good times he had holidayed with Leanne in their little terrace house that over looked Kapparis Bay, on the edge of Paralimni village. "I'm a little frightened as to how I'm going to react when I get over there."

Suzanne looked at the crown of Jacks' head, pitying the man and what he was going through. How he must have loved her. What must it be like to have loved, to be loved so deeply.

"I don't really know what to say, Jacks, you have to face it sometime, maybe it is better sooner rather than later. Are you concerned that Patsy will appear to you again?" Suzanne wanted to get to the real reason he felt the way he did. "When did you last see her?"

Jacks thought for a minute, things had a habit of getting confused lately. "The night she took me to the woods, or so I thought, a couple of days before we discovered her body."

Suzanne picked up on the 'we'; Jacks was quite a modest man, considering his successful career to date and naturally included his team in all his successes. "So nothing since you found her... remains?"

"No, nothing," he answered honestly.

"Then there's no reason you should see her in a foreign land," she assured him, hoping for the best. Suzanne watched him as he raised his head and looked at her with his deep brown, doleful eyes, making her wish she could hug him.

"There's more," he said. "The murder took place twenty-five years ago. He's been out in Cyprus for the past twelve years. Witnesses have got a lot older, and some have died. I'm concerned that I am going to let her father down and not bring this to a successful conclusion as I promised him."

Suzanne realised that Jacks was unsure of himself and that this was very alien to him. The confidence that had carried him and his team through investigation after investigation was deserting him.

"Beware that you do not lose the substance by grasping at the shadow," Jacks mumbled quietly.

"What does that mean?" Suzanne asked, puzzled.

"Aesop's Fables, The Dog and the Shadow," he answered. "I have to be careful not to put too much dependence on this man in Cyprus. There are other avenues that we should be exploring as well."

"You know your business, Jacks. Don't doubt yourself. You found Patsy against all odds, you'll come good," she assured him. "If you are jetting off to Cyprus, it's going to be quite hot. Don't you think a haircut might be beneficial?" Suzanne was determined to move him away from his present mood.

Jacks grinned at her as he swept the hair back from over his eyes. "You might be right there, it is time for a change of style," he answered, glad for the change of subject.

They finished their meal, had a short tiff over who paid the bill, before Suzanne conceded and allowed him to pay. It was ten thirty in the evening when Jacks pulled up outside her apartment, and they sat in awkward silence, not knowing how they should part.

Suzanne was starting to get that tingling feeling in the bottoms of her feet when Jacks lent over and kissed her on the cheek.

"Good night Professor," he said simply. "Thank you for a lovely night."

"Good night, Jacks," she smiled, her face reddening as she hurriedly opened her door and got out.

Jacks watched as she closed the door and went up the steps to her apartment, with that awkward but elegant stride showing off her muscled calves. He waited until she opened her door, waved and drove away.

As she got inside her hall, Suzanne kicked off her high heels and went into her drawing room. She sat down in a Queen Anne chair and started rubbing the bottoms of her feet.

I never felt this with the rogue solicitor, she thought, a little concerned but smiling happily to herself.

The next morning as Jacks drove into work, he made a stop off. He parked at the rear of some shops and walked through the alleyway to the front of the parade. He spotted the white and red pole hanging outside SID's the BARBERS, and wondered if every barber in England was called Sid, it certainly seemed like it. He couldn't see how busy Sid was because of the high curtain along the main window.

Jacks pushed the door open and entered, empty but for one old man in the chair being shaved. Sid looked round as Jacks entered, immediately grinning from ear to ear on recognition of his favourite policeman.

"Well I never, Jacks, if I live and breathe," he exclaimed. "And I can see by the state of your hair you don't visit any other barber."

"Hello, Sid, how are you?" Jacks asked as the old man in the chair looked round to see who was commanding his barber's attention.

"Sit down, I'll be with you as soon as I've finished here."

Thirty minutes later, Jacks left the barber's minus the shock of hair over his right eye and with it cut well above his collar.

Arriving at the Yard, he exited the lift and went through the doors to the main office, and self-consciously strode across to his own office on the other side. The incident room was full. It went deathly quiet as he passed through, with everyone looking at him, surprised at his smart, short haircut. He opened his door and was about to step in when Diane let out a loud wolf whistle. Allowing himself a smile, Jacks closed his door shutting out the laughter of the room.

Mike and Bobby tapped his door and came in.

"Don't say a bloody word, you two," he barked, noticing the broad grins on their faces.

Later that morning, flanked by Bobby and Mike, with AC Carstairs in attendance, Jacks addressed the whole murder squad which had now swelled to twenty personnel. No one was left under any illusion that he expected hard work, dedication and results whilst he was away.

When he was back in his office he made a telephone call to Dhekelia Army Base in Cyprus. He was put through straightaway to Divisional Commander Redmond of the SBA, the Sovereign Base Areas police.

"How can I help you, Chief Inspector?" he asked obligingly.

Jacks explained that he was coming over to Cyprus overnight, and would be visiting the base in order to interview Derek Blandford, who was a civilian sports instructor on the base.

"Can you tell me what for?" Redmond enquired politely.

"Yes, sir, I can. I want to interview him over a murder that took place over twenty-five years ago. He was the victim's sports teacher at the time."

"Is he a suspect, Chief Inspector Jacks? Do you want us to take him into custody?" he asked helpfully.

"No, Commander, that won't be necessary. I would rather you didn't mention anything to him, but make sure he's available for me to interview." Jacks looked up at Mike who had just entered the room, and waved him to a seat.

"I will certainly make sure he is available. Do you need picking up at the airport and accommodation on the base?" The man was eager to please, and Jacks was grateful.

"Again, that won't be necessary, sir. I will have transport and my own house in Paralimni. I will be staying there during my visit with my sergeant, Detective Sergeant King." Jacks said his goodbyes and put the phone down.

"All set then, Governor?" Mike asked cheerfully.

"All set, and from tonight its plain old Jacks, okay?"

***

That afternoon, Jacks walked through the graveyard and placed flowers on Leanne's grave. There were other bouquets placed neatly on the grave from his parents, Maddie and Ron, and a few friends that had remembered the anniversary of Leanne's death.

"I can't believe that we have been apart for a year, love. I can't believe that I have survived without you. I am going to the house in Cyprus tomorrow. The case is taking me out there. It is going to be hard without you, Leanne, very hard. I will find Patsy's killer, sooner or later, I'll get him," he vowed.

FIFTEEN

The airport was bustling, but Jacks had seen it a lot busier. Their police driver had picked them both up in turn and dropped them right outside terminal five. They checked in at precisely eight thirty in the evening, and noticed that the overhead screen was showing the British Airways flight was on time. They watched their baggage disappear alongside the check-in desk, and slide on the running belt behind.

"Let's get a coffee before we go through passport control, Mike, it's going to be a long night."

"Okay, Guv, but after that I think I would like something a little stronger to help me sleep on the plane," Mike replied.

"What did I tell you before we left? Jacks not Guv, all right?"

"Sorry, old habits…" Mike was interrupted by his mobile buzzing in his pocket. "Mike King," he said into the mouthpiece. He listened to the caller and started to smile as he looked at Jacks.

Jacks was puzzled, why the wry smile?

"He'll be pleased and surprised. I'll see you in a minute in the Café Nero." Mike closed his phone down and slid it into his canvas jacket pocket.

"Who are we seeing in the café, Mike?" Jacks asked, thinking he could do without any surprises at this late hour.

"You'll see soon enough," Mike answered, grinning like a school boy.

They entered the café, didn't wait to be greeted and made their way over to a table alongside the far wall, where they promptly sat down under the disapproving eye of the foreign-looking waiter. The waiter slowly and deliberately made his way over to them, but was overtaken by Suzanne Kaine, who reached the table first.

Jacks intended to ignore the waiter for his previous look of disapproval, so hadn't noticed her buzz by.

Suzanne stood over the table, Mike coughed loudly and Jacks looked up, having caught her perfume. He was surprised and it showed.

"What on earth are you doing here?" he asked incredulously.

"Thanks, Jacks, you certainly know how to make a girl feel wanted," she said with her hand on her hip, feigning annoyance.

Jacks sprang to his feet, wondering what she was doing here; surely she couldn't be travelling with them.

"I'm sorry, Suzanne, but you have really taken me by surprise," he said, as he eyed a still-seated Mike with disapproval.

"Nothing to do with me, Jacks, I only knew when I took that call," he protested.

Suzanne realised what Jacks was thinking and quickly jumped in to prevent any misunderstanding.

"It's all right, I'm not actually coming with you. I thought I would give you a few notes to take with you about the sort of character your killer may be." She handed Jacks a large manila envelope with his name scribbled across the face of it. "Are you going to invite me to sit down or not?" she challenged.

Jacks took the envelope offered. "Oh, please, please sit down, Suzanne. I'm sorry, forgive my manners." He moved in to allow her to sit on the outside of him. "Can I get you a coffee, or would you like something stronger?"

"Coffee's fine, thank you, I'm driving. Hello, Mike," she smiled down at him as she sat down.

"I've just remembered I have to make a couple of calls before we take off," he said diplomatically. "I'll do it in private in the main hall."

Jacks didn't say a word and watched him get up and leave. He turned to Suzanne, "Sorry about your reception, I'm pleased to see you. It's just that it was a surprise to find you standing over me, that's all."

"That's fine, I understand," she smiled at him as she patted his hand.

Her hand was cool. Jacks returned her smile.

"Thanks for the notes. You do realise that I can't sanction this on an official level though, don't you?" he said honestly.

"I'm helping a patient out," she responded, trying to sound professional. "All part of the treatment, Jacks."

Jacks noticed Mike hanging about at the entrance to the café and beckoned him over.

"Better let him get his coffee while it's hot," he said to Suzanne, with a knowing smile.

"I never took my cousin as the diplomatic type," she grinned. "On the contrary, he normally puts his foot in things."

"Oh, he's like that in private life as well," Jacks laughed as Mike arrived.

"Like what as well?" he asked as he sat down. "Is this at my expense?"

"Certainly, that's very nice of you, Mike," Jacks quipped.

Mike looked at them both in turn, they were grinning at each other. "Ha, bloody ha. I didn't mean the drinks."

Jacks and Suzanne had another awkward parting just before he and Mike went through to passport control. They were both conscious of Mike's gaze as they stood looking at one another.

"Thanks for the notes. I'll study them on the plane," he said self-consciously to her, as he held out his hand.

Suzanne smiled nervously as Mike looked on, amused at her discomfort.

She held his hand and smiled at him. "My pleasure, Chief Inspector, all part of the service." She felt her feet start to tingle and hoped he was going to kiss her.

"I don't know what's wrong with you two," Mike laughed, as he went straight up to Suzanne and gave his cousin a kiss on her lips. "That's how to say goodbye."

Jacks realised he was jealous and felt like wrenching his sergeant away by the scruff of his neck, but instead stood by, smiling sheepishly.

***

The captain apologised for the delayed take off, although it was only by ten minutes. He assured the passengers that they would easily make up the time on the way over.

As they crossed the channel to France, Jacks opened the envelope. He studied the very concise report and was surprised at Suzanne's insight into a sadistic criminal's mind. When he finished, he handed the report to a waiting Mike.

Mike read it through and eventually placed it back in its envelope.

"Phew!" said Mike. "Who would have believed she could come up with things like that?"

"I think your cousin is quite a lady, and certainly knows her business. Quite frightening really, isn't it?" He took back the envelope, placing it in his attaché case before sliding it under his seat.

Jacks slept fitfully and uncomfortably by the side of his unconscious friend and colleague who, at this point, he envied for being able to sleep the way he did.

He thought of Cyprus, and the happy times he and Leanne had spent there with their adopted Greek Cypriot family. He was going to find it hard meeting them, it was bad enough when he telephoned to let them know of her death. All of them absolutely worshipped Leanne.

His thoughts were interrupted by the professional voice of the captain, telling them they had begun their descent into Larnaca.

Jacks nudged Mike until he was wide awake.

"Where are we?" He asked, looking through bleary eyes.

"We are following the coast down to Larnaca, should be about another ten minutes to landing. You've had a very good flight, Mike," Jacks offered.

"Can never sleep on these blasted flights," Mike complained

Jacks smiled to himself as he looked out of the window as the plane banked, flew out over the bay of Larnaca and headed back in to the airport before starting to straighten up for the landing. The landing was smooth and the Cypriot passengers applauded the captain for his skill as they always did.

They went through passport and customs, collecting their cases from the baggage hall on their way through. As they went through the exit of the airport, the heat hit them. It was hot this September in Cyprus.

Jacks searched the waiting faces until he saw a grinning bear of a man who waved at them.

"Yassoo, Andoni," Jacks shouted, as he dropped his cases by his side.

Mike looked on as his boss hugged and kissed this unshaven beast of man on both of his cheeks, this was a side to Jacks he had never imagined.

Jacks stepped back. "This is Mike King, Andoni, a friend and colleague of mine."

As Andonis came up to him, Mike was a little concerned he was going to get the same treatment as his boss. He held out his hand and was relieved when Andonis took it and shook it warmly.

"I am pleased to meet you, Mike," Andonis grinned as he spoke in perfect English, before turning back to Jacks and grabbing him in a bear hug again. His manner changed as he said, "I am sorry to hear of my princess's death, Jacks. I cannot understand the pain you must be going through. Maria wants to see you as soon as you can make it to our house."

Jacks gritted his teeth as a lump came into his throat, which he found hard to swallow. This is what he had feared most of all, he knew that coming back here, with all the wonderful memories, was going to be an ordeal. Mike sensed and felt his pain but could offer nothing to his friend.

Andonis broke the awkwardness as he released Jacks. "Your car is parked in the tourist area. I'll take you to it."

He grabbed Jacks' bags and led the way. Jacks and Leanne had been getting a hire car from Andonis ever since they purchased the house, becoming firm friends and being accepted by all the family.

They parted company with Andonis in the car park, after Jacks had promised to call round and see his family before returning to England in a few days' time.

He decided to give Mike the scenic route home, instead of taking the motorway to Paralimni. They went through the old town of Larnaca, before taking the coast road heading towards Famagusta on the east coast. It wasn't long before they picked up the signs to Dhekelia.

Jacks entered a new roundabout and took the road sign posted to Ayia Nappa, taking them up past the army base. This part of the road was British Sovereign territory, and was policed by the British army with Turkish and Greek police employed by them. The check point post at both ends was empty as they passed through and continued on their way to Paralimni.

"No guards," Mike commented.

"They only man the posts on heightened tensions or on exercises," Jacks explained as he continued. "We'll get home and freshen up and come back later. It's still only seven o'clock."

They drove through Sotira, the last village on route, before entering the outskirts of Paralimni, where they turned off to avoid the village centre, going down a couple of back roads to Jacks' house.

Jacks pulled up on to the paved area at the front of the small terraced house, with roses lining either side intermingled with jasmine bushes. He turned off the engine. It all looked exactly the same as when they were here last.

"Lovely, what a smashing pad," Mike said, as he got out and stretched his legs.

Jacks sat where he was and stared at the number three on the front door. Oh, Christ, why had he come? Why didn't he stay in a hotel or at the army base? Mike opened his door so he had no other choice but to get out. Jacks took out his key and inserted it into the gleaming brass lock on the white door, and opened it right back to the holding catch set into the marble floor.

The inside was immaculate. The floor gleamed from the kitchen right through the dining area to the lounge. The drapes were pulled back, showing sliding windows which revealed a good size patio, leading to a small garden. From there you could see the deep blue sea about a quarter of a mile away, glistening in the morning sunshine.

He went to the windows and pulled the left hand side one back until it was over the other half. A warm gentle breeze wafted in, lightly lifting the damask covers on the armchairs and settee. The only things missing were the flowers normally positioned on the dining table, which were usually put there for Leanne.

"The place looks good, Jacks, no housework for us here," Mike said, as he brought the cases in. "Where do I plant these?"

"Up the stairs. You are to the left, I'm at the front with a view. It looks as if Stavroulla has been busy. I think Andonis must have told her I was coming." Stavroulla was a Cypriot who had lived in London for most of her life, before moving back to Cyprus on the death of her husband. Jacks and Leanne had employed her to look after the house, but over the years she had become almost family to them.

"I noticed her car wasn't on the drive opposite. She must be out," Jacks explained.

***

Two hours later, they had showered, changed into suits and were on their way back to the army base at Dhekelia, where they arrived at eleven o'clock. They drove through the main gate leading to Alexander barracks, and stopped at the guardhouse. Jacks showed his warrant card and asked for Divisional Commander Redman.

The sentry looked down the pad he was carrying on his clip board. "He is expecting you, sir. Follow the road round and you will see Divisional Command HQ on your left," he directed without a smile.

An orderly was waiting for them as they arrived outside the offices, and they were shown into the commander's office.

Redman was a typical red cap. Straight up and straight down, military through and through, he was aged about forty, fit and athletic, short hair and a small, greying, trimmed moustache over his thin lips.

He got up from behind his desk, and Jacks realised he was over six feet four in height, as he came round to greet them.

"Chief Inspector Jacks, I presume, and Sergeant King," he asserted rather than asked.

"I'm Jacks, this is Detective Sergeant King," he replied, taking the outstretched hand being offered. He stepped to one side as Mike shook hands with him.

"Redman," he said in a no nonsense and matter-of-fact manner. "Please be seated, gentlemen. Tell me how you want to play this."

Jacks liked the man, although he was army through and through. To the point and get on with things, rather like himself, he thought.

"Thank you for accommodating us, sir," he started. "Where is Blandford now?"

"He's taking a PE lesson in the gym. I have two of my officers waiting nearby to snaffle him for you. Would you like him brought here?"

"Firstly, what can you tell me about the man, sir?" Jacks wanted the feel of his man as he was now.

"He's the last man I would have thought to be in trouble with the law, let alone something as serious as this. Married, with two grown up daughters who live and work in England. His wife's name is Kathy, he is devoted to her. He works hard, is very punctual and conscientious, and is very popular with both service and civilian personnel. We couldn't want for a better member of staff."

"As you say, sir, he doesn't really fit, but stranger offenders have been known."

Redman reached for his radio. "Would you like me to get him now, Chief Inspector? I would like to get this nasty business out of the way."

"Thank you, sir, that would be ideal," Jacks replied as Redman picked up the radio set off of his table and spoke into it.

"Just escort Mr Blandford to my office, no need to say why," he ordered the officer on the other end.

Two minutes later, Jacks and Mike heard boots approaching the office, followed by a sharp tap on the door.

"Enter," called out Redman, as the door opened instantly to admit Derek Blandford, flanked by two Cypriot police officers.

Jacks looked at the photograph he had in his hand. It was Blandford all right, twenty-five years older, thicker set and his blonde hair thinning, but it was him.

Jacks and Mike got up to face a very puzzled and worried man.

"This is Detective Inspector Jacks and Detective Sergeant King of the Metropolitan Police, Mr Blandford. They want to speak to you about a matter some years ago, back in England." He didn't wait for an answer as he turned to Jacks. "All yours, Chief Inspector." Redman and the other two officers left the room.

Jacks moved round to the other side of the desk and addressed Derek Blandford. "Please sit down, Mr Blandford."

"What's this all about?" Blandford protested.

"You were invited to sit, now bloody do it," Mike barked at him.

Blandford reacted immediately, and sat down in the chair vacated by Jacks. Mike joined Jacks on the other side of the table, standing to his left side.

"Are you Derek Blandford, and did you used to teach physical education at Sunningdale School in 1989?" Mike asked.

Blandford was worried, what on earth was this? What was he being accused of? "I was the sports master," he answered, looking up at Mike.

Jacks was observing him as he spoke to Mike. He was definitely nervous, but was he guilty? "Mr Blandford, did you know a girl by the name of Patsy Kerridge?"

Blandford reacted with his mouth and eyes wide open. "Why? Why do you want to know that?"

Mike leant over the desk and was in his face. "Just answer the questions, Blandford. Did you know her?"

Blandford looked appealingly to Jacks, but Jacks just sat there looking at him, waiting for his answer.

"Yes, I knew her. I taught her. She was a future star of both track and field. She was going places," he stammered.

"Mr Blandford," Jacks waited until he looked him directly in the eyes, "did you ever meet Patsy Kerridge outside of school hours, or anywhere else but the school?"

Blandford started to really panic as he looked from Jacks to Mike, before blurting out, "She went missing didn't she? We thought she had run off with someone. You people questioned me at the time, along with other teachers."

"Do you want me to repeat the question, Mr Blandford?" Jacks asked, looking at him with menace clearly showing in his eyes. "And I would be careful to tell us the truth. We haven't come all the way here on a whim."

Blandford thought about his options. "Okay, I did meet her, a couple of times. Well, it was three actually, but it was quite innocent. I didn't arrange it, she was just there."

"Where?" Jacks pushed. "Where did you meet her, and how?"

He searched his memory, deciding to tell Jacks the truth, no matter how it sounded. "I was walking my dog in the woods behind our house one early evening. A path led from the village, across a stream, and out to the main Sunningdale road. As I went to go over the stepping stones in the stream I spotted her walking towards me. I was surprised to see her and I asked her where she was going. She told me she was taking a short cut to the village because the bus didn't go there. I had no reason to doubt her and walked back with her as she played with my dog."

"And the next time?" Jacks asked.

"Same thing really, I did think it a little odd that it should be at the same time, but then I thought, 'well it must be the bus times'." Blandford was looking straight into Jacks' eyes; he was either a very good and cunning liar or he was telling the truth.

"You say you met her three times, Mr Blandford. What happened on the last walk?" Jacks watched him carefully to see if his manner changed.

"Well, when it happened a couple of nights later, I got a bit suspicious as to why she was going to the village, so I asked her who it was she was visiting. She couldn't think of a name and it began to dawn on me that she was there to bump into me. Kids get these silly crushes on their teachers, so I shouldn't have been surprised, but she was attractive and quite mature, and I was happily married. I didn't want my wife getting even the faintest hint of this, so I took her to task about it and warned her that it should not happen again, or I would have to report it."

"How did she take the rejection, Mr Blandford? Was she angry, upset, or what?"

"No, Chief Inspector, she was a little sad and disappointed, but then she told me she thought she was being followed wherever she went. Well, I thought this was just another ruse to get my attention, so I didn't take too much notice of it."

"Did she say who she thought was following her?" Jacks asked.

"She was a bit vague, said a man dressed in army fatigues was hanging about the playing fields when they were doing sports. No one else complained, and there were no other reports from any of the other girls, so I don't think it was followed up. She also told me she thought he had followed her onto the bus a couple of times. Anyway, I didn't want anything happening to her, so I escorted her back to the road and waited for the bus to pick her up. I didn't see a soul."

"We believe Patsy went missing on the evening of the seventeenth of September 1989. Can you tell me where you were on that day, Mr Blandford?" Jacks asked. He didn't expect a positive answer straightaway, who remembers where they were twenty-five years ago?

"I told one of your officers some three weeks later where I was," he protested. "Surely it's a matter of record?" he queried.

Jacks looked at Mike, surprised by his reply. "Tell us again, please, Mr Blandford," Mike requested, helping Jacks out.

"My wife was quite an athlete in those days, and represented Ireland in the Europeans. We were both in Dublin the whole week Patsy Kerridge went missing."

Jacks couldn't believe his ears. He was seething and trying not to show it. "Are you still married to her?"

"To Kathy, hell yes, I would never leave her. We've been in love ever since she moved to England from Cork when we were teenagers."

"Okay, Mr Blandford, I think we are done here, and I am sorry to have troubled you. I would like you to jot down where you stayed in Dublin, and what flight you took over there and back. Can you do that for me, please, and let me have it before I return to England?"

"Certainly, Chief Inspector. I'm relieved that it has been as simple as this. I was always worried in case I would be implicated somehow in her disappearance. You haven't said, but you must have found her. Was she killed?"

"I am afraid she was, sir. We found her remains in a shallow grave in the copse not far from the stream, hence why we had to speak to you again."

"Oh my God, that's awful. Such an attractive girl. Is there anything else I can do to help, Chief Inspector?" Derek Blandford showed true regret, but was also relived he had been cleared.

They watched Derek Blandford from the large open window as he left the building. Mike looked at his governor, wondering what was going through his mind. "You were very easy on him," Mike stated. "Any particular reason?"

"He didn't do it," Jacks answered bluntly. "We'll go through the motions, we'll check his alibi out, but it's not him.

Even Suzanne's profile screams that. Blandford has been married for over thirty years and still in love with his wife. Our killer is a sadistic, bad-tempered, violent control freak who goes berserk if he doesn't get his own way. No way will he have been married to the same woman all this time."

***

Jacks thanked the commander for his accommodation and they left the base at one thirty in the afternoon.

"We'll get back to the house and change into more suitable clothes, Mike, and then we will go swimming at a little beach in Pernera. Tonight I'll take you to a restaurant Leanne and I have used on the first night since buying the house," Jacks said as they got into their car.

***

At eight o'clock that evening, they drove into Protaras about three miles from the house. Jacks took the crescent route bordering Fig Tree Bay and the many tourist hotels, bars and gift shops, emerging at Diva's restaurant at the far end. He parked the car and they walked back to the restaurant to be spotted by Kyriacos, the co-owner, as they approached the entrance. Kyriacos didn't say a word as he walked straight up to Jacks, embraced him, kissing him twice on both cheeks. His partner, Fordes, joined them and gave him the same welcome.

"Words are not enough, Jacks mou, we are all so sorry."

"Kala efkharisto, Forde, I wish Leanne could be here," he thanked him in Greek.

Mike watched all the waiters leave customers at their tables and come over in turn to greet and kiss Jacks on his cheeks. Jacks would have normally responded but stood stiffly to attention trying to keep things together. The customers watched puzzled and mesmerised by the scene, thinking that the local mafia had come to call.

"I think it would be nice to sit down now," Mike said, trying to break the awkwardness for Jacks.

"This is Mike King, a very good friend and colleague from England," Jacks introduced Mike to them all.

Mike shook hands with them, grateful that they didn't want to kiss him as well, before being led to a table. They ate well whilst chatting with the waiters. At the end of the meal there was no sign of any bill being presented.

"Tonight is on the house, filos mou, my friend," Kyriacos added in English.

After dinner they said their goodbyes and left the restaurant. Jacks drove back towards Paralimni, before turning off and heading towards the beach area.

"Just one more visit before we go home, Mike."

"How come you know so many people and have so many friends here?" Mike asked

"I don't know. Leanne and I have more friends and adopted family here than I have ever had in England. Maybe it's because I am more relaxed her. Maybe I can look for the good in people rather than the bad. I don't know. Perhaps it's the people themselves," he answered philosophically.

As they arrived outside a tavern in Penera, Mike looked up at the bar sign and laughed. "Only Fools and Horses." He read out loud.

They parked beside the yellow three wheeler car, a replica of the Trotter's vehicle from the TV series, placed as an advertisement outside the small bar and restaurant. On entering the bar, they were immediately spotted by Lambros, the owner, who was standing behind the counter with his elder brother, Petros. Jacks has known these two for many years. Petros also had a bar with the same name in Protaras along the coast.

"Jacks, welcome. What can I get you?"

"Hello, Lambro, it's nice to see you. Mine's a pint of Keo, Parakalow."

"I'll have the same please," Mike said.

"Hello Petro," Jacks embraced the elder brother as he came to greet him. He resembled and spoke more like a college professor than a bar owner.

The waitress by Lambros' side started to pour the drinks as he came round to greet Jacks in the same way as his brother, and the staff at Divas.

"If there is anything you want, anything I can do, Jacks, just say the word."

"Thank you, Lambro, I'm fine, really I am."

Mike stayed sober, unlike Jacks and Lambros, who joined him in a serious drinking session. It was left to Mike to drive and find the way back to the house whist Jacks slept the deep sleep of an inebriated man.

***

Early the next morning, Mike woke to the sound of voices downstairs. He put on shirt and shoes and descended the marble steps to the kitchen, where he was greeted with the smell of freshly made coffee. He looked through to the patio where the voices were coming from and made his way through to the lounge. As he stepped out from the large glass open windows, the brilliant sun hit him full in the face causing him to shield his eyes.

"Good morning, sleepy head." Jacks said cheerily.

He had no right to feel so good, how does he do it, thought Mike.

"This is Stavroulla who looks after us, she lives opposite. This is Mike."

Mike held out his hand to the woman sitting opposite Jacks sipping coffee. She was dressed all in black, the mark of a permanent widow in mourning, in her late fifties, with her jet black hair pulled back and tied in a bun. Stavroulla put her coffee down on the white round table and took the hand offered.

"I am pleased to meet you, Mike, welcome to Cyprus. I hope you enjoy your stay." She said in perfect London English, learnt in her many years spent living in London with her late husband.

"Thank you. It's a pleasure to meet you, I've heard a lot about you," He responded.

Stavroulla finished her coffee, made her excuses and left the two of them for the day.

"Well I think a bit more of what we had yesterday would be good, Mike, we could do with topping up. What do you say?"

"I think I can do without any more booze for today, Jacks, if that's okay?"

"I meant the beach. Let's get down for a bit more sun and exercise, eh? Then we will meet my adopted family in Zafeiros restaurant later."

"Have you let your friend know what time to expect us?" Mike asked, remembering that Jacks said he would phone.

"All done before you woke up. We'll get to the restaurant about one. They'll probably dawdle in any time after that. Whenever a Cypriot is late, the time is always referred to as, 'Cyprus time.'"

At twelve forty five, they made their way off the packed beach to the promenade. It had been built for the tourist industry with EU money and stretched from Pernera all the way to Protaras and Fig Tree bay. As they walked, they passed hotels and small kiosks offering anything from fresh strawberries and ice cream to massages and tanks of fish that will eat the dead skin from your feet.

Mike noticed the Shirley Valentine boat berthed at the small jetty. On the beach in front of the hotel, was an awning with a queue of about thirty tourists, mainly Russians, waiting to board. Jacks spotted the Cypriot owner, Kyriacos, and Jean, his English wife, and waved to them as they spotted him.

"I can't stop, I am due at a restaurant," he shouted as they acknowledged him with Jean blowing him a kiss.

"More friends," Mike smiled. "Just how many have you got over here?"

"Jean is a true 'Shirley Valentine,' having come to the Island as a tourist," Jacks answered. "She couldn't have met a nicer guy. They make a great couple."

They arrived dead on one o'clock and Jacks was surprised to see the whole family had already assembled on the green manicured lawn out front of the restaurant, and just a few short metres from the sea.

Jacks caught his breath as he thought he saw Leanne standing behind the family, only to see it was an English tourist, standing with her husband and some friends a little way off.

"You okay?" Mike asked, hearing the intake of breath and thinking it was a reaction to seeing his adopted family.

Jacks, with his jaw set firmly, merely nodded and went forward to greet the throng.

The owners, Kyriacos and Andreas, followed by Christine, Andreas' wife, came to meet him. Skevos, Leanne's favourite waiter, was standing to one side and nodded solemnly as jacks acknowledged him with a raised hand. They had just enough time to say hello before he was mobbed by his whole adopted Cypriot family.

Zafeiros, together with Divas restaurant in Protaras, were Jacks' and Leanne's favourite dining places. They had never been made more welcome anywhere.

Mike couldn't believe the warmth of these people towards his boss, it was no wonder he and Leanne had loved coming to the island and had bought the house. They stayed all afternoon and into the early evening before Jacks made his final tearful goodbyes to them all. They walked back along the promenade to where they had left their car before heading back to the house.

The next morning, they travelled to the airport for their journey home. It had been a fruitless journey, other than to eliminate Blandford from their enquiries, but he was glad he had come and laid some fears to rest. Jacks wondered how things were progressing back in England.

SIXTEEN

Whilst Jacks was interviewing Derek Blandford at eleven thirty in Cyprus, it was only nine thirty in England.

Bobby McQueen and the rest of his team were examining the scant paperwork from the missing persons file, and contacting the personnel who had anything to do with the initial enquiry. There hadn't been a lot of work done initially, and even less on any back up. Bert Kerridge, at first accompanied by his wife before she died, then later forlornly on his own, tried to keep the enquiry alive.

"Everybody seems to have just given up on her, Bobby," Diane said ruefully. "How could they just forget her and write her off?"

Bobby looked at the bewilderment in Diane's eyes, and realised that it could have been any one of them who was over loaded and too busy to chase up a simple missing persons case. "Who knows, Diane, workloads, apathy, who knows? I'll tell you what though, we can make a difference now. Get Len and his team to go and see every police officer whose name is on the file. You and I will go back again and interview the driver and the conductor of that bus, and we will also go and see Mr Kerridge again, no matter how painful it's going to be."

Diane, for the first time, felt energised and that she could make a difference. She turned to the room full of officers and shouted out, "Listen up you lot, here's what you have to do."

***

John Darke, the elderly bus driver who Bobby had interviewed previously, but appeared too old and frail to remember anything about his time twenty-five years ago, was in the back garden of his small terraced house in Twickenham. He was dead-heading his roses, making sure they would bloom time and time again.

Hearing the doorbell, John knew by the time it took to reach the door the visitor would have left, so he carried on dead heading. A few minutes later, Bobby and Diane opened his back gate and entered his beloved garden.

He watched, puzzled, as they approached before recognition came to him.

"You're that copper who came a few days ago, aren't you?" John asked, squinting as he tried to make out Bobby's companion. He was unkempt and hadn't bothered to shave for a few days,

"DS McQueen and DC Plant," Bobby explained, showing his warrant card that he knew Jack Darke couldn't make out. "We need to ask you a few more questions, Mr Darke."

John Darke looked a bit panicked at this. "I told you all I knew then, young man. My memory isn't what it used to be, you know."

"That's all right, Mr Darke, we won't take too much of your time," Diane chipped in. "What lovely roses for this time of year," she added, watching his eyes light up at the praise.

John thought for a moment as he looked Diane up and down. "Well, my girl, if you want to waste your time on an old man like me I had better make you a cup of tea, hadn't I?" he offered.

His kitchen was neat and clean, like his garden. They were surprised at the cleanliness of the surfaces, including the cups they had their tea in. John's general untidy appearance with his clothes, as well as his lack of grooming on his receding hair, belied the inside of his house.

"Is there a Mrs Darke?" Diane asked, as she looked round the kitchen.

"No, Beryl died some fifteen years ago now, bless her heart. She used to love the roses, like you, young lady. We spent many an hour tending our little patch and visiting gardening exhibitions."

"John, may I call you John?" Diane asked politely.

"I would like that, yeah, please do," he said, with a glint in his eye.

Bobby was more than happy to take a back seat on this. Diane seemed to be building a rapport with the old devil, and he appeared to like the ladies.

"You know we found a girl's body in Brackenbridge Copse, don't you?" Diane asked.

John nodded and looked over at Bobby. "He told me," he said simply.

"Well, she got on your bus a few evenings when David Trent was your conductor. She used to get off at the stop that led across to the copse to Brackenbridge, and would walk through the copse to the village. She wore a very bright yellow dress and was very attractive, John. Now you have an eye for a pretty girl, don't you?"

John Darke was trying to think, and looked at Diane as if she was trying to trap him. "I never touched any young girls, never in my life," he protested.

"No, no, no, John, no one is saying you did. There's nothing wrong in appreciating something or someone pretty, is there? We all like good lookers, John, even I have an eye for a handsome man." Diane was putting him at ease, as Bobby looked on with eyebrows raised and a silly smile on his face.

"Well I did think about this when the big fellah came last time, and I seem to remember a girl in a yellow dress that David Trent pointed out to me. I couldn't really tell you what she looked like. He used to chat to them all because he had to deal with them. I think I remember him saying that a young army bloke who got on the bus quite fancied her, but I can't remember anything else, even if I knew anything at the time. I do remember Trent being a little scared of him, although he tried to laugh it off."

"Okay, John, but if anything else comes to mind you phone me, yes?" Diane handed him her card. "Anything at all, John, no matter how small."

Bobby and Diane took their leave of John Darke, with Bobby having to duck quite low through the small terrace door.

Once outside, Bobby looked at her. "So you fancy good lookers do you, Diane? I'll have to let the lads know when we get back."

"Piss off, Bobby, there's no good lookers amongst you bloody lot anyway." Diane got into the car, laughing loudly.

An hour later they pulled up outside the home of David Trent. The house was a modest, semi-detached property with a very small paved garden area in front. David Trent answered the door, and they were led into the lounge-come diner. He was a little nervous, wondering what more the police wanted of him.

Bobby had decided that, after her success with John Darke, Diane should lead with the questioning.

"I'm Detective Constable Plant, Mr Trent. You already know DS McQueen, don't you?"

David Trent nodded. "How are you, Mr McQueen? I thought I had told you and Chief Inspector Jacks everything I knew." He obviously wasn't happy with another visit to his home.

Diane didn't wait for a response from Bobby and moved straight to the point of their visit. "Mr Trent, we have just interviewed John Darke and some things have come up we need to clarify."

Trent looked back at Diane. "I thought he was too elderly to remember anything," he replied, a little puzzled.

Diane pressed on. "He remembered you pointing out a pretty girl in a yellow dress, who had got on the bus and that you also mentioned a man, an army type, who seemed to be paying her some attention."

"I told you all this before, and repeated it at your office in New Scotland Yard. The man had a series of star tattoos on his ear, right ear I think it was. He had short cropped hair, dressed in army fatigues and wore boots. I thought he looked army, but there again you can get kitted out like that at the Army & Navy stores in any town," Trent said quickly, as if to get it over with. "I can't tell you anymore because I don't know anymore," he pleaded.

"That's okay, Mr Trent," Bobby interceded to try and calm him down. "We are just checking on stories and trying to glean any bits of information we can, no matter how small."

"I'm sorry, Mr McQueen, but I really don't know any more. I have thought and thought about that time but the more I do the less I seem to be able to recall."

They parted company after calming David Trent down, and headed for the home of Patsy's father, Bert Kerridge. They were stabbing about in the dark, but they needed to keep pushing if they were going to get any sort of break in this case.

Bobby's mobile phone rang, Diane, who was driving, glanced across at him as he answered it and listened.

"McQueen," Bobby answered, as he looked across at Diane. "Hello, Guv, how's it going?" Bobby turned the volume up so that Diane could listen in.

"Not good this end, Bobby, I think we have more or less ruled Blandford out of this," Jacks capitulated, adding, "I have emailed over some details of his alibi to you that I would like checking out with the Irish sports body."

"I'll get on it when I get back, Guv. I'm out and about with Diane at the moment. We are re-interviewing everybody involved in this. We are just off to see Bert Kerridge, after seeing the bus driver and the conductor."

"Do you have any developments of interest?" Jacks asked.

"The same thing comes up every time, including from the bus driver, who couldn't remember much before. Diane got him talking, you know what a little charmer she can be." Diane scowled as she caught his eye.

"They all describe a soldier-type, dressed in fatigues. I think this individual is our main suspect, although we are interviewing all the teaching staff as well."

"Well done Bobby. I take it Miss Charming is listening in?" Jacks laughed. "We'll be back tomorrow, early evening. Can you get us picked up? I'll send you the details of the flight."

"Will do, Guv, no problem," Bobby said, as he ended the call.

Diane turned to Bobby as he ended the call. "Where do we find a soldier-type dressed in fatigues that can be around during the day and the evening?"

"Presumably, if he's not kitted himself out at the Army & Navy Stores, any local barracks at the time," Bobby suggested. "We'll start making enquiries at military establishments tomorrow."

***

Bobby got home to his wife, Betty, and two children that evening, but he couldn't stop thinking of the mysterious man in fatigues. He was the right age for a squaddie, but where did he live and where were his barracks? First thing in the morning, he would put the team to work on it. He played with his two children before they went to bed and then sat with Betty in their lounge.

"How's the case going?" she asked a distant Bobby.

"Sorry, love, I was miles away. It's where to start looking for a soldier in the Sunningdale area twenty-five years ago. Would they have used a particular pub in the area?" he mused to himself.

237

"Difficult to find that type of location after all this time, Bobby. How about starting at the local British Legion? That's where I would have found my brother most of his time off."

Bobby remembered Carl, her brother, had served in the Royal Engineers. He looked at his wife with a big grin on his face. "You're a bloody marvel, love. That's exactly where I'll start." Bobby slid over to his wife and put his arms round her.

"Steady on, big boy," she protested weakly. "The kids are still awake."

SEVENTEEN

Jacks and Mike carried their bags through the customs hall, overtaking other passengers wheeling their overloaded trollies to the entrance. They looked for their driver, spotting Diane waiting amongst a host of taxi drivers standing at the barrier, with their name boards raised.

"Miss Charming, how are you?" Jacks hailed Diane, as he made his way towards her.

Diane grinned at the recognition. "I'm well, Guv. You're not very tanned," she quipped.

"Didn't go there for the sun, Diane, hardly saw it," Mike complained, grinning at her.

They picked up the M4 motorway out of the airport making their way easily through traffic to London. Diane dropped off Jacks at home first, and continued on her way with Mike.

It was getting dark as Jacks looked at the house, remembering the happy times when he had looked forward to coming home to Leanne. He felt no sense of joy or home coming as he turned the key in the lock and opened the front door. He dropped his case in the hallway before picking up the mail on the inside doormat. He altered the thermostat, instantly operating the gas boiler to heat the house up and to give him hot water for a shower.

Jacks went to the fridge and took out a bottle of cold beer, removed the cap and drank it from the bottle. He took the drink into the hall, placing it on the table before picking up the telephone and dialling Suzanne's number. He listened as the answer service kicked in, but before it could operate it was interrupted.

"Hello, Jacks, good trip?"

"Hello, Suzanne, how are you?" Jacks responded into the mouthpiece as he sipped his beer.

"Never been better. How did it go in Cyprus? Did you find what you were looking for?"

"It was a no go. He didn't fit your profile in the least, and as it happens he had an alibi anyway. He was in Ireland the whole week Patsy went missing."

Suzanne felt a little disappointed for Jacks. "So where do you go from here?"

"We start again on other lines of enquiry," Jacks replied giving the standard answer.

"Did you want to come in for another session?" Suzanne asked hopefully.

"No." Jacks' reply was sharp. She worried she had pushed him.

"No, not another session in your office, but we could meet for dinner one night this week," Jacks found himself saying without thinking, regretting it straightaway. Would she accept? he wondered.

"That would be lovely," Suzanne said far too quickly she thought, as she felt her feet going through the same old routine. "When did you have in mind?"

"I have a series of meetings at the Yard tomorrow morning," Jacks answered, relieved that she had accepted the invitation so quickly. "I'll ring you at your office around midday, if that's okay?"

***

After the call had ended, Suzanne kicked off her shoes and massaged the bottoms of her feet. The tingling sensation, although very pleasant, was getting stronger every time she had contact with this man.

"I can't wait until tomorrow," she murmured out loud, grinning to herself like a school girl.

***

Jacks was in his office at seven thirty the next morning, and watched through the glass screen as the murder squad drifted in. He was impressed, the whole team had assembled before eight o'clock.

Mike and Bobby were talking to each other, before looking over to Jacks behind the window and making their way to his office.

"Morning, Guv," they both said in unison.

"Good morning, sergeants two," Jacks said cheerily, as they grinned at one another at the old Jacks appearing this morning. "Right, Bobby, what have you got for me?"

Jacks listened to Bobby's report on the interviews of ex-police personnel and teachers who had anything to do with the case all those years ago. He didn't envy the laborious and thankless task he and the team had undertaken whilst he was away.

"Something interesting came up though, Guv," Bobby continued. "It was my missus Betty who came up with the idea. She suggested that we start with the British Legions in the area. Her brother was in the army and spent most of his leave in them."

"Have you been along there?" Jacks asked.

"Oh yes," replied Bobby. "And I'm going back tonight. They have a large meeting once a month when a lot of the old stagers assemble to discuss old times. I asked if there would be any who had served in the nineties, and I was told there would be dozens of them."

"That's cracking thinking, Bobby," Mike chipped in.

"Yes, well done. We'll come with you, if that's okay?" Jacks queried.

"Okay, Guv. Diane's due to come as well, if that's all right?"

"Miss Charming is always welcome, no problem." Jacks was pleased the team had not only been working in his absence, but had been thinking as well.

Later that morning he reported to AC Carstairs, bringing him up to date on the enquiries so far.

"Well at least you've eliminated him from your enquiries, Jacks. You can press on now. It does sound as if this army-type is a good suspect, and again you need to run him to ground, even if it's to eliminate him from enquiries."

Carstairs smiled at Jacks. "I have every confidence in you in tracking this killer down. All I ask is, be aware of the budget constraints we have."

***

That evening, Jacks, Mike and Bobby, driven by Diane, arrived at the Twickenham branch of the British Legion in Popes Grove. They walked through the entrance and were met by the club's secretary, a man in his early fifties, who bade them welcome. They had to sign in to comply with the rules and laws of the club, as well as health and safety, before being shown to the main hall. There was already quite a gathering, with the meeting being well attended.

Jacks turned to the secretary. "Thank you for allowing us in, Mr Secretary. I wonder if I could impose on you a little more?" Jacks smiled disarmingly at him.

"What else can we do for you, Chief Inspector?" he asked politely.

"Could I address the meeting when everyone has assembled?" Jacks requested.

"Only too pleased, Chief Inspector. The members will be thrilled to have a senior officer from Scotland Yard address them," he beamed with delight. "I'll do the introduction when you are ready, if you like?"

"That would be extremely good of you, and very helpful," Jacks added.

The members were being chivvied along from the bar, gradually filling up the hall. The secretary went up on to the stage and addressed the meeting.

After twenty minutes of Legion's business, he nodded to Jacks, the team made their way up the steps and stood to one side.

"Tonight, ladies and gentlemen, we have a very distinguished guest, who some of you will have seen on television lately. The people I am going to introduce to you are top detectives from Scotland Yard's murder squad," he boasted. "Please give a warm welcome to Chief Inspector Jacks and his team."

As Jacks and his team strode out to the centre of the stage the members gave them loud applause, followed by one member giving a wolf whistle directed at Diane.

Jacks held up his hands and nodded in appreciation until they quietened, and then he started. "I take it the wolf whistle was for my lovely detective, and not for me." He smiled as the hall laughed and Diane curtsied. "But if it was for me, I'll see the member later." This brought further laughs before Jacks got down to business.

"Twenty-five years ago, a young girl called Patsy Kerridge was murdered, and we found her body a few weeks ago in Brackenbridge Copse. For those who don't know where the copse is, it's on the main bus route from Twickenham to Sunningdale. We believe Patsy was on her way by bus, and got off at the copse to walk through to the village. She was brutally attacked and murdered there. We are trying to trace anyone who had any connection with her at that time. We also believe a young army type was on the bus and got off at the same stop. We need to trace this man and eliminate him from the enquiry. He was between twenty and thirty years of age, with short black hair and dressed in denim-type camouflage clothing. He also may have had three small stars as a tattoo on his right ear. Now anyone that thinks they know this man, or can help us with our enquiries, we'll be in the bar after this meeting. Any small bits of information could help, so don't be shy on coming forward." Jacks looked round at his team, as Bobby stepped forward.

"Good evening, everyone. I'm Detective Sergeant McQueen, and would just like to add if anyone knows of any person using the threatening term which includes 'like a bullet in the brain', we would also like to interview that person," he said, as he glanced at Jacks.

"Thank you, Detective Sergeant. Please rack your memories, people. As I said, anything can help, no matter how small."

The secretary led the way off the stage, and they made their way to the bar.

"Steward, give these gentlemen what they want and let me have the receipt," the secretary ordered. "I'll be in my office, Chief Inspector, if you require me for anything further."

Jacks thanked him for his welcome and allowing him to address the assembly, before taking the pint offered to him by Mike.

"Not you, Miss Charming, you're driving," he asserted.

"Thanks, Guv, I am aware. This is just a tonic water with ice and lemon," Diane countered, frowning at her new title. "What's with the 'Miss Charming', Guv?" she asked.

Jacks winked at her. "Better Miss Charming than the Dragon Lady, eh, Diane?"

The members were trickling into the bar and ordering their particular drinks. Jacks watched them, waiting for any signs of recognition that they might know something.

A young man of about twenty five years of age stood next to them with a ten pound note in his hand, waiting to order.

"Bullet in the brain," he said, as they all turned to look at him.

He couldn't know anything at his age surely, Jacks thought as he said, "Have you heard it said before?"

The young man turned to him and replied, "Yeah! It comes from Ricky Martin's 'Livin' La Vida Loca'. Something about cocaine and like a bullet to the brain."

Mike shook his head. "No, no, that didn't come out 'til 1990, and anyway, it was 'bullet to the brain' not in the brain."

The man shrugged his shoulders, attracted the steward's attention and ordered his drink before moving off.

"Didn't know you were a Ricky Martin fan, Mike," Bobby laughed.

"I'm not particularly, but if you wanted to dance with the girls it was a must at parties and dances," Mike grinned.

"Chief Inspector Jacks, can I have a word?" A man of about fifty, still looking quite fit, with his black hair showing signs of greying at the temples, spoke to him in a Geordie accent. "My name is John Holmes, and I'm an ex-para," he stated proudly.

"Yes, Mr Holmes, do you have something for us?" Jacks summed the man up. Still army through and through and probably would be until the day he died.

"I remember a man who used to use that term whenever he was threatening someone. He would say something like, 'you cross me you won't feel a thing, it'll be like a bullet in the brain'."

Jacks felt the adrenalin start to rush through them all as they transfixed on this man in front of them. "Excuse me, Mr Holmes," he said as he turned to Mike. "Go and have a word with the secretary and see if there's a private office we can use."

Mike turned away to do his bidding, as Jacks turned back to the ex-paratrooper.

"Can you give us a little of your time tonight, Mr Holmes? It could be of the utmost importance."

"Of course I can, sir, no problem. I seem to be marking time these days, only too pleased to help."

"Just call me Jacks, no need for the 'sir'. Is it all right for me to call you John?" Jacks wanted this man at ease and on his side.

Mike came back, accompanied by the secretary of the club. "You can use my office, Chief Inspector. I've about finished for the night. The steward will lock up for me later." He turned back on his heel. "This way, gentlemen," he invited.

The office was adequate, but not especially spacious with five adults crammed in. Jacks sat down in the secretary's chair, with John Holmes seated next to him, whilst the others sat just in front of the door and the other side of the desk.

"Right, John, tell us your story. How do you know this man?" Jacks asked, as Diane prepared to take notes.

John shifted in his seat, conscious of the eyes on him; he cleared his throat and started. "As I said, I'm ex-para, having served for twenty-two years with 2 Para, and coming out in 1995. I ended up as a warrant officer. My duties took me from the Falklands to Northern Ireland under Operation Banner, and it was in Northern Ireland I encountered who I think is your man. His name is Mark Smith, and he joined us over there as one of the replacements for men who had suffered injuries in a bomb attack. I didn't like the little shit right from the start, but unfortunately he was assigned to me. I was a sergeant back then."

He looked round the intense faces, pleased that he had their undivided attention, and continued. "He was a sadistic prick, and at the first opportunity would cause trouble with the locals, both Catholics and Protestants alike, whenever he felt like it. He would purposely insult the local women to antagonise the menfolk, but always took care to see that he had his back covered. Even his mates couldn't stand him in the end."

Jacks held his hand up to say something. "John, when did he join you in Northern Ireland?" he asked.

John thought back as if he was seeing Mark Smith arrive at the barracks for the first time. "He arrived first in June, but then went on leave for some reason, coming back in late September 1989. By the spring I had got rid of him back to Blighty."

"Why was that?" Mike asked. "Why did you get rid of him?"

"Because he was a bloody liability, that's why. Firstly he gets a tattoo on his ear that can be clearly seen, and secondly, and more importantly, he was out on patrol one evening when he came across a young catholic couple kissing and cuddling in an alleyway. He had to start insulting them, until the lad had no choice but to face him. Smith smashed his face in with the butt of his weapon and, when the girl jumped on him to stop him he turned on her as well. He not only smashed her cheek bones but was trying to break her neck when the rest of the patrol pulled him off. I only found out the true story after I had got rid of him. They closed ranks as brothers always do, even if one of them doesn't deserve it. When I found out the extent of the girl's injuries I wanted to charge him, but the CO said no and shipped him back home. When I eventually returned to the UK, he had been thrown out of the service for insubordination amongst other things."

"Aren't 2 Para based in Colchester in Essex? How did this Mark Smith come to be in this area?" Mike asked.

John Holmes smiled knowingly. "The parachute regiment was based in Aldershot in those days. They moved to Colchester in 2003, after I was demobbed. Anyway, your little shit was a pikey, from the traveling community if you like," he added, not wanting to be branded a racist or worse. "I believe he came from this area, as well as across Kent and Hampshire. I think the clue is in the name Smith, don't you?"

"John, if I arrange to have you picked up and taken to our head office, would you mind making out a full statement of everything you know on this man, including dates, etcetera?" Jacks wanted the man to have time to think.

"What, up to Scotland Yard? You bet I'll come, I'll drink out on that for weeks," he laughed.

"Not until I give you the go ahead, John. In the meantime, I would like you to keep all of this to yourself. Don't tell a soul, not even the club secretary." Jacks looked sternly at him, demanding his answer.

"No problem, Jacks, I'll keep quiet, not a word to anyone. By the way, I think I have some photographs of Smith with some of the lads. I'll look them out for you."

Jacks couldn't hope for more. "That would be very helpful, John, thanks."

***

At eight o'clock the next morning, the whole team was assembled in the main office. Diane was reading out the notes she had taken the night before at the British Legion club. When she had finished, she gave way to Jacks.

"Right, Diane," said Jacks. "Get on to the Parachute Regiment, give them Smith's details and ask for a complete record. I want it picked up by courier today."

Diane was pleased she had her name back, Miss Charming was wearing a bit thin. "Right, Guv, I'm onto it."

"Bobby, CRO records, associates and anything else you can dig up," Jacks instructed, as Bobby slid off his chair and went to his phone. "Mike, you and Len have a word with the local police stations and councils, and see if you can pin-point what bloody tribe this man belongs to. Can you also arrange to pick up John Holmes and get him in here for his statement, and don't forget the photos. Everyone else get trawling through any witness statements and see if anyone else mentions anything that can tie this bastard in to the case."

A few minutes later, Jacks was sitting in front of his boss, AC Carstairs, and reporting his latest discovery.

"Well done, Jacks. I knew you would crack this, and now to find him." Carstairs was a very happy man; for a very limited budget so far, he was going to sort out a twenty-five year old murder, and possibly many other offences committed by Smith.

"Do you want to go public with this, Jacks?" he asked.

"No, sir, not yet at least. He's possibly still connected to the travelling community and will disappear, probably to Ireland and lose himself in the travellers over there. We'll run him to ground, sir, don't you worry about that." Jacks was more positive about this than anything else before in his whole life.

When Jacks got back to his office, John Holmes's statement was on his table, together with a series of photos. John had stuck little yellow arrows on the photographs pointing to the figure of Smith.

Mike had already had the pictures blown up, and Jacks started to take the enlargements out of the manila envelope. He laid them out in front of him on his desk, and examined them in detail.

Mike came into the room with a magnifying glass and handed it to Jacks.

"Look at his left hand," he said, tapping the photo.

Jacks magnified the left hand and noticed the ring; he could clearly see the letter 'M'. He turned the original photo over and noticed the date on the back: 28.06.1989.

Mike pointed out the next picture of Smith, and he noticed the ring was now absent. He turned the picture over, and again noticed the date: 28.09.1989.

"We have the bastard, Guv, we have him cold," Mike said, triumphantly grinning from ear to ear.

Jacks got up and held out his hand to his detective sergeant. "Well done, Mike, and well done John Holmes," he said, as they shook hands.

EIGHTEEN

Later that morning, Jacks stood by Leanne's grave with tears in his eyes. He bent down to tidy away the last lot of flowers that had wilted in the cold, early December weather.

"I'm close, Leanne," he uttered quietly. "Tell Patsy I'm very close. I will have her killer very soon. That I promise."

He should have stayed at the Yard until the results started coming back, but he felt he owed this to Leanne and Patsy somehow. "I'll come back when it's all over, love, and it will be over soon."

An hour later, Jacks entered the main office, which was buzzing with excitement that you only get when progress was being made in such a case.

Mike was sitting in Jacks' office, reading out loud the statement he had just taken from John Holmes.

Bobby listened whilst flipping through a file that had come in from the army, together with the criminal record office's profile of one Mark Smith. As Jacks entered they both stood up, grinning from ear to ear.

"What are you so pleased about?" he asked, looking from one to the other with a distant stare. "Do you have him in custody?"

Mike and Bobby looked at one another with the grins dying on their faces.

"No, I thought not. We celebrate when this bastard's either in the pen or he's dead, do you understand?" Jacks almost spat it out at them. "Let me see what you've got to date. You first, Bobby."

Bobby meekly handed over the file on Mark Smith. Jacks noticed he was born on the 28th January 1968, making him twenty-two years old when he entered the army. He peered at the photograph showing both side and full on profiles, and fixed on the dead eyes staring back at him. Five feet eleven inches tall, powerfully built, swarthy complexion.

Jacks read the file through, noticing the distinguishing marks entered on the file, right ear tattooed with three small stars at the top, and pierced in the lobe, defence knife scar to left forearm, broken nose at bridge.

He continued to read the man's rap sheet, which was quite lengthy. Although there was a catalogue of offences, he had only served two short jail terms for assault and battery, and for stealing lead from church roofs. He had numerous motoring offences and had been banned from driving on the top-up point system.

At the bottom were further details of a violent assault on a female, that hadn't been proven because the victim failed, for whatever reason, to identify him as her attacker. He looked for an address for Smith but most showed NFA, meaning no fixed abode, against all offences, except one.

The one address given was early on in his offending, a caravan park in New Malden.

Travellers site, thought Jacks. He looked at the photographs of the girl's battered face and immediately thought of Patsy.

Bobby and Mike watched the darkening mood of their boss, and wondered what was coming next as he opened up the army file that had been delivered by courier. The same dead eyes met his, Jacks already hated this man. He was dishonourably discharged from the army in 1992 for going absent without leave twice, insubordination to an officer, and stealing army property.

Jacks looked up from the file and addressed Mike. "Your turn, what have you got?"

"Len and I went to the caravan site in New Malden, which is semi-permanent now. The residents were anti us straightaway, but when we mentioned Mark Smith's name they were a little more forthcoming. The upshot of it all is he's banned from ever going near the place on pain of death. They were genuine, Guv, they meant what they said, although they wouldn't give a reason. We pushed Job Smith, who assures us he's not a relative, and he tends to think he heard about Smith moving round the Brighton area in Sussex, but wouldn't give us anymore on that. I telephoned Brighton CID. They said they knew of him, and believed he operated between a site in Worthing and another just outside of Hove. They are going to make a few discreet enquiries with their narks down there." Mike sat back not knowing if this was enough for his boss.

"Well. Well done, Mike, and you too, Bobby. I am now going to get warrants out for Smith's arrest, and I think we may as well prepare to join our friends on the south coast."

Jacks telephoned Suzanne and left a message with Isabelle, her secretary, who now recognised his voice when he called.

Should that worry me? thought Jacks, feeling a little disloyal to Leanne, who he still loved so much. He pushed it to the back of his mind as a civilian clerk knocked gently on the window of his door. Jacks hadn't even noticed her arrival, and beckoned her to enter.

"Good Morning, Chief Inspector. My name is Susan Briggs from Process. I have your warrants for both the search and arrest of one Mark Jacob Smith," she said, smiling breezily.

"In that case, Susan Briggs, I am a very happy bunny, thank you." Jacks took the envelope from her, waited until she left the room before closing the door.

He opened the envelope carefully, and studied the warrants to make sure that everything was correct. The last thing he needed now was any mistakes in the paperwork. Bobby and Mike were watching him through the glass partition, and saw the satisfied grin on his face.

Jacks looked up to see them watching him, as he beckoned them to come in.

"We have our warrants," he said happily. "We can enter any premises on suspicion that Smith is connected in any way, and we can arrest him on sight. I want the whole squad assembled, made aware of the scope of the warrants, and brought up to date on all information."

Bobby and Mike congratulated Jacks, and were about to leave when he stopped them.

"One other thing. Smith is very violent and no doubt he is going to be armed. He may get tipped off by the travellers, although I have a very strong belief they would top him themselves given half the chance," he warned gravely, the smile having disappeared from his face.

As Bobby and Mike left the office, Jacks' mobile buzzed on his desk, the vibration causing it to swivel on the polished surface.

"Jacks," he said, as he opened up the set.

"Hi," Suzanne's cheery voice answered. "You rang and left a message."

"How would you like to go out for dinner tonight?" Jacks asked tentatively, not knowing whether he was being a bit forward.

Suzanne didn't even think about it. "Lovely, same as before?"

"If you're happy with that, great," Jacks responded with relief.

"Pick me up at eight, I'll be waiting for you."

Jacks closed his phone, still feeling a little guilty that he was looking forward to seeing her again.

***

Arriving home early that night, he found his mother and father entrenched in the house. As he entered the hall from the front door he could smell the polish, and a fresh herb smell from oodles of potpourri having been placed around the house.

"Hello, Mum, Dad." He smiled at them in turn as he looked round. "Been busy then," he quipped.

"Just thought we'd help out a little. We know how busy you are," Mum answered. "Dad's tidied up the garden and cut the lawn. I've done the housework, the washing and the ironing."

"How long have you been here?" Jacks asked, incredulous at the amount of work having been done.

"Since nine o'clock this morning," his dad answered. "Your mother hasn't stopped all day, and now it's time for us to go."

Jacks couldn't thank them enough, or persuade them to stay for a while, and waved them off as they drove away. He was a lucky guy, especially as he had summarily shunted them off the last time they were here.

***

Jacks pulled up outside Suzanne's apartment, dead on eight o'clock, dressed in a freshly laundered, crisp white shirt, thanks to Mum, under a Lovett green corduroy jacket. He watched her close the door and descend the steps between the black-painted, wrought iron railings. She was dressed in a short, dark blue jacket over a cream-coloured blouse, a cream coloured skirt, which finished just above the knee, and white high heels, setting off the muscle tone in a her well-formed legs.

Jacks liked what he saw, and immediately felt a pang of guilt again as she reached for the door handle he had already opened for her.

"Hi, Jacks. You look very handsome tonight, your new hairstyle suits you." She smiled radiantly, as she became aware of her feet starting to tingle.

"Thank you, kind lady," he answered, trying to keep his eyes off of her legs as she swivelled them into the well of the passenger seat, and slammed the door. "You're looking very good yourself," he added warmly.

Jacks signalled, looked into his off-side mirror and pulled out into traffic. He still had his eye on the mirror when he saw another car pull out, forcing its way into the traffic behind him.

The other vehicle took up station behind, following at a safe and discreet distance.

They arrived in Leicester Square and turned down a little street to find a parking spot. The road wasn't busy, and Jacks signalled to pull in after looking in his rear-view mirror.

"This looks like a JSH," Jacks said as he began pulling in.

"What's a JSH?" Suzanne asked, puzzled at the term.

"One of your cousin's little jokes. Jacks Size Hole," he answered, smiling as he kept his eye on the rear-view mirror and noticed the vehicle pull in three cars behind them. He didn't give her chance to answer before he leant over her.

"I want you to get out of the car and keep low, so that anyone in a car behind cannot see you."

Suzanne looked at his change of mood and, knowing the man, she opened the door and slid out without argument. Jacks, keeping low, followed silently.

"Get back in, Suzanne, and don't come out until I tell you, is that clear?" Jacks urged quietly.

"You're worrying me, Jacks," Suzanne whispered.

"Do as I ask you. It'll be okay." And with that Jacks disappeared behind.

Suzanne tried to spot him in her side mirror, sliding down and across the car until she could see him. He was keeping low and moving fast towards a vehicle behind. She watched him wrench open a car door and disappear inside it.

Jacks was in the vehicle like a flash, to the shock of the male driver inside. He leant over and grabbed at the keys in the ignition. The man recovered slightly and tried to stop him taking them. Jacks jabbed his elbow up and back into the man's face, sending his head back against the rest. He instantly withdrew his hand as blood started to ooze from his nose.

"You, bastard," he exclaimed, holding his nose. "You've broken it."

"Why are you following me?" Jacks snarled at him, ignoring his whimpering and searching his features for any sign that he might know him.

"I'm not," he replied, and got another slap across his face with the back of Jacks' hand for his trouble.

"I'll ask you one more time," Jacks offered harshly. "Why are you following me?"

"I'm not, I was following her," he blurted out. "I was following Suzanne."

Jacks was a bit surprised by this turn of events, believing this man was connected somehow to Smith, although, looking at his smooth, middle-class face and sandy-coloured hair, he didn't really fit.

"Why are you following her? What have you got to do with her?" he demanded to know.

The man took a handkerchief from his pocket and tried to stem the blood flow before answering. "Up until a few weeks ago I was her fiancé," he said, perplexing Jacks further. "She broke it off when she found out I was still married."

"So, why are you following her?" Jacks asked, staring right into the man's eyes, not caring about his marriage.

The man was aware of the menace in Jacks, and said quickly, "I just saw her waiting in the window as I drove past, and wondered with who and where she was going."

"Do you have some identity on you?" Jacks demanded.

The man reached into his top pocket and handed Jacks a card. Jacks looked at it as he turned on the overhead light. A solicitor by the name of Alan Jenkinson was on the card, with offices just off Mayfair. A heavy-weight with that address, thought Jacks.

"Yes, I'm a solicitor and you have seriously assaulted me, and that could be very serious for you," he whined, hoping this man would get out of his car.

Jacks grabbed him by the throat, forcing Jenkinson's head back against the seat's rest. "Let me tell you as it is, mister," Jacks whispered, as he stared directly into the man's eyes. "We have laws on stalking. It is, as you probably know, a criminal offence punishable with a jail sentence and, for you, automatic striking off from your profession. Still think my position is serious?" he said behind clenched teeth.

Jenkinson remained quiet for a few moments before, saying, "Can we just forget this? It won't happen again, I promise you."

"You bet it won't, mister. If it happens again I'll arrest you, and use a lot more force than I have tonight. Do you understand?" Jacks snarled, as he asserted a little more force to the throat.

"Yes, I understand, it won't happen again," he whimpered.

Jacks let go of his throat, satisfied he had put his message across, opened the car door and got out, slamming it shut. Without as much as a glance back, he strode up the pavement to re-join Suzanne, and heard the vehicle start up behind him.

He opened her door. "Shall we go in?" he invited, as if nothing had happened

Suzanne got out looking cross. "What was that all about, Jacks?" she almost demanded. She watched as the other car went past them, and recognised the driver. "Alan?" she said. "The bastard was following me?"

"It's sorted," Jacks said in a business-like manner. "You won't have any more problems with him. Let's go in."

Over dinner, Jacks assured her that there was nothing she had to explain, what was in the past was in the past, and had nothing to do with him. He had no call over her anyway, being unsure of just how he felt towards her.

The conversation eventually turned to Mark Smith, with Jacks informing her just how accurate her assessment of the killer had been.

They enjoyed their dinner and each other's company. Suzanne was relieved that Jacks didn't think less of her because of her stupidity with Alan.

Jacks was about to order coffees and a liqueur, when his mobile phone vibrated silently in his breast pocket.

He opened the phone as he looked apologetically at Suzanne. "Jacks," he sighed, as he listened to the caller. It was Mike King, in a very agitated mood. "Slow down, Mike, for Pete's sake, slow down. What about Bobby?"

"He's been shot, Jacks," he exclaimed.

"Where the hell are you?" Jacks shouted into the mouthpiece, as the whole dining room hushed and looked at him.

"Just outside Godalming, at a caravan site. Smith was here, but got away after shooting Bobby in the legs."

"Why wasn't I contacted over this? You're off our patch, for God's sake."

Suzanne watched and listened, Jacks was clearly irritated and angry over this.

"How is Bobby?" he demanded to know.

Mike was attempting to compose himself, trying to regulate his breathing. "He's hurt pretty badly, Guv. He was hit in both legs, he's been taken to Guildford Hospital."

Suzanne, aware of how serious the conversation was, rose from her chair and went to reception. Antonio had heard the commotion, guessed it was police business and had already started to prepare the bill.

Suzanne took out her credit card but Antonio declined it as he handed her the bill.

"I will see Jacks some other time. Just go, he will need to get away," Antonio said simply.

Jacks was already on his way to reception when Suzanne met him. "Go, Jacks, I'll make my own way home," she offered.

"I'll drop you, Suzanne. I have to go out that way anyhow," Jacks stated determinedly.

He dropped her off outside her apartment, had a quick glance round just in case the solicitor had found some nerve, and waved to her as she disappeared in his rear-view mirror.

***

He got to Guildford Hospital just before midnight and drove up to admissions, parking just before the area where ambulances dropped off their patients. He slammed the large POLICE sign in the front windscreen of the Volvo, and sprinted to reception.

Jacks was shown down to the area near the operating theatre, where he saw numerous police in uniform.

Mike was leant against a wall, morose and feeling very sorry for himself. He saw Jacks coming down the aisle towards him and pushed himself off the wall, walking towards Jacks with his hands outstretched.

"We tried to contact you, Guv, but you didn't answer your phone," he started to explain.

"Never mind that now, Mike, how is he?" Jacks was more concerned with Bobby than any cock-ups, at this stage anyway. He noticed an officer coming down the hall, who was receiving due deference from the other officers; he recognised him from his time served in the Surrey Constabulary before joining the Met. Jacks noticed from insignia on his epaulettes that he was now a chief superintendent.

"Hello, Jacks. Should be under different circumstances, but I'm pleased to see you," Chief Superintendent Rose said, as he offered his hand.

"Hello, Greg, it's good to see you as well. Are you in charge here?" Jacks shook his hand warmly; they had a good relationship when they had worked together.

"Only over uniform, my son," Greg beamed. "It goes without question you handle all other matters relating to your murder."

"Thanks, Greg. You'll have to excuse me, I want to see how my boy's doing." Jacks turned to find a nurse who could tell him who was in charge.

The solemn-looking consultant's name was Mr Burrows. "I am afraid his legs have been pretty mangled, Chief

Inspector. He is going to need so much care for a very long period."

Jacks almost bit his tongue at this devastating news. His thoughts immediately went out to Bobby's wife Betty. "We'll know more when we have the x-rays," he added.

"Thank you, Mr Burrows. Please do what you can for him." He turned to Mike. "Have you contacted Betty yet?

"Yes, Guv, I phoned her after I got hold of you. She's being ferried down by uniform. I'm sorry, Guv, I really did try to contact you, honest." Mike was almost in tears.

"Not the time, Mike. If it's anybody's fault, it's mine," Jacks assured him, thinking of earlier when he dealt with the solicitor back in Leicester Square. I could murder that bastard, he thought. "Let's find a quiet space to talk. You can tell me everything."

They found an empty side ward, went in and sat down. "Tell me," Jacks requested sternly.

"We got a call from Godalming CID that Smith had been seen at a caravan camp just outside of the town. We tried to contact you, but couldn't raise you."

Jacks didn't respond, so Mike continued. "AC Carstairs gave us the okay, so we drove down to Godalming Police station, hooking up with CID, who also laid on uniform to attend."

"Who else did you take down with you?" Jacks interrupted.

"Diane and Len from our squad," Mike said, adding quickly, "both of them are all right, Guv, it's just Bobby that copped it. Anyway, we entered the site at about nine, it was already pitch black. There were only three vans parked on the site. Bobby went to the rear of them with two uniform guys, whilst Diane, Len and I started to rouse the inhabitants by banging on the doors. We heard some shouts coming from the back, followed by two loud explosions that echoed across the site. We rushed round in time to see Bobby being held in a sitting position by the two uniform guys. The Surrey lot spread out and heard a vehicle start up in a lane running adjacent to the site. Smith had parked his vehicle well out of the way, and drove off at speed. Surrey uniform gave chase but they lost him south of the town."

"He'll make for the Worthing area," Jacks stated. "Have you put out an all points on him for Sussex, Surrey and Kent?"

"Yes, Guv, and for Hampshire, too, just in case," Mike added. "SOCO is on the caravan site, plus we have two travellers in custody on suspicion of helping a wanted criminal."

"Where are they?"

"Godalming nick, Guv."

"Right, you stay here, Mike, I want Bobby looked after. Wait for Betty, and make sure she gets every assistance possible. Contact the Federation Rep and make sure he gets down here tomorrow. Also, contact Bobby's lodge, the Masons will want to help. I'm going down to Godalming to see what I can get from these two monkeys."

Jacks left the hospital, and drove twelve miles down the A3100 to Godalming police station, arriving just twenty minutes later. He showed his ID to the night desk officer, who called CID.

Detective Sergeant Miller came to meet and escort him to their offices. The two travellers had been separated, and were sitting in different rooms, each attended by two CID officers. They had not been talking.

The officers stood up as Jacks entered the room. The first traveller looked on apprehensively as he sat in front of a desk.

DS Miller spoke to the officers. "You can take five, lads, we'll take it from here." They both left the room.

"I'm Jacks, Chief Inspector Jacks from Scotland Yard, and you, you bastard, tried to murder one of my officers tonight and have crippled him."

"Not me, sir, definitely not me. I was in me caravan at the time," he snivelled under Jacks' gaze, whose hatred for this man was quite clearly showing. He was now more worried than ever.

"You have been harbouring him, a wanted murderer, a child sex attacker and murderer," Jacks spat at him. "What's your bloody name? We'll find out through fingerprints anyway. Save me time, you bastard, and you may just sweeten my temper."

"No comment," the man said.

Jacks' fist arced round, smashing sideways into his jaw, hurting him but not knocking him unconscious. There was a hell of a crack as it connected, and sounded in the room next door.

"I can keep this up all night if I have to. You had better start talking," said Jacks coldly, as he straightened the man up in the seat for a further strike.

"All right, all right, there's no need for violence," he screamed, as Jacks pulled his fist back ready to strike again. "As you say you will find out sooner or later anyway. My name is Harry Smith, no relation to Mark Smith," he added guardedly.

"What is the name of the man next door?" Jacks demanded still with his right fist ready to strike.

"Gordon Black," Harry replied without resistance.

Jacks thrust his face into Harry's. All Harry could see was the blazing anger in the deep brown eyes, which seemed to be alight with fire. He had never been as frightened of anyone as much, not even Mark Smith.

"Now tell me where this bastard Mark Smith has gone, and I warn you now, you set me wrong and I will bury you."

Harry Smith believed him instantly. "He's probably gone to Worthing. He has a woman on a site down there," he stammered. "I swear I didn't know about the girl he murdered, honest I didn't. I knew he had a sawn-off shotgun, but I didn't dream he would use it against a copper."

"You write down the details for this nice sergeant, and they had better be correct." Jacks turned on his heel and went next door.

Gordon Black was terrified. He had heard the smack of Jacks fist hitting Harry and the howl of pain that followed.

"Out, please, you two. I don't want any witnesses to this."

The two detectives got up, shrugging their shoulders, they looked at poor Gordon with pity in their eyes and left the room, shaking their heads. The door slammed shut behind them as Gordon Black jumped in his seat, nearly messing himself.

"What do you want to know?" he offered meekly to a menacing Jacks standing over him.

"Everything there is to know. Let's start by you confirming your name."

Ten minutes later, Jacks had gleaned all he could from the two travellers. It was pretty obvious that Mark Smith had nowhere else he could go. These two hadn't dared let any of their fellow travellers know that he was with them because of his violent behaviour to one of the girls, who had ended up fighting for her life in hospital.

Jacks made a few phone calls, summoning his team to join him at Godalming. He also telephoned Brighton CID, appraising them of the situation and told them not to act until he and his team were in attendance.

By four o'clock in the morning, his whole team was assembled in the incident room at Godalming CID. Mike brought everyone up to date, including how Bobby was doing and that Betty, his wife, was now at his side.

Diane had brought two extra pistols for Mike and Jacks; everyone was armed. They set out in a convoy, escorted by Surrey police, with blue lights flashing and horns sounding as they approached the Surrey-Sussex border, where the traffic cars of Sussex took over. They drove on down to the coast in morning half-light, killing their sirens as they entered the outskirts of Worthing. They silently approached a lane leading down to a small caravan site off a beaten track. The convoy came to a halt, and everyone automatically got out and went to the rear of their vehicles. They had done this before, the bullet-proof vests were put on as well as the black baseball caps which were emblazoned with the POLICE logo.

"Check your firearms, and make sure your safety catches are on. Only remove them when a target presents itself, or you feel you or your colleagues are in danger. I want no accidents today." Jacks watched the line of police, and then summoned the tactical firearms unit forward.

"You lead, skipper," he said to the uniformed sergeant, who carried his Heckler & Koch across his chest. "I have the loud hailer, and all men are carrying high-powered lights. Let me know when you are satisfied you have it all covered."

"Roger that, sir," he said simply, as six uniform marksmen went forward with the murder squad and Brighton CID following behind. The marksmen skirted the caravans that were silhouetted in the half-light.

Jacks could almost smell Mark Smith, and was sure he was here. He waited for the firearms sergeant to signal him that they had the whole place covered, and started to move in with his men.

"Don't get in the way of the marksmen," Jacks whispered to his team, as they started to veer off to cover each caravan. "They are more important to this operation that any one of us."

There were four caravans in all, but only two of them seemed to be occupied. No dogs, thank God, thought Jacks, as he and Diane felt their way round the van until he came to the caravan's door. Mike had taken up station and found the entrance to the second van, which had a small lorry attached to it.

Jacks put the loud hailer to his mouth and turned it on. "Mark Smith, this is the police," he shouted through static, listening to the distorted echoes as they reverberated round the clearing.

All the lights were suddenly turned on, showing the scene vividly. A curtain twitched and began to open slowly in the caravan that Mike and Len Baines were guarding. They both straightened their arms and pointed their pistols at the window, making sure they didn't impede the marksmen behind them.

"Come out, Smith. We are armed. There is no place left for you to go."

Nothing stirred as the firearms unit started to close the distance to the vans. Mike and Len banged on the side to rattle the occupants.

All of a sudden there was a scream from behind the door. Mike stepped back quickly, dropping to one knee. Len, standing slightly to one side behind him, afforded him covering fire.

"I'm on me own," the female voice screamed in panic. "He's not in here."

"Then come out now," ordered Jacks over the hailer. "Come out with your hands above your head. If you do not, we will open fire." he was not going to take any chances with his men.

He watched the entrance, but something nagged at him. He's not in here, echoed in his head, did that mean he was somewhere else on site, in this caravan in front of him, for instance? Jacks tapped Diane, and indicated with his pistol to the caravan they were in front of.

The other door opened and everyone's attention was drawn to the figure of a woman coming slowly down the steps, with her hands clasped tightly round her head.

Jacks shouted into the hailer. "Get down on your knees now."

She complied, falling to her knees as if she had fainted. Two firearms officers rushed forward and secured her arms behind her back.

Jacks, still alert, turned his attention back to his vehicle. He became aware of some movement inside the lorry in front of the van that the woman had emerged from. A figure was climbing silently out of the window, missed by everyone who was watching the woman or the second caravan.

Jacks turned his light towards the lorry in time to see Mark Smith running towards the tree line at the edge of the clearing.

"There he bloody well goes," he screamed, as every attention was focused on the fleeing figure, that had now reached the cover of the bushes and trees surrounding the site. There was no point in firing, the chances of hitting him were slim indeed, instead, everyone took up the chase led by Jacks.

Diane over took him. She was blasted fit, Jacks thought, not thinking that anyone would get in front of him, let alone a slip of a girl.

"Hold back, Diane," he shouted, throwing his hailer to one side.

Diane was not holding back for anyone; this killer had severely hurt her colleague, and she meant to have him. Jacks fought to keep up with her as they both flew through the undergrowth and bushes in hot pursuit. She seemed oblivious to branches slapping her in the face as she raced on.

They spotted Smith breaking cover in front of them, fleeing desperately across the field; unless he was super fit, they had him cold.

Diane was still in the front as they steadily gained on him. Jacks watched in horror as Smith suddenly stopped, turned and brought his shotgun up to his shoulder. Jacks made a supreme effort and dived at Diane's legs, just catching her heels, bringing her down as the shot whistled over them, grazing the back of Jacks' head.

He ignored the pain and the blood trickling down the back of his neck. "You okay, Miss Charming?" he quipped.

"I'll give the bastard 'Miss Charming'," she said in a shrill voice that showed her tension.

They both scrambled to their feet and set off again in pursuit of their quarry with Jacks' stamina now showing as he pulled slowly away from Diane. He reached the edge of the field just fifteen yards behind Smith, and jumped the low hedge into the lane.

Smith was now only ten yards away, and Jacks shouted to him. "You might as well give up, Smith, you're going nowhere. Stop or I will shoot."

Jacks stopped and raised his arm, ready to fire. If he didn't stop he was going to shoot, and shoot to kill.

Smith didn't actually stop, but threw himself to one side, rolled and came up with the shotgun ready to aim. He was fast, but Jacks was ready for anything and had kept the target in sight the whole time. He squeezed the trigger aiming for the man's chest and watched him slump forwards with the shotgun going off harmlessly into the ground in front of him.

An explosion came from just behind Jacks' right ear, making him duck as he watched Smith's head jerk violently backwards, as a bullet from Diane's pistol hit him in the forehead.

Jacks went forward slowly, as Diane came up to his side. They both had their weapons aimed at Smith's body, automatically obeying their training although they both knew he was finished.

Jacks was trembling slightly as he looked down, seeing the stain of blood oozing from his chest, and then the neat hole in the man's forehead. Smith's lifeless eyes were wide open as if he had been surprised.

"You all right, Guv?" Diane asked, noticing the blood on Jacks' neck. She turned to face him, as Jacks noticed with surprise she looked as cool as the proverbial cucumber.

Jacks grinned at her. "Never been better, Miss Charming. You could say I have seen the most amazing *PLANT* of my whole career, right between his eyes." he quipped.

"How very droll, Guv," she smiled. "By the way, how about calling me Diane or DC Plant, or anything rather than Miss Charming?" she asked.

"You've got it, detective. Diane it is from now on," he conceded, as the firearms unit and members of the murder squad caught up with them.

NINETEEN

Jacks was sitting by Bobby's bedside when Betty walked in. He started to rise, but she signalled him to stay seated.

"Stay where you are, Jacks, no need to get up for me."

"I'm sorry, Betty. I wish to God this hadn't happened," Jacks said quietly.

"It's not your fault, you silly man," Betty smiled, using Leanne's term of a mild rebuke. Leanne and Betty had been friends ever since Bobby and he had joined the Met.

He smiled sadly, taken aback and a little surprised at the phrase used.

"The doctors say it's not as bad as they first thought, and with lots of care and therapy he will be able to walk. Knowing Bobby he'll be running about in no time," she added bravely.

Jacks got up and went round to Betty, taking her in his arms and holding her tight. He kissed the top of her head, and said, "If there is anything, anything I can do…"

Betty was about to respond, when Bobby woke up. "Hey, you two, how long has this been going on behind my back?" The Hampshire accent was back, and so was the humour.

***

An hour and a half later, after fighting through heavy traffic, Jacks arrived at the Yard just as his mobile rang. He answered in his usual curt style. "Jacks."

It was Suzanne. "How are you, Jacks? I saw you yet again on the news. You seem to be making a habit of getting on television. Are you thinking of changing profession?" she laughed.

"Ha, ha, bloody ha!" Jacks mocked. "I'm surrounded by comedians, even in my personal life."

Suzanne immediately picked up on the 'personal life' bit. Did she dare to hope that Jacks felt the same about her as she did about him? She was about to respond when Jacks spoke.

"I've just arrived at the Yard, Suzanne, and I'm late for a meeting with the AC. I'll have to ring you back later. I've a feeling it's going to be a very busy day."

"That's fine," a disappointed Suzanne accepted. "I'll wait to hear from you."

Suzanne was cheered by what he said next.

"Keep this evening free, I'll book at Antonio's."

***

AC Carstairs couldn't have been happier, or nicer, as he welcomed a belated Jacks into his office.

"Sit down, old chap, I'll order some coffee for you," he enthused heartily. "We have a press conference arranged for eleven o'clock this morning, and I want you to field the questions. Would you like biscuits with your coffee?"

Jacks' face must have dropped as Carstairs added, "Oh come on, for goodness sake. You will have to get used to the press, Jacks, no matter how irksome you find them. Apart from being expected of the investigating officer, it is good PR for the Met."

Jacks shrugged his shoulders and groaned, resigned to the fact that he would have to join the blasted circus once again. "No biscuits thank you, sir," he said quietly.

How he hated this part of the job; he would spend the next few weeks being recognised by all and sundry, some of whom wanted to shake his hand, buy him a drink or slap him on the back. This did not sit well with the private and modest man that he was.

"Okay, sir, but it must be brief. The team and I have a lot of work to do, not just on this, but on Bryan Payne's murder and robbery trial as well."

"Good heavens, man, you have all the resources of the Met at your disposal," Carstairs answered. "Stop using excuses and just prepare for the press meeting."

***

At eleven sharp the press meeting started, with Carstairs flanked by Jacks on one side and Diane on the other. Jacks got through it, but couldn't remember a word he, or anyone else, had said.

Later that day, both Diane and Mike accompanied him to the mortuary for Smith's post mortem. There were no surprises, both shots would have proved fatal, but at least Gregory was polite to both Diane and Mike, although he was a bit aloof with Jacks.

***

Suzanne made her own way to Antonio's, getting there just after eight o'clock that evening.

"Good evening, Miss Kaine," Antonio beamed. "Jacks is on his way and will be here soon. I'll show you to your table."

Antonio, although he had loved Leanne, had taken to Suzanne and hoped that the relationship was going to be permanent. Jacks needed someone in his life, he thought.

Suzanne had only just sat down, and was sipping her dry Martini and soda when she saw Jacks arrive. She became aware of her feet starting to tingle.

I hope it doesn't show in any way, she thought, smiling a greeting to him.

"I'm sorry I'm late, Suzanne," he apologised. "Loose ends and traffic, I'm afraid."

"Is your phone likely to go this evening?" she asked, frowning at him.

Jacks took out his phone, making a very visible effort of turning it off. "Not now it isn't," he said, raising his eyebrows and smiling.

Oh, how she loved his smile, she thought as her feet carried on tingling.

Later on that evening, instead of dropping Suzanne off at her apartment, Jacks accepted her invitation to coffee, and entered her home for the first time.

He loved what he saw; nothing too pretentious but plenty to show her exquisite taste in decoration and pictures on the plain pastel walls.

Jacks felt awkward, as did Suzanne. Neither knew what to do, or how to behave towards one another. They made light conversation, just managing to stay away from the subject of work and any personal relationships.

As Jacks eventually got up to leave, Suzanne went to him. She stood square on and looked him in his eyes; the tingling was too strong to ignore.

"Blast you, Jacks," she said, as she grabbed him and kissed him full on his lips. His first reaction was to hold her even tighter, and to return the kiss with some passion. He then froze and gradually but firmly pushed her away.

"What's the problem, Jacks? I know you feel the same as I do," Suzanne said, with a feeling of hopelessness. "Is it because you prefer to chase criminals, or is it still Leanne?"

Jacks tried a half smile with another quotation immediately coming to mind. "Brigands demand money or your life! Whereas women demand both." He saw her crestfallen face, immediately regretting his flippancy. "I'm sorry, Suzanne, I don't know how I feel. I am drawn to you, what man wouldn't be? But... maybe it's too soon... maybe it's me. Oh, for Christ's sake I don't know," he stammered, unsure of just what he was feeling. Leanne was still very raw in his mind, causing him to feel such guilt; it confused him.

Suzanne stared at him with sorrowful eyes as she understood what he was going through. "I do understand, Jacks, but I'm not going to apologise, or give up. You know how I feel about you, I can't stop my feet from tingling when I see you," she blurted out, and was instantly sorry that her secret was out.

Jacks was even more puzzled now; what did anything have to do with tingling feet? First he gave a hesitant laugh at the revelation, but then said, "Don't apologise to me, Suzanne. I have probably sent out confusing signals, because I don't know what I truly want. Well I do know what I want, but I don't know if it's right or not."

Suzanne took hold of both his hands and squeezed. "We'll give each other space and time, Jacks. Let's see if we can work it out and see how you feel then."

Another awkward goodbye followed as Suzanne, without any hesitation whatsoever, kissed him on his lips again.

Jacks had a very puzzling ride home that night; he couldn't stop thinking of her tingling feet. "Tingling feet," he murmured. "Whoever would have thought it?" He smiled as he thought to himself, that's a good thing, right?

***

The date was set for the inquest for Mark Jacob Smith. The verdict was justifiable homicide.

That afternoon, the inquest was concluded on Patsy Kerridge, with a verdict of homicide by one Mark Jacob Smith. The evidence presented was not only compelling, but irrefutable. Not one person from the travelling community bothered to attend.

Patsy Kerridge's body was released to her family, and the funeral was arranged. Bert Kerridge had approached Jacks and requested his permission for Patsy to be buried next to Leanne. He had no objection and thought it was fitting, seeing it was Leanne who had set him on a course to find her first and then catch her killer.

***

After the church service, they all assembled at the graveside for the internment. At the front on one side was Bert Kerridge, supported by his family and friends, with uniformed police in line behind them.

Jacks stood with his team and Suzanne on the other side of the grave. They felt for poor Bert Kerridge, who tearfully handed the ashes of his late wife to the undertaker to be buried with his daughter.

After the service the police waited for the relatives and friends to leave for the wake. Bert Kerridge approached Jacks, stood in front of him and then hugged him without saying a word. As he broke free he saw Mike and Bobby, went over and silently shook their hands, and then he was gone.

"Right you lot," Jacks addressed his team. "We have one more thing to do. All of you back in your vehicles and follow me to Brackenbridge Copse."

Suzanne, carrying a holdall he had given her, was as perplexed as the rest of his team but, like the rest of them, she went along without question.

Half an hour later, they were all assembled at the site of where they had found Patsy's body.

"I would like you all to say a silent prayer for Patsy here," Jacks said quietly, as they all obediently bowed their heads in silence.

Afterwards, Jacks looked up at them all and said simply, "Follow me."

They arrived at the stream, and Jacks stood with his back to the babbling little brook and faced his team.

Suzanne stood amongst them, wondering what the heck this was all about, but his people seemed to be just as lost.

Jacks looked at Diane and smiled. "Step forward slightly, Diane," he ordered.

Diane did as she was told very warily, wondering what her boss was up to. Suddenly, Jacks threw out raised arms to his sides, and shouted, "This is for you, Miss Charming."

With that, he allowed himself to fall backwards, splashing down in the cold waters of the stream. The team couldn't believe what was happening, and it was sometime before they all burst out laughing at the figure of their governor, almost fully submerged in the water.

Bobby, on his crutches, nodded to Mike, who grasped what he had to do. He went behind Diane, lifted her up in the air and threw her into the water to join her boss.

There was nothing gallant about Jacks; as he saw her hurtling through the air, he quickly dodged to one side and watched as she landed, back first, in the water.

It wasn't long before most of the team, watched by Suzanne and Bobby on the safety of the bank, joined them in the water.

Jacks eventually made it back to the bank, followed by his team. Once they were all safe on the bank, Jacks laughed at the sight of them.

"You are some stupid people. You are going to catch your deaths," he jibed. "Suzanne, my bag please."

He opened it and took out a towel and some dry clothes. "What the hell are you lot going to do?"

***

281

A dry Jacks and Suzanne made their way back to his house. It was the first time she had seen it, and she wondered what it was like inside.

As they entered the hall and went through to the lounge, she was struck by the similarity of décor to her own apartment in town. Leanne's mark, she thought, probably not him.

"We'll have some tea and then I want to go back to the churchyard and have a quiet spell with Leanne and Patsy, if that's okay with you?" he asked.

"Are you asking me to come with you, Jacks?"

"Of course I am. Do you want to?" Jacks said, as he took her hand, kissing her gently on the lips. "You'll have to be a little more patient with me, Suzanne. I have feelings running all over the place."

"I know that, and I understand," she said sincerely.

***

They got back to the church just before it started to get dark. They stood at the graveside, and Jacks searched for Suzanne's hand.

Praying silently, he stooped to pick up a rose off the grave, hoping with all his heart that Leanne understood. Surely she would understand, he thought.

Suzanne tensed and gripped his hand tightly. Jacks straightened up, looking at her, alarmed by her sudden nervousness. It was then he noticed two figures on the other side of the grave, and the reason for Suzanne's alarm. Leanne and Patsy were standing together and smiling at them.

"Be happy, Jacks, she's right for you," Leanne whispered, as she and Patsy gradually disappeared before their eyes.

"Oh Christ, Jacks... I can't believe what I've just seen... tell me I wasn't dreaming it... please?" Suzanne stammered, searching his face for an answer.

Jacks didn't answer; he just stood there with tears rolling down his face. Eventually, he said under his breath, "Goodbye, my love," as he realised the finality. Leanne was letting him go. For once he couldn't think of one quotation to fit the occasion.

EPILOGUE

As Jacks and Suzanne were leaving the graveyard, the moon came out from behind the clouds which had gathered, showering the graves and stones in a ghostly light. They drove away, disappearing up the narrow lane, leaving the graveyard to its deathly silence.

A few minutes later, two figures gradually materialised from the mist at the side of the freshly covered grave. They still held one another's hands as they looked across the churchyard to the vehicle disappearing up the moonlit lane.

A third figure gradually appeared on the other side of the graves, and stared hopelessly at the vehicle disappearing down the lane, before turning to Leanne and Patsy.

"Will they help me, do you think?" the stranger asked beseechingly.

"What do you think, Leanne?" Patsy asked.

"I don't know," Leanne answered. "We can always ask them."